SILV

Over 100
Great Novels
of
Erotic Domination

If you like one you will probably like the rest

New Titles Every Month

All titles in print are now available from:

www.adultbookshops.com

If you want to be on our confidential mailing list for our Readers' Club Magazine (with extracts from past and forthcoming titles) write to:

SILVER MOON READER SERVICES

Shadowline Publishing Ltd
Box 101
City Business Centre
Station Rise
York
YO1 6HT
United Kingdom

Telephone: 01904 525729
Fax: 01904 522338

NEW AUTHORS WELCOME

Please send submissions to
Silver Moon Books
Box 101
City Business Centre
Station Rise
York
YO1 6HT

Silver Moon is an imprint of Shadowline Publishing Ltd
the print publishing division of the Convecto Media Group
First published 2009 Silver Moon Books
ISBN 9781-904706-75-5
© 2009 Martin Jayne

THE SLAVE BUSINESS

BY

MARTIN JAYNE

All characters in this book are fictitious, and any resemblance to real persons, living or dead, is purely coincidental.

THIS IS FICTION - IN REAL LIFE ALWAYS PRACTISE SAFE SEX!

CHAPTER ONE:

A NEW ITEM

When the item fresh from the Ukraine had been stripped and bound and set in position, a secretary placed the printouts relating to her on the desk of the CEO of Domino Import-Export, James Walpole.

"Ah, thanks, Ms McGillicutty, I was wondering where they'd got to."

Walpole took a sip of coffee and glanced through the file. The documents included all the essential facts and statistics relating to the new item.

On the first page were three photographs, one frontal, one side and one rear view, of a naked girl, blonde and blue-eyed, standing erect with her hands at her sides in front of a screen marking her height. Beneath the photos were the words:

Item 1420 renamed Honey: Katrina Petrovna Sabyenye, k.a. Katya. Aged 21. Height 5 feet 3 inches (1.6m); weight: 105 lbs (48kg). Graduate in English, Yalta University. Native language: Russian; fluent in English; fairly fluent in Ukrainian. Education – there followed the details of the item's education and qualifications. The item had provided those herself when applying for the post advertised, supposedly as an interpreter. The item's passport was in a wallet attached.

On the remaining pages of the document were body measurements each with an accompanying photograph illustrating the relevant part: breast, waist and hip measurements; cup size; length and depth of vagina and its elasticity; breadth of posteriors and length of posterior cleavage; elasticity of anus (very tight as it happened, but that would soon change); length of legs and circumference of thighs; detailed measurements of the head and neck which had been taken with a pair of callipers. These latter measurements were necessary for the fitting of the branks: the rubber occlusion helmet and pony bridle which were being prepared.

On the next page were general remarks on stamina and bodily type. There was a blank entry for Walpole's comments, and boxes for him to tick. He had to decide on the type of slave the item might be best fitted to be trained as. There were four non-special types: firstly, general, that is to say, all round curvaceous. (This was the type Walpole preferred himself and thought of privately as "bouncy". Walpole was inclined to place Honey there); secondly, big buttocks; thirdly, big breasts; fourthly, legs and crotch. Then, many well-paying customers had delicate and unusual tastes, and the reserve price for items that satisfied their requirements was set very high, so there were many specials: pony-girls, milk-cows, bitch-girls – and there were other, even more abstruse types, which were only traced, procured or trained when there was a particular demand from a customer: for example, enormous breasts (the item Honey was obviously not suitable); the type with huge posteriors extracted from the deserts of Southern Africa (ditto); the type immobilised in a rigid transparent plastic frame; the type totally encased in a skin of shiny rubber, with only the crotch parts exposed; large muscular women trained as female wrestlers. Walpole decided it would be premature to decide on a type for item Honey right now – more data was needed. There was no rush. In any case, they would have to see what the market pressures were towards the end of Honey's training.

Finally, there was a page describing Honey's current personality – "current" because the whole point of the training program was to transform it. However, the current personality wouldn't need to be transformed too much, because the slave item was essentially submissive as it was. Another point didn't escape Walpole's attention. While the item was still in Yalta there had been an informal lunch after the interview for the (fictional) job as interpreter. During the course of it, item Honey had said she wanted to have lots of babies. That sort of detail was important, because it helped Domino target likely buyers.

All in all, very promising, Walpole thought. Now it was time for an inspection "in the flesh" so to speak. One of the perks of the job.

*

Walpole knocked and entered the office of the director of training, adjoining the suite of training rooms in the basement of the Agency building.

"How's the new item coming along, Vicky?"

Victoria Stratton looked up from her work and smiled. She was a woman in her early thirties, dressed in a dark business suit and shoes to match, with a rather expensive Victorian brooch pinned at the throat of a white chemise. She might have passed as the headmistress of a private girls' school.

"Very well, James. She made the usual rumpus to begin with of course, before anaesthetic was administered by the medic, but she's been put in position and all's ready for the preliminary orientation and induction. She's been given a contraceptive. The posteriors are well-presented, because I know you like taking slaves that way. She's been immobile and silent for the last hour or so. We used the silencing equipment."

Walpole nodded. The silencing equipment was a device invented by one of Domino's IT boffins. Electrode clamps were attached to the item's breasts and clitoris and a dildo electrode buried deep in her rump. A directional microphone connected to a computer running a voice recognition program picked up the slightest sound the item made, even a grunt or a sob, resulting in the item receiving electric shocks. They were not powerful enough to do the victim any serious harm, but caused a sharp pain which caused further noise and further pain. Then the voltage was automatically increased slightly until it reached a level judged to be the maximum the victim could endure without suffering permanent damage. Eventually the item learnt to be absolutely silent no matter how much pain was experienced. The procedure could be reversed, too, if that was required – the victim would be shocked unless she made a noise.

"I think now's the time for you to visit the item. In one very essential matter, you're equipped to train her and I'm not."

Walpole smiled and made no comment, even though he realised Victoria Stratton was being rather disingenuous. It was well-known within the Domino organisation that Stratton enthusiastically employed a strap-on dildo on all appropriate occasions, and quite a few inappropriate ones. Frequent violations of the items were a necessary part of their training, of course, and most of the staff of the Domino Company believed in mixing business with pleasure.

"Lead on, then."

Stratton took an electric prod which was hanging by her desk on the wall, and led Walpole to the cell containing item Honey. It was the first phase of photo shoots and DVD footage for Honey. Clients liked "Before and After" comparisons. It convinced them that the item had been properly trained. Prods were often used before shoots because they didn't break the skin and left the item more photogenic, unlike more conventional instruments of chastisement. Although of course sometimes a prospective buyer requested the sight of a well-tanned rump.

*

"Hm. Well it seems you've been your usual efficient self, Vicky."

Stratton smiled at the compliment. "Thank you James. It's nice to know one's efforts are appreciated. Would you like to…?"

"No," Walpole said. "A CEO should be prepared to delegate. I'll just stand aside and watch."

"Very well."

Honey was on a table whose height could be adjusted by a pedal. A casual observer might think the item was poised there of her own free will, for the bonds that held her were not immediately apparent. She was kneeling on the table, head down, posteriors high and presented for punishment, hands held behind its back, legs wide apart. The electrode dildo was plunged in its anus, and below that, the depilated sex was also presented for all to see. Electric leads from the dildo led along the anal cleavage and the vagina and joined those at the sharp-jawed clitoris clamp. They were taped up round the belly and disappeared out of sight. It was a painful, and extremely humiliating posture, deliberately so, of course. Walpole saw the bonds because he knew what to look for. Almost invisible wires in flesh-coloured plastic surrounded the lower thighs and continued up round the back, to where the hands were attached. Other wires were attached to ankle cuffs, splaying out the legs. When he moved to the side of the table he could see that wires attached to tit-rings pulled the slave's boobs severely downwards and surrounded the thighs. Other thin wires surrounded the back of the knees and were attached to the slave collar.

Stratton switched off the silencing equipment and then said: "What's your name?"

"Katrina Sabyenye. Katya."

"Wrong!" Stratton switched the silencing equipment on again. With a grin, she dug her prod directly into the item's sex , and swivelled it around. Then she pressed a button in the handle of the prod, delivering a sharp electric shock. There was a howl, and then another howl because of the electric shock from the silencing equipment, and then silence.

Stratton switched off the silencing equipment, rather satisfied the howls had subsided so quickly. "Good. You're learning. Now, let's try again. What's your name?"

"I'm an item."

Stratton persisted. "Tell me you name."

"I was told… I can't remember." Then she broke out: "This isn't fair! I'm a free woman! You can't do this to me."

Again the equipment was switched on. Stratton pushed her prod into the anal cleavage just above the obtrusive dildo, and shocked the item there. This time though, there was no howl. The item had learnt to endure its pain in silence.

"You are called Honey. What are you called?"

"I'm called Honey."

"Why is that answer, though correct, unsatisfactory?"

"I… I don't know."

Honey's breasts received the ministrations of Stratton's prod next, and they were shocked six times each, because Stratton wanted to make the item scream. She was gratified with a howl eventually, and then another one, because the pain from the electrodes of the silencing equipment was too much for the item to bear. But the last shock was endured in silence again.

"You will address me as Madam, do you understand?"

"Yes, Madam."

"So, tell me your name again."

"My name is Honey, Madam."

"That's very good." She would make a submissive slave yet, this girl. Training her would be a delight. "You're intelligent, Honey. Well done."

"Thank you, Madam."

Victoria Stratton's panties were moist, but she noticed that there was a bulge in James Walpole's trousers, and thought it politic to let her boss have first pick of the cherries. There was no hurry. There would be plenty of time to ream Honey's snatch over the next few months.

"Now you're going to have the privilege of servicing a man. Make sure you're polite and call him Master and thank him properly afterwards."

"Yes Madam," Honey said miserably.

Stratton winked at James Walpole and handed him the prod, patted Honey's rump and left the room, to allow James to get on with the business of shafting the item in private. The CCTV cameras were not switched on when Domino's boss went to work.

Walpole went over to the keyboard of the computer and with a few deft keystrokes changed the settings. Then he lowered the table, and poked the prod hard into Honey's sex, and then said: "Listen, bitch. You needn't be shy. I want everyone in the building to know I'm fucking you." (The training rooms were sound-proofed, but the item was not to know that). "I've reprogrammed the equipment. When I switch the machine on again, it will shock you if you're not screaming with joy. And when I'm finished with you, you'll thank me, do you understand?"

"Yes, Master."

Walpole unclipped the electrode at the item's clitoris, switched on the machine, and then rammed his cock up Honey. She screamed with joy. When he'd finished, she thanked him profusely.

He replaced the clitoris clamp, lowered the table again, slightly, and pulled the dildo out of the anus. It left a gratifyingly large cavity, which his penis could enter with ease. He gave the item an anal poke, and her joyful screams echoed through the training rooms once again.

When the item had thanked him properly, he replaced the anal plug, and moved round to the front. He raised the table until her mouth was at waist height and made her suck his erect cock, shocking her from time to time with the prod if her tongue was not energetic enough. Soon she drank a large quantity of his come, and when he withdrew, he yanked her up by the hair, and was amused to see quite a lot splattered all over her face. The item succeeded in being joyful about that, too, on pain of more electric shocks. After that, time to ream her snatch again...

*

Walpole showered in the washroom adjoining the training rooms, and then called Stratton on the intercom.

"I've finished. Please carry on."

*

The strap-on sported by Victoria was a prick-shaped steel rod, coated with corrugated rubber, longer and thicker than any man's penis. She went round to the front of the item and yanked up her head by the hair, so Honey could see what she was going to get, and could see too, the long studded rubber strap Victoria was holding. Victoria chuckled at the expression on her face.

"You're going to really enjoy your fucking, aren't you, my little slut?"

"Yes, Madam."

"You're going to squeal with joy and thank me for all the pleasure I'm giving you, aren't you?"

"Yes, Madam."

"Because you don't want to feel this strap across your bum, do you?"

"Oh no, Madam."

"This is being televised and highlights may be shown to prospective customers. And we want to be seen at our best, don't we?"

"Yes, Madam."

"Are you sure? You don't sound very enthusiastic. You do want me to fuck you, don't you?"

"Oh yes, Madam."

"Hm. I think I detect a certain insincerity in that response, Honey. There's something about the tone of voice which suggests a lack of total commitment. I'd better show you what the strap feels like, just so's you'll know what will happen if you don't try your best."

With that Victoria walked round Honey, and landed two hard cracking spanks on her prominently displayed posteriors.

"How are we feeling now?"

This question was the first that demanded more than a "yes" or "no". Perhaps for that reason the item hesitated. There was a swish and another resounding slap.

"I asked you a question. Well?"

"My bottom – "

"You're in no position to be prim, with it sticking out like that. Let me hear you call it your arse."

"My arse is burning, Madam. It's – it's very sore."

"Is it? Good. And after only three strokes too. Just think what it would be like after thirty. Your backside isn't the only thing that's going to be sore either, by the time I've finished with you."

During the course of the next eighty minutes or so, Honey got a thorough seeing-to, penetrated in both rear orifices, beaten and electrocuted countless times. She was expected to squeak and gurgle her appreciation and thank her trainer throughout. Domino's philosophy was that it was not enough for a slave to be humiliated; she had to revel in her humiliation; not enough for her to be forced to obey; she had to passionately long to be obey. Honey wasn't at that stage yet, but by the end of her training she would be.

Afterwards, two assistant trainers released the fine wires that were holding the item in her magnificently degrading head-down, bum-up posture. Victoria could see scarlet lines where the wires had dug into the item's flesh. Then the item was lifted to her feet, and her ankle cuffs were locked together. She was forced to wear a steel gag, a bar in the shape of a W. The middle part plugged into the mouth, and the two outside pieces of flexible thin steel squeezed against the cheeks, and were padlocked together at the back of the neck. The mammary and anal electrodes were removed, but the vaginal one remained. It was plugged into a socket on a steel belt fitted with a crotch piece to which a dildo prong was attached. The belt was locked in position.

"I'm afraid you won't be able to play with yourself for a while, slut, even though you might want to, with that dildo up your cunt," Victoria said. "But there, I suppose even you've had enough sex for one day. The belt won't stop you excreting, if you need to. While it's on, you'll have to remember to do exactly what you're told, otherwise...."

Victoria pressed a device she was holding in her hand, which looked a bit like a mobile phone or pager. The item yelped, lurched double and almost fell.

"Hm. Perhaps that setting was rather high. I'll never get used to these damn things.... There, how's that?"

The item yelped again, but didn't move this time.

"Yes, that seems about right. O.K. Remove her cuffs and take her to the gym. You can't lie around having sex all day you know – very bad for the figure. What you need is lots of healthy exercise. I'm rather busy – you're not the only item in the world, so I'll leave your physical training to Mr Burns here." Victoria handed the device to one of her assistants.

Honey was marched into a gymnasium, where there were about thirty other slave items, naked except for steel gags and belts just like Honey's. There followed ninety minutes' strenuous exercise. After that, the slaves were soaped and hosed down in cold water. It didn't do to allow slaves too much comfort. Honey wondered whether there was a danger of the belts shorting out, but they seemed to be water-proof.

Then, with the gag removed, Honey was led into a chamber where there were three other slave items. They were all naked except for the belts, of course.

This was to be the next phase of Honey's training.

CHAPTER TWO:

ENSLAVEMENT

Katya had been very happy with the well-paid job as interpreter she had landed. She hadn't expected the interview to be so easy. The interviewers had hardly bothered with her educational qualifications, but seemed to be much more concerned with her appearance and personality. In fact she'd had to take a personality questionnaire, and apparently the results had impressed her future employers greatly. She'd had to take a medical, too. The only thing she didn't like about that was the many photographs they insisted on taking of her while she was standing against a screen in the nude. She had wondered whether the photos were really necessary, but she didn't have much choice about it if she wanted the job.

Her first apprehension had come when they told her not to bring anything but hand-luggage with her on the flight.

"It's unnecessary, everything you need will be provided by the firm, and we will need to dress you in fashionable clothes. Our customers are impressed by such things."

It seemed a strange request, but the job was well paid, and if they were going to pay for new clothes as well...

The mild apprehension turned to a definite conviction that all was not well when she reached her hotel in a side road near Earl's Court in West London just as night was falling. It was run down and seemed to cater for economic migrants and backpackers from Australia and Africa. That in itself didn't cause alarm, even though Katya had been expecting accommodation rather more up-market. After all, she wasn't paying for it, so why worry? The manager showed her to her room, and closed the door behind her.

Katya kicked off her shoes and flung herself on the bed

travel fatigued. She dozed off for an hour or so. When she awoke she felt rather hungry and decided to explore the area and see if she could find a not too expensive restaurant. But then it seemed to her that there was something odd about the door. It was only when she tried to open it that she realised what it was: there was no handle. She pushed the door. It wouldn't give. She was locked in!

She tried shouting, but with no result. She put her ear to the door, but couldn't hear a sound. When she had first arrived, there had been quite a considerable noise of traffic and some North Africans arguing volubly with each other in Arabic in the lounge, but now there was not a whisper. The room was evidently sound proofed. She went to the curtained window opposite, in the hope of opening it and yelling for help. But it was a single pane, lacking sash cord or latch. Moreover, when she drew the curtains back she found the glass was frosted, so she couldn't attract the attention of anyone in the street. This called for desperate measures. She looked round for something heavy, and her eye fell on the kettle in the kitchen annexe. She hurled it at the window with all her force. It bounced off with a clang. The kettle was slightly dented, but the window unmarked. There was nothing for it after that but to sit it out and await her fate. She didn't have long to wait.

Because she was unable to hear the approaching footsteps, the two men who burst into the room came without warning. Before she knew what was happening, each held her firmly by an arm, and she was thrown face down on the bed. She felt a knee in her back, her skirt was thrown up, and her panties pulled down. There was a sharp pain in her backside, and then she lost consciousness.

*

She woke up, aware of being surrounded by some rough material, with her hands buckled behind her back in a belt.

Her rump was still smarting. She guessed she'd been injected there with some anaesthetic. She was evidently enclosed in a sack, and judging by the engine noise and vibration, was lying on the floor of a motor vehicle. There was a ball-gag in her mouth, forcing her jaws open as wide as they would go, and her legs were tied. There was something else.... As she recovered complete consciousness, she realised to her horror that her pussy and bum hole were both stopped with objects large and unmoveable. Unmoveable, because a tight cord ran between her legs from the front of the belt to the back, cutting into her slits before and behind and holding the horrible plugs in place. She also realised that she was naked. They must have stripped her while she was unconscious.

She felt dirty, humiliated. But she was also sexually aroused. She felt her juices leaking out. Those paradoxical feelings were to grow, in the coming months of her training, into a masochistic lust which would cause her to betray herself, bring about the destruction of Katrina Sabyenye, and the creation of willing slave item Honey.

*

"Stand to attention, bitch!"

Katya had no choice but to obey, if she didn't want the man to poke her belly with the electric prod he was carrying. She was still naked, gagged, with her arms pinioned, but the belt and cord had taken off and the plugs removed.

"Head up high, shoulders back, tits out, that's better! Now, quick march to the square frame over there, left, right, left, right. Head high! Left, right, stomach in, left, right, left, right, halt!"

A chain from each of the four corners of the frame was attached to one of Katya's ankle or wrist cuffs, and the petite blonde found herself yanked off the ground, with her arms and legs stretched out and her naked sex available to her persecutors, although it seemed they weren't interested in that just then. Her legs, arms and pubes were depilated and rings inserted through piercings in her clitoris, nipples and nasal septum. A swab of some kind of anaesthetic cream was wiped on each area before the piercing tool was pushed through her flesh, but even so she felt a sharp pain, especially when her clitoris was done. Her nasal piercing made her eyes water terribly and by the end of the procedure she was bewildered and sobbing, her body one huge ache as the effects of the cream wore off. The men ignored her entirely and left her to hang in the frame for a while until someone came along with a long-handled sponge and wiped her down with soap, and then dowsed her with cold water from a hose-pipe.

Katya was led to a steel cubic cell, about four feet on each side, which looked exactly like a large safe except for small grill at one side. It was in this dark cell that she was left until her training began the next day.

*

The Domino London training centre was an unobtrusive Victorian block off a busy high street in Dalston, in North London. The casual passer-by would not give a second glance at it. There was a sign across the door in large red capital letters:

PRIVATE: AUTHORISED PERSONNEL ONLY

CCTV cameras were directed at the door, which was usually bolted. No respectable member of the public had ever given a thought to the Domino Import-Export Company, but if they had, they would have wondered how it managed to make a profit, since hardly anyone was ever seen going in or out of its doorway in daytime. It was true that occasionally a limousine drew up nearby, and a person important enough to have the chauffeur hold an umbrella over him if it was raining, or someone in Arab dress, might enter the building. But London is a very cosmopolitan place where people keep themselves to themselves, and in any case, in that commercial district there were few neighbours.

Domino's slave-market had a virtual existence; although sometimes real "in the flesh" events were laid on for customers. But mainly Domino's business was done through a secure website. A customer could browse until he found a slave item which met his or her requirements, and then put in a bid for the slave. All members had to place a returnable deposit of two million dollars, and pay an annual membership fee of ten thousand dollars, which in itself was likely to cut out nosy journalists and policemen. Passwords and PINs and a very sophisticated firewall kept would-be hackers at bay. Then members also had to agree to be vetted by Domino's security wing, which was very efficient. Before any deal could be struck, the customer's circumstances were evaluated. If an item was going to disappear into a middle-eastern harem, or a remote ranch in Texas, that didn't present much of a problem. If, on the other hand, the customer was a Tokyo salary man, or a Wall Street arbitrageur, or a City of London broker, there might be difficulties. In that case, Domino's security wing would insist on a surveillance before a deal finally went through, and give advice (completely free of charge) on how to keep the item safe and sound.

Wives of first-time buyers were often a problem for Security. Sometimes, if the customer was into bondage, domination, discipline and sadism, his wife would be masochistic anyway, attracted to him in the first place for that very reason. Then it was a simple matter to suggest she receive further training in Domino's "dungeons" and "playrooms", at a small extra cost to the husband. The word "dungeon" suggested fantasy, and "playroom" suggested – well – play. Domino's training rooms were neither fantastic nor playful, as the female would eventually learn to her cost, but many wives had been trained up into obedient slaves in them over the years. Sometimes the customer wasn't interested in his wife being returned. Then she would be taken in part-exchange. Domino would put her through a rigorous training programme and transform her into a saleable asset. If she was not attractive or young enough to be sold on the slave e-market, she would have to earn her keep as a prostitute in some country far from her own. Over the years, downmarket slave-prostitution had become a very profitable side-line for Domino.

Domino also did a brisk trade in pony girls, and running pony clubs in many countries. Pony girls could fetch quite considerable sums if they had the right physique and stamina. Honey had been considered in that light, not as a racing mare or a hunter of course, rather as a little show pony, though even there usually taller girls were needed. Walpole was inclined to think she wasn't suitable in that rôle, but time would tell.

Of course, not all customers were dominants or sadists. Some were perfectly straight and simply wanted an attractive, obedient sex partner.

About ten per cent of Domino's slaves were male. Some customers were gay, and the wealthy heiress or businesswoman who required the attentions of an obedient toy boy, though comparatively rare in the past, had become more common in recent years, as more and more women broke through the "glass ceiling" and acquired real wealth.

Slaves had once come mainly from various Asian and Latin American countries, but in more recent times many had also been taken from Eastern Europe, in exactly the way Katrina Sabyenye had been.

CHAPTER THREE:

CRIME AND PUNISHMENT

After her enforced P.T. session, a trainer, a Mr Short, led Katya by a leash attached to her collar to yet another room in the training suite. Like the other girls there, she was naked, as usual, except for her belt, and on all fours. This training session was held in a fairly large room, better lit than most in the suite, with steel-tube-framed chairs piled up along one wall. However the slave items were not allowed to make use of them. They were ordered to rest on their forearms so their rumps were presented for an electric shock delivered in the anus by a prod in the event of any of them fidgeting.

The woman who had tormented Katya with a strap-on dildo, and whom Katya had heard a man call "Vicky", was sitting on one of the chairs, holding a coil of light chain in her lap. She handed a length of it to one of the other trainers, who threaded it through each of the items' nose-rings. Counting Katya, there were four of them. It was then looped back and through a steel ring that slid along the chain, forming a noose.

The woman called Vicky pulled the noose tighter, so that all the slave items were yanked by their noses into a close circle, where each was pressed against her neighbour and all sense of private space was lost. Slaves weren't allowed any private space, it seemed. Then the woman leant down to her handbag by the side of her chair and took out the pager she had used earlier to administer a shock to Katya's clitoris.

"There now, we're face to face and can examine each other properly. Listen carefully to what the other items say. At least one is an insincere hypocrite. Although she pretends to be an obedient slave item, she has a false belief in an inner self which she fantasises is essentially free, and only temporarily enslaved. She secretly gives herself airs of superiority which cause her to resist correct training and the appropriate attitude of humble subservience. It is for all of you to find which of you is the hypocrite. You will stay here on your knees in this circle until you come to a unanimous decision. All of you, including the culprit, must agree which item deserves severe punishment. Until you do that, you will not be allowed off your knees and you will not be fed or watered. Do you understand?"

The items chorused: "Yes, Madam."

Katya wondered how long it would be before she was given something to eat. The mention of food had brought the realisation that she hadn't eaten for twenty-four hours. She wondered if the other girls had been similarly starved. But the first one to speak didn't look hungry at all.

"You, the fat cow, Daisy, introduce yourself. Tell us your slave type and training and future prospects, if you know them."

The girl referred to was indeed very fat, and her breasts were very swollen. She smelt strongly of urine. Nevertheless, with her curly brown hair, large, broadly set cow eyes, rosy cheeks and delicate complexion, she was pretty in a chubby sort of way. Her mountainous posteriors showed evidence of having been recently spanked, though with something flat, not a cane or a whip. Katya, who was not quite as innocent of the motives of her persecutors as she had been only a day ago, guessed they must get some sort of perverse pleasure watching the girl's behind wobble when a strap or paddle impacted it.

"Thank you for giving me permission to speak, Madam," Daisy said, in a Polish accent. "As Madam has said, I am item Daisy, milk cow type. I have been trained as a milk cow for six months now, my trainer says, and I'm progressing satisfactorily. I am kept in a pen all the time, except when I'm taken out to be soaped and hosed down, or when a master or mistress wants to play with me." (Play! That's not how I would describe it, thought Katya.) "This is necessary, because my future buyer wants me absolutely passive, and says I'll probably spend my life chained to a bed post, so I have to get used to confinement. I'm fed very frequently, six times a day, and I'm given half a kilo of feed each feeding time. I have to eat it all up within a few minutes or my trainer presses my face in the feed and spanks me hard. In the early days of my training I'm ashamed to say I used to refuse to eat even then. Whenever I did that, I was given another beating, which I thoroughly deserved of course, and then force-fed. After I'd more or less got used to my feeding schedule and stopped being disobedient, I was given hormone injections and was milked frequently. At first there was little milk, but my udders now provide enough milk each day for the tea and coffee of all the senior staff here, and my trainer says that I shall soon be able to give more," Daisy said proudly.

"Let me see," said Mistress Vicky, if that's what her name was, Katya couldn't be sure, "how much longer are you with us now?"

"Just a day, Madam." There was excitement in Daisy's voice. "My new owner has already bought me, more or less, and it's just a matter of going through the formalities. The only other important thing that remains to be done is that I need to be branded, because my owner wants me branded on my arse and he wants to watch that being done, so he's coming here tomorrow."

"Well, that's certainly a clear and concise account of your training history, Daisy, and perfectly accurate. Just one more question: does your new master intend you to be a breeder?"

"I've never had the honour of being addressed by him directly, Madam, but my trainer says he is thinking of making me one, yes."

"The rest of you, you have heard what Daisy has had to say for herself. I hope you've been listening to her tone of voice, as well as the content of her words. Do you think she's the hypocrite? Is she the one we have to punish?"

There was general consent that Daisy was not the hypocrite. Not at all, thought Katya, she's been thoroughly and efficiently brainwashed by these people who seem masters of that art.

"Good. So we'll go on to Black Beauty. Item 1411, Black Beauty, it's your turn to describe your training."

Black Beauty was the sort of girl, thought Katya, whom any normal man would want to bed. She was quite tall, just under 1.8 metres, with dark lustrous hair and an olive complexion. Katya guessed she came from one of the southern Slavic countries. She had a beautiful symmetrical face and a curvaceous figure.

"Thank you for giving me permission to speak, Madam," Black Beauty said. "I am slave item Black Beauty, type pony girl. I was obtained by Domino six months ago, according to my trainer, it's difficult to keep track of time here, and like Daisy I'm nearly at the end of my training."

Why am I being put in with these trained slaves? thought Katya with alarm. She began dimly to realise how this meeting was going to end. "Mr Walpole told me after he first made love to me –" Made love to you! thought Katya bitterly. " – I'd make an excellent pony." There was an unmistakable note of self-satisfaction in Black Beauty's voice. "He said my boobs were probably a little too big, but that problem could be solved by fastening a bar between my tits so they flopped in unison when I ran. He said in any case many of Domino's customers liked their ponies to have big flopping jugs. I was soon put into training and I have to admit I didn't like that at all at first." She's actually blushing, Katya thought. "I had to wear a bridle with a training bit which was very uncomfortable, and the tit bar, and a tight waist strap with studs on the inside." You poor kid, thought Katya. "It took me a long time to get used to the bridle and get used to being given directions by having my head yanked this way or that. The training bit was bad enough, but if I caused displeasure to my trainer I would be made to wear a punishment bit, which was worse, because it had spikes in it. My cunt lips were pierced and little silver chastity rings set in them. I always had a dildo up my cunt, to keep my mind where he wanted it, my trainer said. The worst thing was the light crotch chain attached to the belt which was pulled very tight. It cut into my arse and then came up between my legs through the cunt rings and really made me sore. I cried a lot when I was first put into my harness and had to be whipped thoroughly before I took a common-sense view. It was quite a while before I realised that all this was necessary if I were to become an acceptable pony girl." Oh God, thought Katya, have I got to go through all this? "Then I was put on a treadmill in full harness. To begin with, I was only put on it for two hours a day, because my owners are very merciful and understanding. But now," Black Beauty said proudly, "I regularly tread the mill for eight hours a day. Then I had to be transported to one of Domino's race tracks."

"Where is that? If you don't know, say why not."

"I don't know because I was strapped into a rubber body-bag and had to wear a rubber occlusion helmet, which covered my ears and eyes and gagged my mouth. But it felt like I was being transported in the back of a van or truck."

"Continue."

"They had to find out what kind of pony I'd make: carriage pony, hunter, or racer. I was quite good as a racer but in the end my trainer thought my boobs were too big. So I was trained as a carriage-pony. I was sent to our training farm in Guatemala." Our! She actually identifies with this horrible organisation, thought Katya. Guatemala! This truly is an international corporation. "I was on the track for hours and hours and the whip was applied to my arse every time I slackened. My trainer says that's necessary because my new owner likes using lots of whip, and I shall be whipped to exhaustion pulling a pony-trap on every racetrack that Domino owns. But I'm very fit and quite confident I'm ready to be a first-class pony girl for my new master. I'm going to be sent to him tomorrow."

"Are you going to be branded?" Madam Vicky asked.

"I think so, Madam, but my new owner lives on a ranch in Texas, and I believe he wants to do that himself."

"Hm. Well again, a perfectly clear and straightforward account of Black Beauty's training. I can vouch for its accuracy. But it's not so much the factual content, rather the emotional tone that I asked you to look out for. Is Black Beauty a hypocrite?"

Again it was the unanimous view that Black Beauty was not the hypocrite they were all seeking.

"Well now we come to slave item 1415: Hotlips." As she said this, Madam pressed a key on her pager, and Katya's eyes widened as a humming sound came from between her legs. The prong locked inside her wasn't just a dildo, it was also a vibrator, which Madam could switch on and off at will. Katya's confusion increased as she realised all the other slaves could hear the hum, and would know what was happening to her. Madam gave her a sardonic smile but said nothing to her.

Hotlips had a physique similar to Katya's own: she was of medium height, quite slim but large breasted, with high round posteriors. Like Katya, she was a blonde blue-eyed slave with that heart-shaped Slavic face which Katya recognised. She's probably Russian, Katya thought.

"Thank you for giving me permission to speak, Madam," Hotlips said. "I'm slave item Hotlips, bed-slave type. When

Mr Walpole made love to me –" Oh not that again, thought Katya. "– he told me I was the best cunt he'd fucked for a long time, really juicy, I became very wet really soon, and I would make a really good bed-slave. I'd got really good bouncy tits and a nice bum that he loved to stroke and spank. And wow! did he spank my arse! – usually over his knee with a heavy rubber flogger, until my hole got really wet. He made my arse really sore, and then he would screw me all ways up! He loved to take me doggie style, I believe Mr Walpole likes to do that, then he'd make me suck his cock – he's such a virile man – then he'd screw me in the arse. That was painful to begin with, but I didn't mind it, because after all Mr Walpole is my master. It's true, at the beginning, I was a bit doubtful, but I was soon whipped into submission, and quite right too! Mr Walpole took charge of my training personally, and he's the boss you know, so I felt really honoured –"

"You didn't show it at the time."

Hotlips blushed crimson. "No, begging your pardon, Madam Victoria, I was very contrary and sulky then. I should have said, now I know who Mr Walpole is, I feel honoured that he took an interest in my case, and spent a lot of his valuable time teaching me good manners."

"One may forgive the untruth, since it was unintentional, but it may not be overlooked." So saying, Madam Victoria pressed a key on the pager, and Hotlips let out a squeak and wiggled her bottom as the electrode at her clitoris shocked her. At a nod from Madam, Hotlips's trainer prodded her in the anus, so she let out another squeak.

"I'm very, very sorry, Madam."

"Your apologies are accepted. Continue."

"For a lot of my training I was put in a go-go frame and sometimes –"

"Some of the other slave items here will not know what a go-go frame is. Describe it."

"I was squeezed between lots of steel struts that fitted through two wire panels. The whole frame rotates vertically, and can be locked at any point in its rotation. So I could be put any way up and in practically any posture: head down, arse up, legs spread out, thighs touching belly, arms high behind my back with my tits pushed out and squeezed between two struts; my ankles shackled to the panels –"

"Yes, I think we get the general idea," Madam Victoria said. Hotlips was getting a bit carried away.

Katya wanted to be indignant, but the devilish vibrator prong inside her locked chastity belt was betraying her. She was beginning to feel hot and moist.

"What else did your training consist of?"

"A lot of P.T., and like Black Beauty I spent a lot of time on the treadmill or the exercise bike, because I was expected to be really fit. My ankles were locked to the pedals of the bike, and my wrists to the handle-bars. The handle-bars were low, so my arse stuck out nicely, Mr Walpole said. The back wheel was fitted to an electrical device. If I was lazy and the wheel was turning round too slowly, an electric motor would switch on, and my bare arse would get thrashed by rubber lashes. They whirled round really fast, and went both ways, I mean clockwise and counter-clockwise, so both my arse cheeks got the treatment. I got a very sore bum towards the end of the session, which generally lasted for an hour or so. My arse crack and cunt got sore as well as my arse cheeks, because the seat of the bike was just a cross-piece of two steel rods –".

"You enjoyed it really, though, didn't you?"

"Oh yes, Madam, my cunt got really wet."

"Good. You're commendably frank, Hotlips. I like honesty in my girls."

Hotlips blushed at the praise. "Thank you, Madam. I also had to wear something to correct my posture, which was really bad at first."

"Your posture, or what you had to wear?"

"Both, I suppose. It was a very tight-fitting belt with studs on the inside, a bit similar to what Black Beauty had to wear, except there was a small horizontal projection at the back, which a steel rod passed through. The rod screwed into a steel posture collar at the top, which kept my chin up and head immobile, and ended at the bottom in a curved hook that fitted up my back passage. Wearing it, it was impossible for me to slouch, and my bum was held up by the hook. I soon learnt to walk correctly. I had to walk up and down the room wearing six inch heels, with two books balanced on my head, and every time I dropped them my arse would get swiped with a flogger."

As Hotlips was talking it occurred to Katya that Hotlips would never use terms as precise as those naturally, her English wasn't as good as Katya's. She must have been made to learn by heart a description of the instruments used on her, and no doubt she would have been punished if she got the terms wrong. What cruel mind games these people played. She wanted to feel compassion for the girl, but her sex lips were swollen as the vibrator hummed inside her wet hole, and all she could feel was lust.

"My vaginal muscles had to trained, too, so I had to learn how to squeeze a rubber bulb inserted in my cunt. My muscles down there are really strong now. I've already been sold, and I'm going to be branded and transported later this week. I think an Arab gentleman has bought me, and wants me to have lots of children. I'm really looking forward to serving him."

At that point, Katya orgasmed. Another contemptuous smile from Madam, and little suppressed giggles from the other slaves.

Again, it was the unanimous view that Hotlips was not being hypocritical.

Suddenly, Katya found the vibrator switched off.

"Now Honey, what have you to say for yourself?"

All these slaves were thoroughly brainwashed. There was no doubt about it. She was being set up.

"I'm a very new slave item –"

"She didn't ask your permission to speak, Madam." It was the horrified voice of the milk cow slave, Daisy.

"No, you're quite right, Daisy. She didn't. Do you think she should be punished for that?"

"Oh yes, Madam," all the slave items except Katya chorused unanimously.

"Very well."

Katya felt as if her clitoris was being burnt off as the shock hit her, and then she got another shock in her anus, as her trainer's prod was inserted there.

"Ow! Thank you for giving me permission to speak, Madam."

"But she hasn't apologised for not thanking you in the first place," Daisy said indignantly.

What a cow, Katya thought.

"Quite right, Daisy. More of the same, I think." Again, Katya's clitoris and bumhole received unwelcome attention. "Carry on, Honey."

"I am very sorry not to have asked permission to speak, Madam. I am slave item Honey, I haven't been told my type yet. I was… obtained yesterday. Rings were inserted in my clitoris, nipples and nose – "

"I've told you before about giving yourself airs of modesty, Honey. You will refer to your tits. And you'll call your arse your arse and your cunt your cunt."

"I'm very sorry, Madam. Rings were inserted in my tits, I mean. After that, Mr - er - Walpole, he… made love to me. And then you… trained me, and I went to the gym –"

"How did I train you?"

"You stuck a strap-on dildo up my cunt and… arse. And you flogged me with a strap, and gave me electric shocks."

"Did you enjoy that?"

"No, Madam."

"But at the time you said you did. Why was that?"

"I got electric shocks if I kept quiet or protested, Madam."

"I think the other slave items have heard enough to form a judgement. What do you say, is Honey a hypocrite?"

"She's admitted it, Madam."

"She hesitates before words, because she's thinking what to say to make a good impression."

"She was very rude to you, Madam, not asking permission to speak and not apologising, which shows she doesn't mean what she says when she's being polite." This was Daisy again, on her favourite theme.

"It looks as if the others believe you're a hypocrite, Honey. Are you going to make that unanimous?"

There didn't seem much point in not agreeing. Katya hadn't learnt much, but she'd learnt enough to know that her persecutors would get their way, and if she resisted, the punishment would be greater.

"Yes, Madam, I admit that I'm a hypocrite."

"Then beg to be suitably punished and have your behaviour corrected."

"Please may I be punished and corrected, Madam."

"You may. Your punishment will have to be severe, I'm afraid. You will not enjoy your punishment, but hopefully the lesson it teaches you will remain. The rest of you items here will be able to watch, as a reward."

There was a murmur of excitement and gratitude, which Katya was sure was genuine.

Katya was led out by her trainer to her cubic cell. Over the next day she would be prepared for the punishment theatre, where she would be made an example of before her fellow-slaves, in as spectacular a way as possible.

CHAPTER FOUR:

STEFAN AND TANYA

Tanya took the last rack of crockery out of the washing-up machine, put them in a cupboard, and dried her hands on a tea towel by the sink.

"I've finished the washing-up, Mrs Ellington."

"Oh good. Well, you can go then. Remember, we open early tomorrow, because of the sales. There'll be a lot of customers wanting an early breakfast. So be here by seven o'clock sharp."

"Yes, Mrs Ellington."

Tanya sighed. I suppose I should be grateful, she thought to herself. At least it's not burger flipping. Ellington's catered for the affluent shoppers of Kensington and Knightsbridge, and provided such things as toasted teacakes and muffins (real muffins, not the awful American cakes) and poached eggs on toast for the well-to-do clientèle. It was only that, well, Tanya had a Ph.D. in Economics from Sofia University, and had rather hoped to get a better job in England. But she was not very fluent in English as yet, and would have to wait until she had passed the Cambridge Proficiency Exam before she would be able realistically to aspire to a job that her degree entitled her. Her husband, Stefan, had the same problem. He was working as a plumber, but had a higher degree too – his was in physics.

Tanya pulled her thoughts away from depressing topics and tried to find a bright side to look on. One of the few advantages of a waitressing job was that you didn't have to take either work or the cares of the job home with you. Not that Tanya was going home. As she walked to the rendezvous she felt a surge of excitement and a slight apprehension. She had wanted to go home and change, but Victoria had insisted that wasn't necessary.

"No need to dress up for me, my dear," Victoria had explained over the telephone. "I'm not interested in your clothes. In any case, it's best if we meet early in the evening. Gives more time for fun and games later, doesn't it? - if you still want to play them after we've met and introduced ourselves, that is."

*

Tanya and Stefan loved each other very much, but early in their married life they'd realised there was a problem – a sexual problem. Stefan was deeply submissive, and Tanya was rather submissive too. They'd tried switching – taking it in turns to be dom and sub, and spanking each other's bottoms – but it hadn't worked. Neither had wanted the dominant rôle and found playing it boring and a real sexual turn-off. Moreover, playing at being a slave appealed to neither of them – they both wanted actually to be one. So, despite the real attractiveness each found in the other, neither was able to satisfy the other's sexual cravings.

One day, Stefan came home from work late.

"I've been to a sex-shop in Soho," he explained. "I found this. I think it might solve our problem." He put a magazine on the table. "It's a contact magazine. We can get in touch with a dominant who's willing to master both of us. There are instructions for placing ads here, at the back. It doesn't cost very much."

"But Stefan, I love you. I suppose I might get some sexual pleasure being the slave of a dominant man, but it wouldn't be right. I'd feel I was betraying you. Anyway, you never know what creeps might read a magazine like that. We might attract anyone!"

"The same thought occurred to me. How would you feel about being dominated by a woman, though?"

Tanya thought about it. At first she demurred, but the photographs of leather-clad whip-wielding women in the magazine did rather appeal, giving her a warm, masochistic feeling in the pit of her belly. She wasn't lesbian, she thought… but nevertheless…. The idea of Stefan being enslaved by another woman made naughty ideas she hadn't thought she had run through her mind too….

She looked through the magazine again, and then glanced up at Stefan: "I'll get you your dinner."

All through dinner, Tanya was thoughtful. Then she said, "All right, it's worth a try."

They spent that evening preparing an ad for the magazine. It was quite fun, Tanya thought. They took photos of each other, naked. Tanya lay on her belly, a cushion under her belly, her legs splayed out, giving a good view of her naked backside and her pussy, which in her excitement, was engorged and glistening.

Tanya took a photo of her man standing, holding his erect cock, his balls tight and bulging beneath his fist. Tanya noticed with interest a little dribble of spunk had appeared at the end of his shaft. Naturally his face was not in the photo.

The wording of the ad took some thought, especially as neither of them were proficient in English. They scribbled out drafts on the back of discarded A4 printouts, and eventually came up with the version they sent to the magazine, along with their photographs:

Young submissive couple GSOH, she 23, he 24, WLTM strict dominant lady who knows how to put them in their place and keep them there. BDSM allowed and expected. No fees given or received. London.

Stefan was dubious about the stipulation of "no fees". He thought most of the dominants in the magazine were professionals, and would expect some fee, but Tanya was adamant.

*

A month passed, and there was no reply to their ad. Tanya had almost forgotten about it, well it was a crazy idea anyway, when they got a letter from Victoria:

"I am a life-style dominatrix who specialises in training young submissives. If they're not prepared to pay a fee though, they must allow themselves to be wholly owned by me, and become my property. However, we can talk this through at some neutral rendezvous, perhaps a pub somewhere, preferably in West London."

Victoria included a photo of herself with the letter. She was dressed in a shiny rubber outfit, and was brandishing a long, whippy cane. She was an attractive thirty-something woman, but thin-lipped, with a cruel expression on her face. She was Tanya's idea of a haughty, aristocratic English lady, and her pussy went wet as she contemplated the photograph. I want to be her slave, Tanya thought. Victoria had given a telephone number, and Stefan and Tanya arranged to meet her.

*

Tanya walked towards the rendezvous with some degree of trepidation mingled with a good deal of excitement. It was a rather old fashioned pub called The Rising Sun in an out of the way side street, Hob's Lane, off Knightsbridge. Stefan and Victoria were already there when she arrived, lodged in an alcove. They spoke softly, but in any case there was nobody else in the pub so early in the evening.

The photo had not flattered Victoria. She looked more attractive and much less formidable in the flesh – a rather feminine woman, in fact, the sort a casual observer would expect to pretend to be afraid of mice and not know how to mend a fuse. Appearance was to prove deceptive, however.

While Stefan was buying Tanya a drink, Victoria said, "He's very submissive isn't he? I won't have much trouble training him. You're not interested in enslaving him yourself?" Tanya shook her head emphatically. "Are you sure? A male slave is an asset to any woman."

"Oh no." Tanya shuddered. The idea of dominating a man was repugnant to her. "I wouldn't want to do that. I – I wouldn't enjoy it at all."

"What would you enjoy?" Victoria smiled impishly and lifted a gin and vermouth to her lips.

"Well, I'm submissive like him." That wasn't quite true, Tanya realised. She blushed. She was submissive, and the prospect of being dominated turned her on, but it wasn't the obsession with her it was with Stefan. She could have had ordinary sex with Stefan if he had been able to provide it. "I want to be dominated by another."

"Another man or another woman?"

"Well, a man would be best, I suppose. But I'd feel disloyal to Stefan. And then, a man is likely to be too –er – fierce."

"You mean rough."

"Yes."

"Well, some men might be. But you've no objection to being dominated by another woman? Would it arouse you?" When she saw Tanya hadn't followed, Victoria used simpler English and spoke slowly, "You are happy to be made a slave by a woman? It would make you feel sexy?"

Tanya blushed again, and a slight frown crossed Victoria's face, as if she was wondering whether Tanya had been raised in a nunnery.

"Yes I think so," Tanya said.

Stefan had returned with Tanya's beer in time to hear the last remarks.

"We both are very obedient slaves," he said.

Victoria said nothing and raised her glass as if in thought. "You don't want to pay a fee, I take it. I give sessions to some clients and the usual fee is £60 per hour. I charge couples £80 per hour, which is good value I'll think you'll agree."

The couple looked horrified. "We can't afford anything like that," said Stefan.

"No. Well, in that case, as I said in my letter, I would only be prepared to dominate you on the strict understanding that you regarded yourselves as my property. You'd be slaves twenty-four hours a day, you'd have to do everything you were told, and you'd be caned if you didn't. You might be given a thrashing anyway, just because I felt like giving you one. You'd have no rights, and you'd be locked in a cell when I had no use for you. You'd usually be in bondage, you'd have to wear a slave collar and piercings. You'd perform sexually whenever you were commanded, and when not explicitly commanded, sex would be absolutely forbidden and masturbation severely chastised. So would an erect cock or wet pussy when they weren't supposed to be aroused. Your genitalia would be my property to do what I liked with, just like the rest of you. I'd give you a very thorough acquaintance with my suite of punishment rooms, and you'd find yourselves regularly bound, beaten and humiliated until I was satisfied I had trained you into complete subservience. When that point was reached, you wouldn't want to disobey me in any circumstances, and would be absolutely compliant. After a while I'd get bored with you, since you no longer presented me with a challenge, and sell you on. There are plenty of buyers out there looking for slave flesh, you know."

"But what about our jobs? I am plumber, and Tanya is waitress."

"Oh you'd have to give them up, wouldn't you? Of course it's true, if a slave's a very high earner, I keep him at his job and his salary goes into my bank account at the end of the month. He can't escape because he would only have a little pocket money on him and no credit or debit cards. In any case, I lock him into a chastity belt, with an electrode wrapped round his penis. It can be switched on by a pager link. I say "penis" because high earners are usually male in this stupid patriarchal society we live in. But a similar arrangement can be fitted on a woman. But none of that applies to you, because you've only rather menial jobs."

"Oh." Tanya had been able to follow the gist of what Victoria had said. She was astonished at the cool way she recounted her domination practices. Victoria evidently knew from experience that being frank about her methods attracted rather than repelled her victims. Now Tanya had to decide whether she could endure all that pain and humiliation. If she did so, she knew it would be mainly for Stefan's sake. She wasn't as masochistic as he. She would let him decide.

"There's one more thing. I do work free-lance, but sometimes sell my slaves through an organisation which trains them with the object of selling them to rich customers worldwide."

"Oh, in that case, we couldn't agree to it," Tanya said. "I couldn't bear to be separated from Stefan."

The couple held hands, and Stefan said, "We must always be together."

The expression on Victoria's face was cynical, as if she thought they were a pathetic pair of cooing love-birds.

"Oh I shouldn't worry about that if I were you. Slaves find, after a while, that what they want and what their masters and mistresses want coincide. Not at first, of course. But you'll find that your likes and dislikes will change with time. But I'll see what I can do about keeping you together," she added vaguely. "Maybe I'll arrange for you to have matching slave-collars, or tag your genital rings or something. Although we're into bondage, it's not in our interest to separate couples who are bonded to each other." She smiled.

Neither Tanya nor Stefan were able to follow that argument. They didn't understand words like "tag", and the pun on "bondage" and "bonded" was too difficult for their limited command of English.

"Never mind, dearies. Just take it that you'll soon find yourselves happy doing everything you're told. You might not be able to have sex with each other – sometimes I might let you, though."

Tanya wasn't so worried about not being able to have sex with Stefan. After all, they didn't have sex now. That was why they had advertised for a dominant in the first place. Even so, she was still apprehensive. Would she really want to be owned and controlled by this strange, mysteriously seductive, English lady?

Stefan, however, had no doubts.

"Madam, I shall be your slave. May I kiss your beautiful leather boots?"

"Certainly not Stefan. Not here anyway. You may do so when we get back to my house." Victoria laughed. "The night, as they say, is young."

Stefan had agreed to it! Then Tanya had no choice, she thought. It was evidently her fate to be the slave of this lady, too. She said as much.

"All right. Then if you've made your minds up, there's no point hanging around here anymore. When you've finished your beers, we'll go back to my place."

Stefan drained the last of his beer and Tanya left most of hers (she was not all that fond of alcoholic drinks) and Victoria led them to her car, a Lamborghini. Victoria was evidently a wealthy woman.

*

The Lamborghini purred up the drive of the large square house set off the road somewhere near Wimbledon village. The garage doors opened automatically at the same time that a bell rang in the house, telling the servants that their mistress had returned. Before Victoria and the two young foreigners reached the side-door of the house it too was opened by a young woman – a pretty, buxom maid.

"Welcome home, mistress," the maid said as Victoria swept into the most luxurious drawing room Tanya and Stephan had ever seen.

"Bring me some tea."

"Yes, Mistress. Tea for three?"

"No, just for me. These two won't have time for tea. They'll be too bound up in their work."

When the maid left the drawing room Victoria said, "Time to unwrap my presents I think. Strip naked. Let's see you in your birthday suits."

By the time the maid returned, the two new slaves were standing to attention, perfectly nude, their hands on their heads. Victoria was looking at them judiciously, patting her left palm with a riding crop she was holding in her right.

"Excited are we, Stefan?" she said, flicking the crop over Stefan's erect shaft.

"Yes, Mistress," Stefan said.

"Well, we shouldn't be, should we?" said Victoria, bringing the crop down hard across Stefan's naked backside. "We're only hard when Mistress – gives – permission!" The crop cracked twice across Stefan's cock so it became soft at once. "Maria, stay," she said to the maid. "I didn't tell you you could leave. Now you," she continued, addressing Stefan again, "open your thighs."

Stefan obeyed, and Victoria flicked the crop upwards

between his legs, painfully catching his balls. She repeated rapid upward strokes, so the riding crop became a blur, and Stefan was yelling in agony.

Victoria stopped at last, admired her handiwork and chuckled. "Did you like watching your husband get his balls whipped, Tanya?"

"No, Mistress," Tanya said, still standing to attention with her hands on her head, her legs trembling slightly.

"Liar!" Tanya's rump was stung with the riding crop and then the crop was pushed into her sex-slit. "Of course you did! You'll always make sure you like everything I do to either of you from now on, won't you?"

"Yes, Mistress."

"Stefan, your balls have gone blue. Thank me for beating your balls, Stefan."

"Thank you, Mistress."

"I suppose you do want to keep them, don't you?"

"Yes, Mistress, of course."

"There's no 'of course' about it. If you want to keep them you'll have to be on your best behaviour from now on. Any objectionable machismo and I might decide you have to learn to use your bottom as your principle erogenous zone."

"Maria, hoik your skirt up, turn round and bend over. That's right, right over. Touch your toes. Stick your nose between your knees."

A large dildo had been plugged into Maria's anus.

"Maria is trying to make her anus more sensitive. Aren't you, Maria?"

"Yes, Mistress."

"Yes. Tell the two slaves here about the discipline regime I've given you since you were enslaved."

"Mistress shafts me with a strap-on dildo in both... my passages. By degrees I've been introduced to thicker and longer dildos."

"Have you enjoyed that?"

"Not at first, Mistress, but I get an orgasm every time now, especially when you spank my arse."

Tanya was several inches taller than the woman who presumed to dominate her and suddenly it was all too much. She went up to her, slapped her about the face, kneed her in the belly, and said, in Bulgarian: "Stefan, I think we'll go. This woman is a pervert. Get your clothes on."

"Yes, you have to put your clothes on before you leave, don't you?" Victoria said through gritted teeth. Though she hadn't understood the words, Tanya's meaning was clear enough.

Victoria seethed with anger. That was very rare with her. Chastising a slave was a happy experience which sometimes aroused her sexually and often amused her. Occasionally it was desirable to simulate anger, but she hardly ever felt it. Indeed, it was dangerous to lose one's temper, one might damage the slave, and slaves were valuable livestock. In any case, the affection she showed Maria was quite genuine. She grew to have an affection for most of her slaves (who were after all just domestic animals) so much so that parting with them at the auction always pulled at her heart strings a little. But this Tanya cow inspired nothing but rage and loathing.

While the Tanya slave was struggling into her clothes, Victoria took a cell phone out of her handbag and called for assistance. She was pleased to see that the male animal had remained obediently standing to attention, hands on head. Perhaps he realised that his partner's desperate attempt to escape would not succeed, perhaps he had taken to heart the warning of possible castration if he was disobedient.

Within a short time, a broad-shouldered muscular slave entered the room. He was naked, except for the chastity belt which curtailed the activity of an enormous cock, and from which hung handcuffs and a gag. He easily threw Tanya to the ground belly first, sat on her, and applied the handcuffs and the gag, which was soaked in ether. Then he ripped off the skirt and panties she had managed to put back on.

"Take her to the punishment suite."

The unconscious slave was thrown over her assailant's shoulder, and carried out of the room.

Stefan and Maria were still in the postures they had been ordered to adopt. Victoria was pleased with them, and said so.

"Well done, especially you, Stefan. You resisted the temptation to obey your wife, who's just a slave – and a female slave is just tits and arse and a cunt on legs, and isn't to be obeyed of course. Maria, you may get up and leave the room. Stefan, I promised you I'd let you kiss my boots, didn't I? As a reward, you may do it now. Get down on all fours. Make sure to lick them thoroughly: remove all the dirt."

She sat down in an armchair next to a side table where Maria had put the tea things, and poured herself a cup of tea. She sipped it, with one leg crossed over the other, while Stefan licked her shiny, black, thigh-length leather boots.

As Stefan was eagerly enjoying his reward, Victoria said: "Hunk, the slave who dealt with your wife, wasn't always the strapping chap you saw just then. He's been beefed up with steroids and testosterone and plenty of weight-lifting exercises and running on a treadmill. I had his cock enlarged too. There's a big demand for he-man types, and he'll fetch a great deal at auction I daresay. In the meantime he acts as my guard and minder." Victoria looked at the slave cowering at her feet thoughtfully. "Would you like to be transformed, Stefan? Would you like to be a big strong boy with a huge cock? Or maybe a sissy boy with a tiny cock? You'd make your mistress lots of money if you were."

"I – I'm not sure, Mistress."

"No, well, perhaps the idea needs time to get used to. When I transform a slave, he always wants to be transformed, because he always wants to obey me. And why do you think that is? Why do you think big, muscular Hunk obeys a little woman like me? Stop licking for the moment and tell me what you think the reason is."

"I suppose it's because of the chastity belt, Mistress. Does it have an electrode in it like you mentioned when we were in the pub?"

"Well, yes it does, but that's not the real reason." There was a pause. "No ideas?"

"No, Mistress."

"It's simply that he believes he's a slave and has to obey, and so do I. Deep down, he wants to obey me, and he knows he has to. And I want him to obey, and I know he has to, too. Do you understand now?"

"I think so, Mistress."

"You're the same, aren't you, Stefan? You know you have to obey me as well, don't you?" When Stefan readily agreed, Victoria added, "Every slave comes to realise she's not just playing a rôle or doing something out of a fear of punishment. She's a slave because her inner nature is servile, and she can't be anything else. Tanya will come to that realisation, too, sooner or later, probably later, but I'll break her eventually, be sure of that."

*

Over the course of the next hour or so, Victoria gave detailed instructions to Hunk and to Rex, another similarly endowed slave. Tanya and Stefan were set in position for the first stage of their training, which, after what had happened, would obviously have to be Tanya's punishment.

Tanya was doubled – hanging by her wrists and ankles from a single hook in the punishment cell. Her head was forced between her legs by rubber straps, and she was gagged with a metal bit coated with rubber that dug deeply into her mouth, forcing her jaws apart. A tight chain looped round her torso and legs. Tit-rings were clipped to it, so her boobs were squeezed painfully through her legs. A long thick dildo had been rammed without lubrication into her anus, and a vibrator that might have served a mare was thrust deep into her sex, buzzing and chuckling.

The brutally shafted vagina, the anus stretched and tortured, breasts squeezed and pulled by newly-emplaced tit rings, and above the whole, a face goggle-eyed, gagged and red-cheeked: in such a way had the rebellious Tanya been reduced to a humiliated whipping object. She was able to see that for herself, moreover: a long mirror had thoughtfully been placed opposite her.

Against the opposite wall of the cell, too, a ball-gagged Stefan was mounted in a stiff rubber surround which sealed his feet together and reached up to his thighs – a sort of boot for both legs. Steel bands, connected to a steel pole behind him, surrounded his naked body, and his forearms were also tightly bonded to the pole. A posture collar kept his chin up and head forwards. The whole effect of his restraints was to keep his legs, torso and head stiffly erect. They were not the only things kept erect. He had been injected with Viagra, so that his penis was ramrod stiff and inserted into a vibrating ring lined with Velcro, fixed on another pole in front of him.

After having them set in position, Victoria had left them alone in the cell, so their predicament had plenty of time to sink in. When she revisited her slaves, the warm smell of sex was in the air: spunk was dribbling from Stefan's wet cock, and Tanya's juice was running down her vulnerable naked buttocks. Victoria took this in gleefully. How she enjoyed dominating and controlling slaves! Her earlier anger had long since disappeared.

"Ah, it's always a pleasure to help a young couple have satisfying sex together. Now, Stefan, you're going to enjoy this evening. You'll be able to witness your wife being caned and shafted. While she's treated to the cane and my strap-on, Stefan, I want you to show your appreciation of your wife's just punishment. I want you to frig yourself off – just so that your wife knows you approve of her treatment at my hands. I want to see lots of spunk spurting out of your cock as your wife is caned and fucked – but not before, mind you, be sure to wait till you get the order. If you don't wank yourself off, you'll be caned as well. Do you understand? – I'm sure you do."

A collection of canes were hanging on a rack along a wall of the cell. Victoria inspected them, and then selected one, four and a half feet long, of gleaming rattan, notched every six inches or so, and about a quarter of an inch thick. She swished it about in the air, as if to test it, and then squared it carefully against Tanya's bottom.

"I think this one will do, don't you, Stefan? Show me your appreciation of my choice."

There was no reaction from Stefan, at first.

"I gave you an order, Stefan." Very quietly, Victoria added, "Do you want your balls caned again?"

Immediately Stefan began plunging his penis in and out of the ring, and the end of his cock became moist once more.

"That's right, Stefan. You've got the idea. I knew a connoisseur of canes like you would approve of this particularly long one. It's the official type used for judicial canings in Singapore. Now you just have a good wank. No one should let affection for a wife stand in the way of his enjoyment. Don't come until I tell you though, or you'll have to have your cock and balls caned. They'll be caned if you're not stiff and caned if you come. Life's not fair, is it, Stefan?'"

Victoria stood a few paces back from Tanya, raised the cane behind her back, then ran up and delivered the first blow. The cane came swishing down across Tanya's rump, level with her anus, leaving a livid red mark. Tanya would have howled, but her gag allowed only a gurgle.

"You've a full view of your punishment, haven't you, Tanya, dear? I'm sure it's gratifying to you to know you're giving some amusement to me and a lot of enjoyment to your lover. How are you, Stefan? Oh, quite well, I see."

Stefan's face was purple as he pumped away.

"I learnt the art of caning recalcitrant slaves from Madam Kwan, you know," Victoria said dreamily, to no one in particular. There was a swish as the cane cracked down again on Tanya's buttocks, and another gurgle. "Madam Kwan is Domino's caning mistress. I think you'll have to be trained by Domino, my dear. There are more resources for dealing with impudent slaves there." Swish! Crack! Gurgle! "Now that's three across the crest of your arse." Victoria paused to contemplate her handiwork. She seemed satisfied. "So far so good. Madam Kwan always recommends one divides the rump into three parts, like Caesar's Gaul," she continued in her self-absorbed way. "The crest, level with the anus, the part beneath the anus level with the pussy, and the first six inches of the thighs or so." Swish! Crack! Gurgle! "Now that's the first stroke across the lower part – actually above, since you're hanging bent double. Hurts more, doesn't it? Your arse will feel like you've been sitting on hot coals by the time I've finished with you." Swish! Crack! Gurgle! "Of course, sending you to Domino means me having to share the profit from your sale with them," Victoria said as if to herself, "but better that than end up with a slave only half-trained. I'd get complaints from the customer then, and that would never do, one has one's reputation to consider." Swish! Crack! Gurgle! "Now the thighs." The cane lashed across the top of Tanya's thighs. Her body contorted and she screamed under her gag. "That's really painful, isn't it? I bet you're regretting being such an insolent cow, aren't you? Well, two more across the thighs, for now." Two more strokes were delivered in quick succession, causing Tanya to writhe in agony, in so far as her bonds allowed. "There, there, didums hurt ums?" Victoria chuckled. "Never mind, my dear, you're a quarter of the way through, now. Only another twenty seven strokes of the cane to go."

Victoria returned her attention to the crest of the rump, which was soon criss-crossed with vivid red overlying cane marks, and then methodically treated the rest of Tanya's buttocks to the cane again, giving each part three strokes and then going on to the next. At the end of thirty six strokes, Tanya's buttocks were raw.

"Well, that's enough of the cane, I think. Now all that remains is to whip your tits and snatch with a scourge and you're sorted."

Victoria selected another instrument of chastisement hanging along the cell wall. Many long, thin rubber lashes were attached to a short wooden handle. Victoria held it above her head, the handle in her right hand and the end of the lashes in her left, and examined the vulnerable target between Tanya's legs.

"Hm, we'll have to have you depilated, won't we dear? I forgot about that in all the excitement. Never mind."

The scourge came down and the thin lash raked Tanya's sex gash, still wet and glistening as the vibrator buzzed away inside it.

"By the way, Stefan, time to spill your spunk, juicy boy."

Victoria swung the lashes of the scourge in a circular motion, catching Tanya's quim as it came round again and again. Tanya broke out in a long gurgling wail. At the same time, Stefan's buttocks quivered, his penis thrust forward, and milky semen splashed across the floor.

Victoria laughed ecstatically. "Well done, Stefan! Tanya, that's a lovely noise! Let's hear more of it!"

*

After Victoria had thoroughly whipped Tanya's tits with the scourge, she felt aroused and so had both slaves handcuffed and gagged and taken to her room. Instead of shafting Tanya as she had originally planned, she gave Stefan an over-the-knee spanking and then ordered him to lick her sex until she came.

"You can watch, Tanya. I promised you two would be together, didn't I?"

As she orgasmed she noticed that Stefan was about to come again as well. She slapped his tool vigorously to cut it down to size. "No, no! We can't have that, naughty boy, can we? What would your wife think? Let me see you hump your wife. Tanya! Touch your toes! Nose between your legs, that's it! Go on, then, Stefan, what are you waiting for? Do it!"

She lashed him across the backside with a rubber flogger. Stefan was soon vigorously humping away, to the great amusement of his new mistress.

Then she rang for Hunk, and had them both removed to separate slave-pens for the night.

*

The next morning the two slaves were gagged, and fitted with slave collars, handcuffs, and manacles that were fastened together on short chains. Then they were deposited in the boot of Victoria's Bentley and transported to Domino's London training centre, which was to be their home for a while. Tanya became "Bimbo" but Stefan's new name was reserved until Victoria decided whether to transform him into a sissy she-male or a strongman.

CHAPTER FIVE:

LIFE ON THE FARM

Shortly after the acquisition of Honey, Bimbo, and the male slave item formerly called Stefan, James Walpole asked Victoria to come into his office.

"Ever heard of Lady Marianne de Vere, Vicky?"

"The Marianne de Vere? If it's the one who regularly appears in the society columns, I should think everyone's heard of her. Born Marianne erm, Spriggs, wasn't she? - and then she became a model, I think, and adopted the professional name of Carter. I know she married the billionaire Sir Lionel de Vere. In the circles I frequent, they're celebrated for their BDSM parties. I've recruited quite a few of my slaves there. It's really amazing how many submissive women there are in London. They walk into my dungeons as if they were expensive saunas or massage parlours. And then I enslave them – permanently."

"Yes. I've noticed how successful you are at recruiting slaves for Domino. And you do it free-lance as well, I believe. I've often wondered how you manage to avoid the attention of the law – not that I mind, as long as you keep Domino's name out of it. But the police ought to have been alerted to the disappearance of so many young women, I should have thought."

"You would have thought so, wouldn't you? Far be it from me to suggest anyone was bribed, but…"

"Ah, quite. Well, bribery is a useful instrument of social intercourse. Where would Domino be without it? Anyway, Vicky, Lady de Vere has recently become an online member, and has told us she wants to buy our slaves, particularly hunters and racing mares."

"She's no different from a lot of our other clients in that respect, surely?"

"No. But she's potentially one of our richest clients, and that's saying something, so I think we have to humour her. She could become a valued customer, once we have her confidence. I can see her buying a few dozen of our slaves every year or so. Mainly females, apparently. But she emailed me today to say she's not completely happy about buying online before she's seen the quality of the merchandise in the flesh, so to speak."

"Good Lord. We have a return policy if customers aren't completely satisfied. What's she got to lose buying online? Anyone would think she was down to her last million."

"Well the very rich are often a bit quirky. And they have a habit of being careful with their money. That's why they became rich in the first place, I suppose. As I say, I think we have to humour her."

"And so… how are you going to do that?"

"Well, that's why I wanted to see you. I want you to show her round our training farm in Guatemala. Lady de Vere is particularly interested in hunters and racers, and maybe a few show ponies. Apparently she's willing to fly out there at her own expense – she's taking a holiday as well. Otherwise I should have said no."

"What!? I should drop everything I'm doing and fly out to Guatemala just because some spoilt rich bitch wants me to show her round our farm there? No way!"

"All expenses paid, of course. And you can have a two weeks' paid holiday there after that, if you want. And a five hundred pound bonus."

"Oh. Oh, all right then."

After Victoria Stratton had left, Walpole smiled to himself. Yes, it was true, bribery was a useful instrument of social intercourse.

*

"So here, Lady de Vere, are the fillies who are being trained for hunting." It was early in the morning. Victoria Stratton led the way into one of the stables, which smelt strongly of stale sweat and urine.

"Oh, wonderful!" Lady de Vere clapped her hands. "I can see Domino has the right attitude to training. I might buy a few of these."

"When they're fully trained they'll by offered for sale online. But if you want to put in an offline bid for any of them, I'm sure Domino would consider that."

Victoria had just opened the door of a stable holding six naked women being trained as hunters. There were other stables for the lighter racing mares and the more petite show ponies, but in the initial phase of their training, all types were trained in the same way. The slaves were chained against the wall, three on each side. The hunters were all fine animals with a lot of stamina – tall, with long limbs, broad shoulders and large round breasts, which would be a delight for any purchaser. It was true, the breasts might be a hindrance when the animal was at full gallop, but an appropriate harness would sort out that problem. Their nubs had been pierced with rings – they were for carrying the little bells that would tinkle as they cantered along. Their buttocks were tight and apple-shaped, and their depilated sex-holes, which were all on view, were generally larger than average. Their clitorises were also ringed – they, too, would carry charming tinkling bells when, fully trained, they were displayed at the race course or on the hunting field.

Each slave was kneeling, facing away from the wall. Each ankle was chained to the wall, and each wrist was cuffed to the wall behind too, at the level of the head, so the slave's back had a nicely curved shape, uncomfortable for the slave, but pleasant for anyone contemplating the sight, with tits well presented, and depilated pussies jutting out between splayed legs. The legs were splayed across an enamel basin which took the animal's excrement. One of the slave items was pissing as Ms Stratton and Lady de Vere entered the room.

The fillies were gagged with funnel gags that held their jaws open, so that they were constantly dribbling saliva on their tits, which was certainly amusing to Ms Stratton and Lady de Vere, but the loss of fluid meant the slaves were desperately thirsty.

One filly's tongue was dragged out of her mouth through the funnel gag. A chain was clamped on the tip of her tongue. On the end of the chain, level with her breasts, hung a heavy weight. She dribbled saliva furiously.

"Why that arrangement?" Lady de Vere asked, in an amused tone of voice.

"I imagine her trainer thinks she doesn't use her tongue well enough. All these items are expected to service their trainers sexually."

Lady de Vere laughed. "My, they do make a lovely sight! You know I far prefer mares to stallions. Of course, there's a certain frisson in dominating the opposite sex, and they are stronger – which is useful if you're a serious huntswoman, but in the end, I can't help feeling they're a disappointment in a way, not nearly as graceful."

"We have some very handsome stallions I'll show you later." The customer was always right, but on the other hand, Domino's business was selling slaves of both sexes. "It's time to feed and water them now. I thought I'd show you myself, rather than let the trainer do it. There's a feeder above the head of each slave, as you can see."

Stratton indicated a device which looked at first sight rather like a wall-mounted phone, but the handset was a black, rubber-coated phallic-shaped pipe, and a rubber tube led from it instead of a cord. There were digital indicators nearby that measured pints.

"We feed them on swill. We have an arrangement with

local cafés and restaurants in the area. We run a pig-farm, you see, so we have a convincing cover story. The swill's liquidised, and then all the vitamins, minerals, proteins and calories our animals require for a day's hard exercising are added, if they're lacking."

Lady de Vere giggled. "It must taste disgusting."

"I suppose it must, but they don't taste it, it's squirted straight down their throats. There's no possibility of them refusing their fodder. Look, I'll show you."

Victoria Stratton picked up the dildo pipe from above the head of the nearest slave, and rammed it into her gagged-open mouth, pushing its nine inch length all the way down the slave's throat. Then she flicked a switch, and the whine of an electric pump could be heard as the feed was squirted down the slave's gullet.

After thirty seconds or so, Stratton said: "Now I turn this other switch here, and the machines pumps water into her stomach instead."

The whine stopped for a short time and then started again as the slave was filled up with water. Marianne de Vere looked on delightedly. It was rather like a car's tank being filled with petrol. The slave's stomach began to look distended.

"That seems quite a lot of water."

"About five pints. Their constant salivation dehydrates them fairly quickly in this heat. Anyway, it's amusing to watch them piss as they trot about – and they're going to be doing quite a lot of trotting pretty soon. Now it's time to feed and water the rest. I'd better get a trainer to help me, or we'll be here all day."

"Can I help?" Lady de Vere asked, like a little girl begging her mother for an ice-cream.

"Of course, if you want to. But be careful to watch the quantities. No more than a pint of swill and five pints of water."

De Vere went to work with alacrity, ramming the pipes down the animals' throats, filling them up with swill and water, watching with amused fascination as their bloated stomachs swelled out like taut balloons.

"There, there," she said to one filly, patting her stomach gently. "Was that nice? I think I'm going to buy you."

When all the slaves had been fed and watered at last, Victoria told lady de Vere what the day's next chore was.

"The next thing is putting them in harness. That can be a bit tricky, so I think I do need a trainer to assist me now."

"I'm sure I could do it if you showed me how."

"Watch me and the trainer do the first one, and then maybe you can help with the others."

When the trainer arrived as a result of a call on the internal phone, he and Victoria got to work. Victoria gave Marianne de Vere a running commentary as they went to work on the slave that had been fed first.

"The first thing to do is to unbuckle the slave's cuffs and refasten the arms behind her back. The slave can't take advantage from her arms being temporarily free, because she can't rise from her kneeling position. In any case, the idea of a slave seriously resisting a trainer is ridiculous. These slave items have already been conditioned to think of themselves as animals, and training's really only a matter of enhancing their horsy skills. Now, as you see, short rubber straps bind left wrist to right elbow, right wrist to left elbow. Now, we unlock her ankle cuffs and help her to stand. Whoops-a-daisy! There you are. After a night of kneeling on stone tiles they find it difficult to stand at first." Then she turned to the slave and spoke as if she was addressing a dumb animal. "Have you got pins and needles then? Better do some trotting on the spot. There we go! Higher! Get those knees up!" These instructions were accompanied by a few stinging blows with a riding crop across the slave's thighs. "That's enough! Stop! Now we take off the funnel gag and replace it with a bridle and bit. All horsies have to wear a bridle, don't they? And we'll remember that horsies don't talk, won't we? We know what happens to us if we try to talk, don't we? Nod your head if you understand." Slowly the mare nodded her head. The gag was removed and replaced by a bridle with a ferocious looking bit. "Now then, we know what comes next, don't we horsy? Bend over!" Victoria Stratton held up a long black dildo, and Lady de Vere tittered with glee. "They're plugged front and back, and we coat the dildos with a lubricant that stings like hell. It keeps the beasts frisky, and their minds focussed on their holes, where we want them to be. The dildo in the front has a battery inside it. It can vibrate, to reward, or deliver a nasty shock, to punish. But it's best to start with the back passage. Doing the front first risks them losing control of their bowels. We don't want that, do we, horsy? At least not yet. I push this one up her back passage very slowly. It's hollow, so the mare trains with her anus wide open. So she'll be dumping crap like a B52 soon. Which is what horses do, don't they, horsy? Nod if you agree." The mare nodded, and Marianne de Vere giggled again.

When the mare had been plugged front and back, Victoria pulled tightly on the crotch strap. "I buckle it up tight so it bites into their crotch and makes the dildos even more – what shall I say? – salient. Soon they're skipping around like jack rabbits."

"But with that crotch strap – how do they wee?"

"Oh, they piss through this slit in the strap here, do you see? They'll be doing that a lot."

"I see. How wonderful!"

Lady de Vere was very impressed by everything she saw, particularly the attention to detail evident in all the training practices and the equipment. She examined one of the harnesses hanging along the end-wall. The harness had been designed to completely control the fillies. None of them would be able to do so much as to raise an eyebrow without the permission of her trainer. The tight crotch strap held in place the importunate dildos that nuzzled into those parts of her body which for a free woman were private and reserved. The dildos constantly reminded a slave simply by being where they were, that she was merely a domestic animal, and therefore property, like any other domestic animal. They stung and sexually aroused her. The dildo stuffing her vagina could punish her with electric shocks, or reward her with sexual feelings, and she would accept those feelings, she would embrace them, just like the animal she was. The dildo up her back passage would ensure she shat were she was, like any mare or cow, and over time she learnt to accept she was no better than a mare or a cow.

The rest of her harness was equally controlling. The tight waist strap had pins inlaid on the inner side, to make her life as uncomfortable as possible. When it came to humiliating and causing pain to the slave, no detail was overlooked. Although her treatment was sadistic, the sadism had a purpose. Everything was done to bring the slave to a realisation that she was entirely property, her fate entirely in the hands of her owners. She was not allowed any opportunity to ignore that fact, to explain it away, to lie to herself that really, one day, she would be a free woman again and everything would be as it had been before she knew Domino.

From the waist strap another strap went up between her breasts to a broad leather posture collar, which held her head up. Then there was a bridle, with a thick bit which held her jaws apart. Her breasts were enclosed in tight leather straps, that squeezed them out and prevented them from drooping. A further strap circled the slave item round the top of the breasts pinioning her arms, and shoulder straps were attached to it. There were metal rings on the shoulder straps, the purpose of which Lady de Vere could not guess. There was no metal bar connecting her tits as yet, that would come later, but her tits were pierced with metal rings to which were attached little bells, which tinkled as she moved. These, together with the bell attached to the ring at her clitoris, completed her humiliation.

Locked onto her feet was footwear with iron soles that made a clip-clopping noise as the mare walked or trotted or cantered or galloped along. They were so designed that she was forced to stand on her toes.

*

With Victoria and the trainer working hard, with some fumbling help from de Vere, all the fillies were soon fitted out in their tack, and ready for their morning's exercises. A rope led from a ring on the back of the posture collar, to a ring in the centre of the waist strap of the following slave, and the line of six obedient ponies was led clip-clopping along in single file to the exercise shed.

"They're not exercised outside then?" asked de Vere.

"Not at this stage no. We use exercise machines, you see, which allows us to measure exactly how much exercise has been given and how much energy the slave item has expended, and the machines are quite delicate – and expensive to replace. We wouldn't want them exposed to the elements. Hot sunlight and tropical rain would do them no good at all."

There were four exercise machines, arranged in the four corners of the shed, and in the centre was an arrangement somewhat like a carousel - four arms, that could swivel round, at right angles to each other extended from the top of a central column. Two chains led down from the end of each arm and were attached to the rings on the shoulder straps of two of the mares. So that's what those rings are for! Marianne de Vere thought. The trainer concentrated on these two mares, leaving the other four for Victoria to deal with. He gave one of the mares a slash with his whip across her naked behind, and she began to trot round the carousel, of necessity forcing her partner in servitude to trot too.

"Lift those knees up!" There was a crack of the whip. "That's it, right above your waist! Higher!" Another crack. "That's more like it! Well done, horsy!"

The two mares pranced, knees high, round and round the central column, their tit and clit bells tinkling. De Vere was amused to notice their crotches were glistening with juice. They were actually being sexually aroused by this humiliating exercise. De Vere guessed the trainer had switched on their vibrators with the wi-fi device he was holding.

Meanwhile, Victoria Stratton was exercising the other four slaves on the machines. Here the aim was not so much posing leg-work as forcing the slave item to gallop as the canvas tread rolled backwards beneath her feet. Again, chains descending from the ceiling were attached to the shoulder-strap rings, and other taut chains fastened to the side rails of the machine were locked to rings on the waist strap. It was impossible for the mare to fall over and injure herself no matter how fast she was forced to gallop. De Vere noticed approvingly that Stratton started the slaves off with a slow trot, gradually increasing the speed up to a maximum of ten miles an hour, sustaining that, however, for a very brief time.

At the moment she was supervising an attractive tall girl with long black curly hair – the slave de Vere had said she would buy.

"I increase the speed, and the time they maintain it, gradually as the exercises progress, but we're not trying to produce Olympic athletes here, after all. In an actual hunt they would probably be trotting at four miles an hour most of the time, with an occasional canter or gallop. All these horses were selected because they're the sporty type, so they can easily manage that."

"I notice they're all sexually aroused."

"Yep. Their vibrators are buzzing merrily away. They just love being horses – don't you gal?"

Stratton flicked a tawse playfully across the panting horse-slave's belly. The slave item snorted, and emitted a steaming stream of golden piss. It was such an unexpected, and comical reaction, both dominant women burst out laughing.

Eventually, the two groups of slave items were changed round, the four that had been exercising on the machines being put on the carousel, and vice versa.

By the end of the morning, de Vere had seen enough to convince her that Domino was an excellent source of future slaves. She dined with Stratton in her private rooms, and over the meal reserved her chosen slave to be purchased offline when her training was finished.

When she had left, Victoria phoned James Walpole: "I reckon we have a satisfied customer, James. She'll be buying more of our merchandise in the future, you can be sure of that."

CHAPTER SIX:

MR SUZUKI

The day after her first training session, Katya – she still couldn't think of herself as slave item Honey even though she knew she would betray herself sooner or later and get more grief – was being prepared for her performance in the punishment theatre by her personal trainer, Mr Short. She spent most of the morning being trained how to crawl on a leash attached to her nose ring. The leash was kept short, and pulled up high, so Katya's nose was forced to point ceiling-wards. This meant she couldn't clearly see where she was going, and had to rely on her trainer's directions. It also meant that her back was severely arched, forcing the posteriors to protrude nicely, a sight the audience would appreciate. The directions were given by Mr Short's electric prod. A turn to left or right was signalled by a shock to the appropriate bum-cheek: a prod in the posterior cleavage meant: go straight on; a yank on the leash meant: stop.

"Good girl, that's right, keep that back arched! Bum up! Good, now when I do that," and he prodded her in the rump. "I want rather more of a reaction…. Again…. Well, that's a little bit better, but it's still not good enough. I want to see a much more pronounced wiggle. Let's try again. Maybe if I shock you lower down this time it'll give you the right idea…." Mr Short stabbed the prod into her sex-slit. "That's much better! Well done! Now I'm going to insert the prod in your anus and I want the same movement, a lot of lateral action and rippling nates…. Excellent! That's it! You've got it! Now, kneel up, attention posture, the way I've taught you, hands behind head, good girl."

Mr Short clamped small bells to Katya's tit rings. "You won't have these on during the performance, they're just for training purposes. Right, down in crawl position, and nose up – high!" he yanked the leash. "Now we'll go forward, and remember, lots of wiggling action, rippling bum-cheeks, ready?"

Katya crawled across the floor of the training room.

"That's good, you're getting the idea now. Now, I want you to extend the lateral action up the torso, so your boobs really swing. And we'll take a few turns round the room, really fast. Ready, wait for it, go!"

Katya found the prod energetically applied to her posteriors and vagina, and desperately tried to please her trainer by wagging her backside for all she was worth.

Her trainer yanked her nose. "Halt. No, I'm not hearing those bells enough. You're not concentrating, Honey. Now, this time, flap those jugs of yours and let me really hear those bells. You've got plenty to flap, after all.

After that, she was blindfolded, and she had to circumnavigate plastic bollards just by following the instructions given to her backside by Mr Short's prod.

It took quite a lot of crawling before Katya was doing it to Mr Short's satisfaction, but eventually he seemed to think she was performing adequately.

She was rehearsed in a new slave position, which was apparently one she would be required to take during the performance. She had to stand up, squat down, and point her pussy at an imaginary audience. She was ordered to do this until it became second nature.

For the next stage in her preparation she was ordered into the hands-behind-head kneeling up position facing a wall, on which was blue-tacked a card. The confession she had to learn was printed on the card, and she was given half an hour to learn it. Then it was touch toes, rump presented for a paddling, and she recited the confession by heart. Any mistake, no matter how insignificant, was rewarded with a hard spank. Given this encouragement, it wasn't long before she had the confession word perfect.

Then she was soaped and hosed down.

*

Katya took the kow-tow position before her trainer which she had been trained to do: knees to breasts, forearms flat on the floor before her, nose touching the floor, rump high. She had a grudging respect for Mr Short. He was a very gentle man, and whenever he punished her, which he did frequently, he always seemed genuinely regretful, and to be doing it reluctantly. With one part of herself, she realised that this was yet another subtle mind game Domino was playing. But that didn't prevent her rather liking her trainer. He was a virile man (he had proved it by entering her many times) and she fantasised that one day they would meet, in circumstances rather more propitious, and have a normal relationship, as man and wife, or at least as man and girl friend.

"Madam Victoria has told you, I suppose, that your punishment is going to be severe?"

"Yes, Sir. What will happen? Shall I be caned?" Mr Short had told her that canings in the punishment theatre were the usual way of dealing with intractable slaves.

"Tomorrow. But today, and initially tomorrow as well, you'll be dealt with by Mr Suzuki, our bondage expert. You will be put, I'm afraid, in a very painful position, and then electrically shocked. You will be in pain all the time, but, as Madam Victoria must have told you, you'll be stronger for the experience. I wish my slaves didn't have to go through this, but it often seems necessary."

Katya felt jealous when Mr Short mentioned those other slaves. "Sir, with all due respect, why is it necessary?"

"Good heavens, slave, haven't you understood anything

I've been trying to teach you? You've been condemned as a hypocrite. That's a horrible crime. You've been saying things you didn't mean. You've been lying to your superiors. How can you suppose that anything less than severe punishment is your due?"

Katya blushed. It had been a silly question, she had to admit. "I'm sorry, Sir. I was being stupid. I mean, I should know I deserve severe punishment, I have learnt my confession speech. But can you tell me…."

"More about the punishment theatre? Well, a picture is worth a thousand words, they say, and a CCTV view is worth a thousand pictures. Sit up, at ease position."

Immediately, the half-trained slave Honey sat up, legs bent under her body, back erect, hands behind head.

Mr Short sighed. "No, girl, that's the attention position." He casually dug the prod into Katya's vagina and shocked her. "When will you learn?"

Katya winced at the pain, and blushed. She should know by now. She placed her palms upwards on her thighs.

Mr Short switched on a plasma screen which gave a view of the punishment theatre, which was just filling up with a slave audience. The first few rows of slaves had already been settled in by their trainers. They were sitting cross-legged, naked on the flag-stones, waiting for the show to begin. The males were without their usual chastity belts. Behind the heads of each line of slaves ran a steel rail to which their slave collars were attached by a short rigid rod, so the slaves were forced to look forwards at the stage, and were unable to move from their positions. Instead of being buckled at the back of a belt, as was normal, their hands were all handcuffed at the front of their bodies, so they could play with themselves. The chains between the cuffs were quite long, too, to allow them to clap, Katya supposed. The female slaves had obtrusive vibrators strapped in their genitals, which were humming away. The male slaves had prominent erections. The whole of the slave audience seemed to be in a sort of erotic trance. There was no mistaking its eager expectancy.

"The males have been injected with Viagra," Mr Short explained.

Katya, who was still alive in the mind which was supposed to be Honey's, noted that Domino didn't seem to have any difficulty obtaining prescription-only drugs.

"Sir, it's not usual to allow slaves to…"

"To wank? No it isn't. Quite right Honey. But when they're watching a slave like yourself being punished, there's a point in it. It conditions them, you see."

"But I should have thought… that seeing another slave being tortured would condition them into being sadistic, rather than masochistic, which Domino wants…"

Mr Short considered the matter. "Hm, an interesting point. You're perceptive and intelligent, Honey. Few of my trainees raise that question. Logically, you're perfectly right. How can I explain it? I can only say that's not how the servile mind works. Masochism and sadism are not so far apart. In fact, the slaves empathise with the tortured slave on the stage; she becomes them, they become her, so to speak. They know if they step out of line, the same thing will happen to them."

An electric bell sounded.

"Well, now, Honey, you're the star: it's time for you to take the floor."

*

But, in fact it wasn't, not at first. At first, Honey waited by the wings on all fours, Mr Short holding her by a leash attached to her nose ring.

From the other wing Mr Walpole came on stage to polite applause to usher on "The Magnificent Suzuki, who needs no introduction." At this, a man dressed in black, wearing a mask and studded collar like a mediaeval executioner, walked onto the stage and bowed, and the applause became tumultuous. Evidently most of the audience had seen his performances before.

"Marvellous stage presence, don't you think?" Mr Short remarked.

Katya had to agree, but her attention was taken by an ominous wooden stock set on a rotatable base centre stage, with hinged steel wings spread out and a cross-piece near the top, and projecting screws with eye-holes at the back. At the base of the stock were coils of rope, and on a nearby table there were an electrical transformer and various electrodes. So far, her fate – Honey's fate – was pretty clear, but why that large clock-face with a single hand? In fact there were two: a large one, centre stage, suspended by wires from the theatre roof, facing the audience, and a small one, at the edge of the stage by the footlights, facing up stage.

"Wake up, that's your cue," Mr Short said, giving Honey a sharp prod in the posterior cleavage.

To the applause of the audience, Mr Short led the reprobate slave Honey on stage by her nose-leash, nose high, posteriors up, and made her do a humiliating, prancing, arse-wiggling crawl round the stage several times, frequently digging the electric prod into her pussy and bum cleavage, and touching the nates when he wanted her to go this way or that. She gave out little squeaks whenever she was shocked. This undignified progress brought hoots of laughter from the audience.

Eventually, the prod manoeuvred the slave item downstage to face Mr Suzuki who was waiting for her with folded arms. Before him, the slave item adopted the kow-tow position her trainer had taught her.

"Slave item Honey," Mr Suzuki said, "tell the audience why you deserve punishment."

Honey recited the speech she had learnt: "Master, I have been condemned for hypocrisy. I have been lying to my superiors, pretending to be an obedient slave when in fact I was secretly harbouring notions of superiority. I have gone so far as to resent my owners' right to control me. I am an extremely wicked slave, and deserve painful punishment, which I hope and desire that you, Master, will visit on me."

There were good-humoured jeers and giggles from the audience at this; most of them knew what was coming.

"I see; anything else?"

"Yes Master. I have been guilty of giving myself airs. I have presumed that I have private parts, like free men and women. I have stubbornly refused to acknowledge that my body is the property of my owners, and that I have no right to privacy whatsoever." There were giggles from the audience. "With a pompous self-importance, I have talked about my vagina, my bottom and my nipples, instead of honestly referring to my cunt, my arse and my tits." The audience howled with derisive laughter.

Mr Suzuki turned his masked face to the audience. "What do you think? Should I let slave item Honey off with a warning this time, or should she be severely punished? It's for you to say."

The reaction of the audience was instantaneous, and the response shook the roof: "Punish her! Punish her!"

"Very well. Mr Short, lead the slave to the punishment stock."

The two speakers at each side of the stage gave a drum roll.

Honey was led crawling upstage, so the audience had a good view of her wiggling rear end. There were cheers each time Mr Short stuck the prod in Honey's depilated sex-slit.

When Honey got to the punishment stock, Mr Short

pulled her up by her nose, so she was overlooking the stock, which was only about five feet high, told her to turn round, unclipped the leash from her nose, and left the stage. The show was entirely Mr Suzuki's now.

"Now, squat! Bend your knees and point your cunt at the audience!"

Honey did it at once, without thinking, squatting down, arching her back, and thrusting her sex forward. Disobeying that commanding voice was out of the question. The audience broke out in spontaneous applause.

"That's right... Let's get your throat level with the collar..."

Mr Suzuki gripped Honey by the hair, and yanked her up, and then the slave item found cold steel closing round her neck as the two steel wings at the top of the stock swung together. There was a sharp point at the throat which made Honey keep her head up.

"Good. Head up high, bitch."

Mr Suzuki took each of Honey's slender arms and twisted them back over the crosspiece near the top of the stock. Then he rotated the whole stock on its swivelling base so that the audience could see what he was doing. He took rope, and bound Honey's delicate wrists tightly together, and then stretched them down by tying the ends of the rope to one of the eyeholes of a screw lower down. Steel clamps connected by a short steel rod were secured on the slave's upper arms, forcing them parallel. The pain was excruciating, but Honey didn't dare say a word. Then Mr Suzuki placed a knee against the slave's side, tilting her body to the side of the stock, so the audience got a good view of her rear. A peg was placed in the stock to keep the slave tilted. Humiliation was added to pain when a dildo of elephantine proportions was stuck in the slave's back passage. The audience chortled. Then the peg was removed and the slave slid back into position.

Mr Suzuki got to work on the lower part of Honey's body. The stock was swivelled round again, so the audience could see the slave's naked pussy, and ropes were secured round her waist, tightly cutting into the flesh. There were more chuckles and sniggers as the clitoris was clamped by a sharp-jawed electrode and a huge vibrator stuck in the slave's pussy. Rope was looped down between the legs. Knots were tied in the rope where it would sink into the slave's vagina and anus, holding in the vibrator and anal plug, and then the rope was drawn up again behind to be knotted at the back of the rope circling her waist.

Up to this point, the slave was still squatting, her snatch on view, but although the position was humiliating, the lower part of her body was not in much pain. But now Mr Suzuki drew up the legs, bound the ankles and secured them behind where they were level with the anus. The whole weight of the body settled on the rope digging into the crotch; so it seemed to Honey that she was being cut in half. The only way she could relieve the pain was by trying to heave herself up with her aching backward-stretched arms. The applause at Mr Suzuki's skill in rope work was deafening.

Honey started to scream, much to the amusement of the audience. Mr Suzuki smacked her hard twice across the face with a rubber flogger. There were cheers and laughter.

"Learn to love your pain, bitch. You deserve it, don't you?"

"Yes, Master," Honey said obediently.

"More pain to come."

The stage lights were dimmed, except for one blood-red spotlight, upstage and slightly to the left of the slave item, which caught her dramatically in a back-lit silhouette. Because the stage was otherwise dark, the illuminated clock-face hanging centre stage immediately caught the attention of the audience. The slave item – who still persisted in secretly thinking of herself as Katya - could not see it, of course, but she could see the other clock-face, hidden from the audience, if she strained her eyes downwards.

There was another roll of drums. Both of the clocks began to tick away the seconds. Her confession, or edited excerpts from it, was played back through the speakers at the side of the stage. Simultaneously, Katya felt the vibrator moving inside her, not humming in the usual way, but pumping slowly. She felt her sex-hole getting moist.

The vibrator stopped. Katya knew thirty seconds had passed from the clock-face just at the bottom of her field of vision. Then she heard recorded highlights of unwise remarks she'd made at the beginning of her training programme:

"I'm Katya Sabyenye. This isn't fair. I'm a free woman. You can't do this to me. I have rights. I won't be insulted like this." These remarks were repeated for thirty seconds.

The hand of the clock came full circle. Then the stage lights came up and Honey was convulsed as a powerful electric current coursed through her clitoris for ten seconds while she screamed. Then the cycle repeated itself, and continued to do so every sixty seconds. For thirty seconds she was masturbated, and then after another thirty seconds shocked. The torture was made worse by Honey's knowing exactly when the awful burning shock would come.

The spectacle was far more satisfying for the audience. The spectators were wallowing in warm sexual feelings: vibrators were humming away in vaginas, penises standing straight up stiff as rods were being caressed by shackled hands. The slave audience was happy to know its place, and got a lovely thrill watching the painful and spectacular torment of a slave item that didn't.

*

Slave item Honey had the benefit of seeing her torture in the punishment theatre from the audience's point of view only long afterwards: she was shown the DVD as she was being prepared for auction. Although, as it turned out, the DVD was never used, it was prepared so that it could be downloaded free of charge from Domino's secure website by customers interested in making a purchase.

*

The dramatic lighting, the bondage of the naked body, the slave's submissive recorded confession accompanied by masochistic whimperings as the massive vibrator plundered her exposed sex-hole, the suspense as the hand of the clock neared the minute mark, then the scream and convulsed face – the audience (and the CCTV cameras) took all this in, and thought it was wonderful. Slaves were sometimes allowed strictly supervised conversations with each other, and in them over the next few days it was the unanimous view that Honey's pounishment was one of the best performances they'd seen.

And Katya herself (although she didn't quite know it at the time) was well on the way to becoming the obedient slave Honey that Domino wanted her to be.

CHAPTER SEVEN:

MADAM KWAN

Honey's trainer was lolling back in an armchair in the ward room, legs stretched out and ankles folded on the naked back of another slave item, whose name Honey had not yet learnt. He took a swig from a can of beer, and pointed the remote at a TV screen. A football match was in progress, somewhere in the outside world. Unlike most screens Honey had seen in her time at the establishment she now knew was called Domino, this one was not closed circuit. The slave under Mr Short's heels was new, and had just learnt the "supportive" position: on all fours, forearms and thighs straight, forehead up. She was wearing the standard steel belt, the vibrator prong humming away inside her. There would be a clitoris electrode too, but Mr Short hardly ever used that. It wasn't usually necessary, slaves quickly learnt to obey commands promptly, without having to be punished and told twice. Honey knew Mr Short didn't believe in unnecessary punishment. Necessary punishment, now that was quite a different matter…

Honey was not wearing a belt. Mr Short had removed it to enter her, and had not bothered to secure it afterwards. Honey was lying on a wooden table. Ropes tightly bound her breasts and then leading down bound her arms, and then were secured under the table. Ropes tightened round her belly too, and then round her wrists. They were also knotted together under the table. She was bent double, her thighs caressing her belly, her feet above her head. Ropes from the ankle cuffs stretched down under the table by her head. They at least were not taut, and allowed her to push her aching legs upwards. But if she did so, a lever was engaged under the table, and the sharp-jawed electrodes biting her tits delivered a shock.

Honey's depilated pussy was well-displayed in this position, of course, and Mr Short had taken advantage of that in the previous hour or so since her humiliating punishment at the hands of Mr Suzuki.

After he had finished enjoying her, he had said: "Well done, Honey. You were very popular with the audience. You provided them with the best entertainment they've had for a long while." Then as an afterthought he added: "You know, Honey, this position you're in now is a good way of introducing you to the methods employed in the tableaux."

What could he mean? Honey had no idea. She had asked him, but all he said was: "You'll learn soon enough. For now just be satisfied that you've been a good slave and taken the first half of your punishment well."

"The first half!" Honey yelped in despair. "There's more to come?"

"Of course. I told you."

"But... what, Sir?"

"Dear me, you are forgetful, aren't you? You have to go back into the punishment theatre again tomorrow."

"Am I to be punished by Mr Suzuki again, Sir?" Honey didn't think she could bear that.

"Yes. I told you. Then you're to be caned. By our Principal Cane Mistress, Madam Kwan."

*

Madam Kwan – she had been known by her European name as Mary Kwan and as Mistress Lotus Blossom before Domino had seen her potential and recruited her – had once been an auxiliary nurse in Singapore's chief prison, the Chang Hi. It had been one of her chief duties to assist the Medical Orderly and be present when canings took place, usually ten a week, every weekday morning and afternoon. The offender was ordered to strip naked, and then attached to an A frame: wrists tied with heavy straps at the apex of the frame and legs spread apart and similarly secured. Two further sets of straps pinioned elbows and knees, and a broad strap was buckled tightly round the waist, so the backside was well-presented for chastisement. Mary Kwan had seen numerous male buttocks lashed with the cane. It intrigued her that as the culprits waited for their corporal correction, bound and naked, cocks became restless: they often rose up to full prominence, and sometimes remained erect to the point when the ferocious implement was applied. It was almost as if the offender was conspiring in his own punishment, his stiff prick mute testimony that he was getting his deserts. As the cane lashed his rump raw, Mary Kwan's panties became moist.

She came to England and set herself up as a dominatrix, and made a good living treating her customers' buttocks with the cane. She used, out of habit and familiarity, canes similar to those that had been used on the petty criminals of Singapore: gleaming yellow instruments of finest quality rattan, four foot six inches long, about half an inch wide, and notched every six inches or so. In the same manner as the Singapore offenders, her customers were ordered to strip naked and secured to an A frame.

It gave her enormous satisfaction caning a helpless naked male, and watching the ridiculous behind wriggling, undulating and swelling under successive strokes. She would take two strides to deliver a stroke, and deliver it with full force, the cane arcing down from behind her back. She waited a full minute between each stroke, while the customer was forced to blurt out apologies and thanks, the number of the stroke, and how many more he should receive. As her standard number of strokes was thirty-six (she liked multiples of six) the caning usually lasted about an hour. It lasted an hour or so, because invariably the customer would not thank her profusely enough, or forget the number of the strokes, and how many were remaining. Then he had to be given the stroke again, and an extra one. After the first few strokes the buttocks were raw and cut. At that point, the customer often began to protest, or began to yell, but she ignored that, at least until near the end of the session, when a gag would be inserted in his mouth, so she could get the session finished. She had taken his money before the session (thirty-six pounds – one pound per stroke – was the basic charge, but she always demanded twice that to allow for the invariable mistakes in counting) and if he didn't come back for punishment again – so what? – there were plenty more absurd little wimps queuing up for the bare arse treatment.

There was the added pleasure that European cocks were usually quite a lot bigger than Chinese ones, and Mistress Lotus Blossom was greatly amused when the big pathetic European cocks and redundant testicles swung about limply as each stroke impacted. She often attached little bells to her customer's dick, so that the tinkly sound would bring home to him his humiliating position.

She was a natural dominant. As such, James Walpole realised her potential and recruited her as Principal Cane Mistress, paying her three times the income she had earned working free-lance.

All the male slaves owned by Domino learnt to fear and respect Madam Kwan, but most of the slave items she treated with the cane in her new job were women. She took this new experience in her stride. Indeed, she began to think that treating a female slave to the cane was even more satisfying than punishing a man: a female's arse was broader, and more fleshy, and seemed a natural target. She began to refine her technique. She would give three areas of the posteriors successive treatment: the crest of the rump, level with the anus, the gluteal area below the anus, and the first six inches of the thighs. Caning the areas below the anus in particular had the pleasing effect of causing intense pain, especially as the punishment proceeded.

A caning by Madam Kwan was an experience no slave item would forget.

*

Slave item Honey was prepared for her caning in the punishment theatre the next day. Mr Suzuki oversaw the slave's positioning, but since he wasn't to appear publicly on stage this time, he was in an ordinary T-shirt and jeans, so Honey didn't recognise him at first. But she recognised the voice, and the Japanese accent, and her heart sank. Mr Suzuki delighted in cruelty and humiliation, not like her own trainer, the wonderful Mr Short.

Honey was not wearing her belt, and was naked as usual of course, except she had been made to wear bright red six-inch heels. She guessed that was to show off the muscle-tone of her legs and rear. Her heart had skipped when Mr Short had said her arse was quite delightful. Honey's arms were held behind her back, and fitted into a single leather sleeve tightly bound with straps. Then, before the audience arrived, she was led onto the stage, where the wooden stock was still placed as it had been the day before.

"Move up," Mr Suzuki commanded, and Honey felt an electric shock in her anus encouraging her to do just that.

She let out a squeak and moved up towards the stock until she was about two feet away from it, facing upstage, with her back to the curtain.

"Now bend. Right over."

Honey did as she was bid, and Mr Suzuki came up to her, placed a surgical-gloved finger in her anus, and said: "Good girl. Don't be afraid. Madam Kwan's caning will hurt a lot, but it's only for an hour. A good whacking, and you'll be a different animal. A corrected slave. All right, assistants!"

The leather sleeve was bent upwards, till it was parallel to the stock, and then ropes were tied tightly round the sleeve and the stock at six inch intervals. Other ropes were tightly tied round her breasts, squeezing them into prominence. Honey's head and neck were pressed upside-down against the stock, and she found herself looking upwards at her crotch. She noticed, in a kind of dispassionate way, that her pussy was leaking and her sex-lips distended.

Mr Suzuki saw the direction of her gaze. "Yes. You get a grandstand view of your punishment today. You'll be able to enjoy it as much as the audience. But we have to improve the view by making sure your legs are splayed apart."

A three foot long steel bar, with two metal ankle cuffs at each end, was attached to Honey's ankles.

"Also, we'll have to make sure that sexy arse of yours is well-presented, won't we? No slouching!"

Steel braces were fitted round Honey's knees to prevent them from bending.

"Well, that's an improvement, but the audience will expect to see those pretty posteriors jutting out more, just asking for it. You'll beg for punishment, and your body-language has to suit your words."

Mr Suzuki padlocked a light chain to a metal ring in one ankle cuff, took the chain round the stock, slid it through a ring in the other cuff, pulled tight and locked it in position. Honey tottered nearer to the stock, bent almost double. She squealed in pain, and received a warning slap on the backside.

"No self-indulgence, Honey. You'll have plenty of opportunity to yell later. You're nearly ready, but one more thing has to be added by special request of Madam Kwan."

A foot-long, silver chain was attached to Honey's clitoris ring. Dangling at the end of it was a sparkling silver bell.

Honey looked up at it swinging between her legs,

fascinated. No opportunity to humiliate a slave was lost in Domino, she thought.

"And – oh – I nearly forgot. It would be a pity if you didn't enjoy yourself as much as the audience is going to."

The sexual orifice so humiliatingly presented for the audience's entertainment was stuffed with an enormous, and very visible, dildo.

"Now your bondage is complete, but there's still a little more to do."

An assistant brought a vase containing nettles from off stage. When she caught a glimpse of them, it struck Honey they were the first green growing things she had seen since the day she was obtained from the West London hotel, which was all of – surely more than four days ago? They seemed incongruous in the world of Domino, where natural light never shone. Here, she'd experienced only strip lights, or stage spotlights and footlights, or the utter darkness of her tiny cubic steel cell.

The nettles weren't for decoration, she realised. Sure enough, Mr Suzuki took one from the vase, and with his other hand, opened Honey's posterior cleft. He ran the nettle lightly down the cleft from top to bottom, paying particular attention to the anus, and then patted the depilated mount of Venus and sex-lips with it. Finally he stroked the nettle across Honey's bum cheeks.

"There we are. It'll give you something to think about until Madam Kwan sees to you."

The pain in Honey's upstretched arms and contorted body and the stinging in her arse and cunt, the humiliation she knew she would endure as soon as the curtain rose, the thought of the caning she was due to receive – these seemed unendurable. She began to tremble, muscles spasmed and involuntarily squeezed the dildo, and suddenly Honey gushed and shuddered in orgasm.

"That's a good girl. It's always nice to see a slave enjoying her punishment. You've still got a good hard caning to look forward to, and you won't have long to wait now, I believe the theatre is filling up. I'm sure our slave items are looking forward to seeing you get a beating almost as much as you are. We must have you looking your best for your admirers, mustn't we? I think a spot of blusher on those pretty cheeks."

Mr Suzuki dabbed some cosmetic on the crest of Honey's posteriors, and then held a mirror up so Honey could admire the result from between her legs.

"There you are. Sweet enough to eat. Well, so long for now. I think the curtain's due to rise any minute."

*

After a few minutes, Honey – she could no longer think of herself as Katya, after the treatment she had received at Mr Suzuki's hands yesterday – heard a man's voice on the other side of the curtain, introducing today's show. It wasn't Mr Walpole. The voice was muffled by the curtain, but she was almost sure it was Mr Short. In a way that disappointed her. She had begun almost to believe her personal trainer rather disapproved of her punishment, he was such a gentle man, and Honey knew she was in love with him.

There was applause, evidently for Madam Kwan. It wasn't as tumultuous as yesterday, and Honey thought she heard a few gasps. It seemed the audience was in awe of Madam Kwan, perhaps a little frightened of her.

Honey heard a slight susurrating sound, and saw the footlights illuminating the stage. The curtain was being drawn up.

There were oohs and ahs from the audience, as the sight of a slave so comprehensively humiliated was presented to them. After they got over the first shock, there were sporadic titters and then loud applause.

From between her legs, Honey saw Madam Kwan approach her. She was a handsome Chinese woman in her late twenties, dressed in a red leather leotard, net stockings and red, thigh boots. It was what she holding in her hand that drew Honey's attention, and had been the reason for audience's gasps. It was a notched cane, nearly five feet long. Madam Kwan held it by its elegant silver handle.

Madam Kwan pointed the cane at Honey's backside, pushed it in her anus, and twisted it round. "Tell the audience why you deserve your punishment."

Honey found the words came out in a babbling rush, exactly as she had been taught them, without her having to think about them, as if they were being said by somebody else: "Madam, I have been condemned for hypocrisy. I have been lying to my superiors, pretending to be an obedient slave when in fact I was secretly harbouring notions of superiority. I have gone so far as to resent my owners' right to control me. I am an extremely wicked slave, and deserve painful punishment, which I hope and desire that you, Madam, will visit on me. Also, I have been guilty of giving myself airs of modesty. I have presumed that I have private parts, like free men and women. I have stubbornly refused to acknowledge that my body is entirely the property of my owners, and that I have no right to privacy whatsoever. With a pompous self-importance, I have talked about my vagina, my bottom and my nipples, instead of honestly referring to my cunt, my arse and my tits."

Madam Kwan grinned, and pressed the tip of the cane into Honey's vagina, pushing the dildo further in. "I am going to give you thirty-six strokes. You will count every stroke and say how many remain. Then you will thank me, in a loud and clear voice. Then you will repeat your confession. If you get anything wrong, you'll have the stroke repeated and get an extra one. Do you understand?"

"Yes Madam."

With a contemptuously curled lip, Madam gave the dildo another shove with her cane, and Honey juddered into another orgasm, her pussy dripping juice and her rear end waggling with lust. Madam laughed and there were ironic cheers and laughter from the audience. "You won't be feeling so happy in a few minutes, Honey."

*

In his office, James Walpole looked at the CCTV screen on his desk transfixed. As slave Hotlips knelt on all fours under the desk and took his cock down her throat, he thought: "Honey has got to be the best bed-slave ever!"

*

There was a swish and the cane came down on Honey's posteriors, delivering a burning pain. Honey's bottom wriggled, and the bell suspended from her clitoris tinkled, much to the delight of the audience.

Automatically, Honey said: "One stroke, Madam, thirty five remain. Thank you, Madam."

She blurted out her confession once again. There was silence for a few seconds, and then Honey's recorded voice came from the speakers at the side of the stage, with those horrible words Honey had hoped she would never have to hear again: "I'm Katya Sabyenye. This isn't fair. I'm a free woman. You can't do this to me. I have rights. I won't be insulted like this."

Then another swish, and burning pain again as the cane caught Honey across the rump. The worst thing was, Honey could see it coming from between her legs.

All went according to Madam Kwan's instructions until stroke number eight. Stroke seven had been an unpleasant surprise for Honey, catching her as it did below the anus, level with her pussy. The pain, on the part of her rump less well padded with flesh, had been intense. Nevertheless, she managed to say her piece without a mistake that time. At stroke eight however, which was on the same place, the pain was so awful her words became incomprehensible.

"No, Honey. That won't do. Your counting and confession have to be loud and clear. You'll have to receive the same stroke again, then an extra one."

After a minute, the horrid cane came down again.

"Stroke eight, Madam, twenty eight remain. Thank you, Madam."

"No, Honey. I said I was giving you an extra one. Now you've made two mistakes, so it's two extra ones. It's stroke eight with thirty remaining, understand?"

"Yes, Madam," Honey said miserably.

The audience was too fascinated by this absolute dominance of a completely degraded slave to laugh. They were in awe of the Cane Mistress's obvious power and control, but there were gasps of admiration and a ragged, chinking applause, as chained hands were put together.

During the next hour, Honey continued to make mistakes at fairly regular intervals. By the time Madam gagged her, she had received nearly fifty strokes, and her posteriors were red raw and bleeding.

Madam Kwan finished her off with the remaining strokes due, turned and bowed to the audience. There was silence for a few seconds, as if the audience were taking in all they had seen, and then the applause was tumultuous.

*

After the curtain descended, Honey was released from her bonds, and the stock unlocked from its base and wheeled away, because the next act was due shortly, a cat-fight between two female slaves found guilty of unsupervised conversation. The ring was quickly set up on a mud floor. Cat-fights were always popular with the audience.

CHAPTER EIGHT:

THE TRAINING OF A BED-SLAVE

Immediately after her punishment, Honey received attention from a nurse. She had to lie on her belly on a hard-surfaced hospital trolley while her backside was wiped with antiseptic. That stung, but then her posteriors were thoroughly rubbed with an analgesic cream, she was given a something to make her sleep, and put to bed.

*

She woke up snug in a bed of soft sheets smelling fresh and clean. Wonderful to relate, sunshine was shining in through the window. There was a vase of flowers and a bunch of grapes on a plate on the cupboard beside her bed.

Though she couldn't rise out of her bed (the sheets had somehow been stretched down and severely fastened) she was free to feel her naked body under the sheets. Her rump was still swollen and smarting with her chastisement, but, strangely, that just made her feel libidinous. She twisted her young body round in the bed, feeling sad there was no man to share it with. Inevitably, she played with herself, plunging her fingers into her depilated pussy, dreaming of masterful Mr Short and being whipped by him, and orgasmed just as a nurse came to serve her a delicious meal. When she smelt it, she realised she hadn't eaten for a long time.

The nurse placed the meal down on the table, slotted a board through two supports near the head of the bed, placed the plate of food and a glass of orange juice on it, untied a loop of cord holding the head end of the bed-clothes down, and said: "Sit up, child."

Honey did so.

"Now eat. If you want more, just ring the bell-pull on

your right hand. You can have as much as you like."

"Oh, thank you."

The nurse smiled at her. "You're a good girl. I can tell you, Domino is proud of you. You received your punishment very bravely. A little girl like you, receiving so much cane, it went to my heart, it did. So eat up your meal."

Honey did, without any further bidding. She was very hungry. The nurse looked on, smiling, as she was eating.

When Honey had finished, the nurse said: "Do you want any more?"

Honey didn't, just then.

The nurse gave her two large brightly-coloured pills and a glass of water. "Take these. They'll make you feel happy and relaxed."

Honey obediently swallowed the pills. Soon afterwards, her pussy was moist and she felt an urgent desire to finger it again.

The nurse collected up the plate, knife and fork, and put it on a trolley. Then she wiped Honey's mouth with an antiseptic cloth, put a small bowl on the board beneath her mouth, and scrubbed her teeth with a disposable toothbrush, making Honey spit out into the bowl, and giving her water to swill round and spit out. She put the bowl on the trolley and withdrew the board from across the bed.

"Now snuggle down into bed again, and get some rest."

When Honey had done that, the nurse retied the cords fastening the sheets.

"Well, if you do want food any time, just pull the bell," she told her.

Before she left the nurse tucked a dildo between the sheets. She began to wheel the trolley away, then, seemingly as an afterthought, she turned round and said: "The sheets will be changed regularly. Dreaming of your nice Mr Short, I'll be bound."

*

Honey was kept in the ward for the next two weeks. She was not allowed up except for the regular P.T. which was for two hours a day. There was a great deal of running round the room, with the P.T. master standing in the centre cracking a show-whip, sometimes stinging the legs of a slave who wasn't running fast enough. There were also quite a lot of other exercises, including stretching, star-jumps, jumping over an exercise horse and toe-touching.

The only other occasion when Honey was allowed out of bed was to relieve herself, which she had to do in full view of other patients and staff since slaves were allowed no privacy. Other patients had marks of beatings too. She was forbidden to speak to them, but it seemed by comparison to some of them she'd been dealt with lightly. One pretty brunette taller than Honey, had the livid marks of a heavy bullwhip across her back, breasts, rear and sex, and must have been in great pain at the time of her punishment. Bright red cane marks ran across a male slave's penis and loins. The penis, banded with tight steel rings, was stretched between his legs and padlocked to a piercing at the perineum. The heavy padlock swung between his legs as he walked. No wanking for him, then.

Except during her period Honey was kept on heat by the aphrodisiac the nurse regularly gave her, and spent her time in bed spinning erotic day-dreams involving Mr Short. She fantasised herself placed into degrading and humiliating situations, bound and gagged, and being spanked, caned and whipped by the love of her life, and the fantasy would always end, for the time being, with a juddering, explosive orgasm. She had never had such orgasms, she reflected, in that other life, already fading from her memory, which she had led before she had been introduced to Domino.

*

One day when the nurse came to give her food, she said Honey should feel honoured, because the boss, Mr Walpole, was really interested in her. Honey had mixed feelings about that. Where was her Mr Short? The next morning the nurse released Honey from her blanket bondage.

"Get up, girl." The tone was severe, the solicitude had vanished. The nurse was still full of smiles, but the smiles meant something different. Perhaps, Honey thought, it was back to normal discipline now she had recovered from her beating.

"Now, face the wall mirror and stand to attention. Chin up, breasts out, legs straight and hands behind head."

Honey did what she was told immediately, even though the nurse had no whip or electrode prod to compel her. She was learning obedience.

The nurse held up a hand mirror and showed her the double reflection of her rump. "You see, almost healed except for a few faint bruises. But what do you notice about yourself that is unsatisfactory?"

"There's hair on my cunt and under my arms."

"Exactly. Anything else?"

"I can't see anything else, Madam…" Honey hesitated, did you call nurses "Madam"?

The nurse smiled. "That's all right. Any free woman should be addressed as madam by you. What are you?"

"I'm a slave, Madam. Slave item Honey."

"Your punishment has brought the truth home to you at last. The pain was worth it, wasn't it?"

"Oh, yes, Madam."

The sincerity of Honey's tone was obvious. The nurse smiled a cruel little triumphant smile.

"Good. Now, you were saying that you couldn't see anything else that was unsatisfactory?"

"No, Madam."

"Use your other senses then."

It dawned on Honey what the nurse was hinting at. "I smell of perspiration and urine, Madam."

"Quite true. But no airs of modesty."

Honey trembled with fear. Those dreadful words reminded her of the ordeal she had gone through.

"I'm very, very sorry, Madam. I mean I stink of sweat and piss."

"Yes, and not surprising after all the wanking you've been doing, you little slut. You are a slut, aren't you?"

"Oh, yes, Madam."

"Yes. You've been wanking day and night and fantasising being punished by Mr Short, haven't you?"

"Yes, Madam." It was the simple truth.

"Well at least you know your place. You know what you really are, don't you?"

"Yes, Madam."

"Say it."

"I'm a stinking slave-slut, Madam."

The nurse smiled that smile again. "Very good, Honey. We'll make a tolerably good bed-slave out of you yet, or at least Mr Walpole will. He'll be taking over your training from now on. But you need a shower and massage and a waxing before you'll be ready for Mr Walpole. He'll expect you to look your best. You'll have to be perfumed too."

Honey came from a strict religious family and had never worn perfume in her life. Her confusion must have shown on her face, because the nurse added: "Oh the perfume will be familiar to you. It smells a bit like urine, but it's sweeter and more musky. It includes a pheromone. It'll help remind you of your purpose in life."

*

Honey received the shower, and the soapy suds of the

shower gel and the warm water coursing over her young naked body seemed like heaven. Her hair was washed, combed, and blow-dried. She enjoyed the next part of her preparation too. She had to lie down on a padded leather couch while a masseur squeezed and pumped every part of her body, not excluding her nates, breasts, mons and vagina. Then her arms were strapped behind her head and her legs strapped and splayed apart so her sex was well exposed. She was waxed, and every trace of body hair was removed. Finally, an erotic, musky scent was sprayed on her.

She was ready for Mr Walpole.

*

The receptionist glanced at the trainer leading the naked girl on all fours and clicked on the intercom.

"The slave item is here, Sir."

"Show her in, Ms McGillicutty."

Honey was led, literally by the nose, into James Walpole's office. No longer was it necessary for her to be prodded in the backside with an electrode. Correct crawling had become second nature. She was brought to the sofa where Walpole was sitting, idly smoking a Balkan Sobranie cigarette, and there unleashed. Immediately, without being told, Honey adopted the kowtow position before her master.

"She's obviously well-trained. You've done a good job, Short."

"Thank you, Sir. Er... I've rather a heavy schedule at the moment, so if you don't need me here...."

"No, there's no need for you to stay. Be sure to have your final report on Honey ready for me as soon as possible though, won't you? And then there's that new one...."

"Yes, Petalbum."

"Yes. Get Ms McGillicutty to fit you in for a meeting sometime tomorrow."

"Will do. See you then."

Honey's delusion that Mr Short had some special regard for her was finally shattered as he left the room. Actually, she'd always known the truth, but had hidden it from herself. She even knew, deep down, that her infatuation had been deliberately engineered by Domino. Another of their mind-control techniques. Wasn't there a word for it in psychiatric terminology? Transference or something....

While these thoughts were passing through Honey's mind, James Walpole was silently regarding her with some amusement, occasionally puffing at his cigarette. Honey couldn't see that, of course. Her nose was touching the floor. She was only aware of the silence. Then there was a swift movement, and something was inserted in her anus.

"Feel anything, Honey?"

"Yes, Sir. You've put something in my arsehole."

"Look round and see what it is."

Obediently, Honey did so. She saw blue smoke rising from behind her posteriors. It was a cigarette! It was going to burn down, and then – Honey shuddered with fear.

Mr Walpole laughed. "It'll help concentrate the mind. Nose to floor again. That's right. Incidentally, don't call me Sir. Free men and women do that in Domino, because I'm the boss. You're just a slave, so you will address me as Master. Understood?"

"Yes, Master."

"Good. Now I want you to tell me your name."

Honey was surprised at such a simple request. "I'm slave item Honey, Master."

"No, I mean the name you had before you became one of my slaves."

That name? Oh, God. "I'm – my name was..." Honey shuddered with fear again, but she had to answer, before that cigarette burnt her tail. "I'm – I mean my name was... I think my name was... I was called... K- K-" She trembled in a paroxysm of fear. She couldn't do it, not even to stop the cigarette burning her anus.

"I'm waiting."

"K- K-" The fear made Honey lose control of her bladder. A dribble of urine dripped on the expensive Persian carpet. "I was called... My name was... I can't remember, Master."

Mr Walpole laughed again. "Good. You've passed the test. Well done." Walpole removed the cigarette from Honey's anus and stubbed it out in an ashtray.

Miserably, Honey realised she had better own up to wetting the carpet. She knew she would be punished, but if she didn't confess the punishment would be greater. But the punishment she was expecting didn't come.

"Of course you wet the carpet, my dear. You were very afraid. Understandably so. I have absolute power over you, and you knew that. Weeing was the natural result. Don't trouble yourself about the carpet. It will be cleaned. I may be your master, but I'm not a monster."

Immediately Honey felt a surge of relief and gratitude. No one in Domino had ever addressed her as "my dear" before, not even Mr Short. She began to feel enormous respect for this powerful, generous man.

There was silence again which eventually Walpole broke.

"You're going to be trained as a bed-slave. You don't understand what that means yet. Ask any questions you like, I'll answer them to the best of my ability."

This was another thing new for Honey. Up to now, she'd been given instructions, told what to do, told what was going to happen to her, sometimes, and sometimes she had asked questions of Mr Short, but she was never encouraged to. The first question leapt immediately into her mind.

"Will I be going to the punishment theatre, Master?"

"I shouldn't think so. Not unless you're a really bad girl, and I don't think you will be. You seem to me to be a very well-behaved slave."

"Oh, thank you, Master. I – I suppose I'm going to be punished, though?"

"You'll be put in bondage, and whacked or shocked, if that's what you mean, yes. Nothing that'll make you bleed."

That didn't seem so bad. She thought she could endure it.

"What's a bed-slave, Master?"

"The customer who buys you will be looking for a slave who's a good fuck. Consequently, you'll be trained up in that expertise. Your vaginal muscles will have to be strengthened for example."

"How will that be done, Master?"

"The answer to that question can better be explained through action rather than words."

James Walpole got up. "Head up, Honey. Now you see that side door? I want you to crawl to it."

Honey was impressed. Everyone else in Domino who wanted her to crawl anywhere put her on a nose-leash, or yanked her by her long blond tresses.

*

In the other room, Walpole told Honey to stand to attention. "Hands behind head, chin up proudly girl, it's not every slave who's chosen by the chief of Domino, that's right, tits out, stomach in, clench those arse muscles, back straight, legs straight, I don't want to see any slouching, good! Now tell me what you see in front of you."

Evidently this was her master's private training room.

"There's something... I think it's a dildo, standing up straight, on a rubber base, and there's some electrical equipment behind it, and on each side of the dildo there are metal things... I don't know what they are, Master. There's a tub of margarine there as well."

"Well that's a reasonably accurate description. What you've called the metal things are steel ankle clasps to secure your feet. You squat down on the dildo, you see, and you see a plug there at the back. Now I've told you that, can you hazard a guess as to what the machine does?"

Honey had by now got a fairly good idea. "I think I squat down on the dildo and wank myself off, Master."

"Well that's essentially correct. You will notice however that the top of the dildo is in the form of a rubber bulb. Why do you think that is?"

"I think I'm supposed to squeeze the bulb with my cunt muscles, Master."

"Well done, Honey! You are a clever girl, aren't you?"

Honey felt a blush come to her cheeks. She was proud she could please her master.

Walpole ordered Honey to rub the margarine on the erect dildo and then secured her feet in the steel clasps and strapped a tight belt round her waist with uncomfortable studs on the inside pressing into her flesh. He strapped her hands behind her back to the back of the belt.

"Now squat!"

Walpole fastened Honey's clitoris ring to a thin chain attached to the dildo. The chain made it impossible for her to pull away entirely from the dildo, and when the dildo plunged into her, her clitoris was tugged and stimulated.

"Take the dildo right up you, that's right. Now push down. Right down. No that's no good. The dildo won't budge unless you squeeze that bulb. Try harder. Harder!"

Eventually the dildo was forced down, then sprang up again with some force, driven by an electric motor.

"O.K. Now this plug goes up your back passage."

Honey squeaked in surprise: "What's that for, Master?"

"It's an electrode of course."

Of course. Silly question.

Her pinioned hands couldn't take the plug out. Not that she would have dreamt of trying to.

"You'll get a shock up your arse if you haven't managed

to press the dildo down within a certain time. Now, let me see… your muscles are not very strong yet so I suppose I should be generous. I'll set it at ten seconds. So if you bounce up and down six times a minute you won't get shocked, provided you pump at a steady pace. Get into the rhythm of it. Here we go, start now."

At first the going was easy. Honey squeezed and eased down on the dildo. Then the dildo shafted up her and she was lifted into the initial starting position once more. The slow squeeze and grind and upward pumping action soon induced orgasm, which electronic sensors on the dildo were apparently able to detect. A number 1 appeared on a LED display screen. Walpole watched her and grinned.

"That's the idea, Honey. Slow and steady. A nice grind."

Honey began to perspire, and her love-juices dripped down the dildo. It wasn't very long before a number 2 appeared on the screen.

Walpole chuckled. "Well done, Honey. You're going to have a really happy time over the next hour or so, I can see that. Well, I'll leave you to it for the time being."

And with that, Walpole went out of the room, leaving Honey to be ponderously shafted by the fucking machine.

After about a quarter of an hour and another three orgasms later, though, Honey began to tire. Her legs ached, as they constantly lowered and raised the weight of her body. Her clitoris and vagina began to feel sore. Her internal muscles were tiring.

Suddenly, there was a sharp pain in her backside, and a number 1 appeared on another LED screen. She'd slowed down too much. Desperately she tried to speed up. How long did she have to do this? Mr Walpole had mentioned an hour. She didn't think she could endure it for more than another minute! But she had no choice. The orgasms stopped coming after number 9, but the other LED display inexorably began clocking up shocks. By the time Mr

Walpole returned, she'd been shocked nearly a hundred times.

"Oh dear, that is bad," her master said as he switched the machine off. "Only nine orgasms and all those shocks. That won't do, you know. That won't do at all. Still never mind, your muscles will soon get stronger with regular exercise. We'll have you jumping up and down like a frog in a hot bath before you can say "Jack Robinson", just see if we don't."

Honey had no doubt of that. Domino never seemed to have any trouble forcing her to do and think exactly as they wished.

Mr Walpole released her from her bonds.

"Now it's time for the exercise bike."

Oh not more exercise! Honey didn't think she could stand it.

"Please may I have a little rest, Master?"

"Don't worry, the bike exercises an entirely different set of muscles. You don't need to develop them specifically for your future vocation, but you need to be in good shape. The exercise is good for the vascular system, you know. Helps muscle tone as well. Keeps you slim. It's very good for you in all sorts of ways, you know," he added vaguely. "Well here we are."

Honey remembered a description of the bike from Hotlips' account of it, when she was being tested for hypocrisy by Madam Victoria. In particular she remembered Hotlips mentioning the cruel saddle – if that's what it could be called – just a crosspiece of two steel rods. And then there was the vertically mounted electric motor behind the saddle with its two counter-rotating wheels from which hung eight thin strips of rubber.

"Now hop on, my dear," Mr Walpole said jovially.

Although Honey was not looking forward to her bicycle exercise, it never occurred to her to disobey. Since her punishment at the hands of Mr Suzuki and Madam Kwan, disobedience was simply not an option.

Walpole clicked Honey's wrists into cuffs set in the low-slung handle bars, and her feet to ankle clasps fitted to the pedals. Then he adjusted the seat, raising it somewhat, and adjusted the motors so the rubber floggers would be level with the crest of Honey's posteriors.

"We have to get that rump of yours well-presented, haven't we? There you are. Now, you can't see it from your present position, but there's a mechanism behind you which measures the speed the rear wheel is going round at. Two electrical contacts are flung out as a governor rotates. The governor is geared so that if the speed of the wheel is less than very fast, the contacts will fall together and a circuit will be closed. That starts the electric motor behind your buttocks. Well, I guess you know the rest."

He fitted a newly prepared branks on her head. A clamp-bit fitted with pins flattened her tongue, and a sharp spike under the chin ensured her jaw remained still. He knew from experience the rubber floggers caused a great deal of pain, and he didn't want to be disturbed by screaming. He had quite a lot of paperwork to get through.

*

Walpole exercised Honey for half an hour, during which time her buttocks were efficiently flayed, and juices dripped down from the steel crosspiece cutting into her quim, which was made even more sore than it had been before.

In spite of his work he frequently came back to see how Honey was getting on. The sight amused him. He remembered this girl from the time he had reamed her snatch just after she had been brought to Domino. The resentful Katrina Sabyenye had all but disappeared. In her place was a hot, wet, tongue-clamped slave, drooling and lathered in sweat and taking the lash well, and obedient, moreover, in fact eager to please. Normally training took about six months, but Walpole guessed that this slave would be ready much sooner. She was a natural.

*

"After the cycling exercise, it would normally be time for your exercises in deportment. But you're new, so I'll let you off those today."

"Oh thank you, Master." Honey had no idea what the deportment exercises involved, but she was quite certain they'd be grim whatever they were.

"Well, you know, Honey, I'm almost inclined to thank you. You were a picture working out on those machines. It was most enjoyable watching you. You made my cock really stiff."

"Thank you, Master." Honey blushed with pride. She had given her master pleasure!

CHAPTER NINE:

TRAINING IN DEPORTMENT

Honey was surprised at her rapid improvement the next day and how quickly her muscles had strengthened in such a short time. When she was put on the erect dildo machine that mercilessly plundered her sex, it never occurred to her that there was any irony or injustice in being trained to do what she had been punished for previously. It was perfectly right and proper that she had been punished for disobedience. She hadn't been punished for masturbating. She had been a dirty little slut, wanking without permission.

Her performance had improved remarkably. Only fifteen shocks in her rear this time, and they mostly at the very end, when she was becoming exhausted, whereas she managed sixteen orgasms. Mr Walpole was quite obviously impressed, and patted her bottom affectionately as she was having her tenth orgasm. She felt a warm feeling at her belly, the exhilaration of joyful subservience.

Her improvement on the exercise bike was not so marked, and she still had her rump tanned by the rubber floggers. Still, there was an improvement and she didn't feel quite so tired at the end as she had done the day before.

As before Mr Walpole allowed her a rest, but only a short one this time – then it was time for the deportment exercises.

An assistant trainer called Madam Julia fitted Honey into a strict corset with half cups that held up her breasts without covering them. The corset was rubber fitted over an aluminium frame, and the waist could be taken in by surrounding wires looped round a wing bolt at the back.

"How's that? Uncomfortable is it?"

"Yes, Madam."

Madam Julia twisted the wing bolt. "How's it now?"

"Uh, that's much tighter, Madam."

"Good."

Madam placed Honey into a neck-stretching aluminium posture collar of awesome configuration. A branks was fitted over her head, steel strips banding her crown then dividing at her nose and holding the mouth piece, which was a very long penis-shaped dildo gag. The penis dildo slid down her throat and forced her head up. A steel rod fitted to the base of the collar at the back, went through a hole in a projection from the back of the corset, entered the upper part of Honey's posterior cleavage and ended in a curved hook which was buried deeply into Honey's back passage. It was a magnificently degrading device, lifting up Honey's pert buttocks and forcing her to stand with a severely arched back.

Honey was ordered to sit on a stool. It wasn't easy, because she couldn't bend her back or turn her head to see where the stool was. With directions from Madam, though, she detected the wooden surface with her rump, which began to smart from the flogging it had recently received.

Madam put shoes with six-inch heels on each of Honey's naked feet and helped her to stand again. She tottered and almost fell.

Mr Walpole had been silent all this time, sitting with legs stretched out on the sofa, one arm slung idly over the back. "Good. Now walk forwards. Go carefully."

Honey gingerly walked forwards, and then almost fell.

"Hm. Mrs Collins, I think you had better hold her arm to begin with. Take her for a few turns round the room until she gets used to her bondage."

After walking for a while assisted by Madam Julia, Mr Walpole encouraged Honey to walk by herself.

"Now be careful Honey. We don't want you falling over and hurting yourself. Mrs Collins, keep near her and be ready to catch her."

"He's such a kind, considerate man," Honey thought.

But Honey managed to walk round the room several times without stumbling once.

"Well done, Honey! I'm really pleased with you."

Again, Honey felt that warm feeling in her belly. She loved being an obedient slave, pleasing her master.

"Good. Now we come to the difficult bit. Mrs Collins, the book's on my desk."

Madam Julia nodded, got the large coffee table book, and balanced it carefully on Honey's head.

"Now walk round the room again. If the book falls, Mrs Collins will give you a tit-whipping."

After the first few paces, the book fell to the floor with a dull thud. Without saying a word, Mr Walpole walked over to her and gave her two resounding slaps with the palm of his hand, one on each breast. Then Madam Julia whipped her breasts with a short whip with many tails, each a thin cord with a metal piece at the end. Then the book was replaced on Honey's head.

"Let's try again. Be more careful this time."

After half a turn round the room, the book fell off again. This time, Honey received no slaps from Mr Walpole, but got another tit-whipping from Madam Julia. Her breasts smarted horribly, but her nipples stood up, mute testimony to her getting sexually excited.

Madam Julia's lips curved in cruel smile. "Glad to see you're enjoying your punishment, Honey." She gave each of the nipples a little twist.

After the book fell off the third time, Mr Walpole didn't raise his voice, he never raised his voice to Honey, but she could tell he was really angry.

"I hope your masochistic predilections aren't making you do this deliberately, Honey. I should be really quite cross if I thought that was the case. Then it would be back to the punishment theatre with you."

Honey trembled with fear. She wanted to say, "No Master, I'm really trying very hard to please you," but of course she couldn't because of the dildo gag in her mouth.

After the next dropping of the book and the next tit-whipping, and the tit-whipping after that, Honey thought she was doomed. But Mr Walpole said mildly: "Mrs Collins, the slave is trembling too much for any more exercise to be useful just now. We'll have to wait till she's calmed down a bit. Honey, go and stand in the corner. Face the wall and put your hands behind your head. That's it. You've nothing to fear. I can see that you do really want to please me. We'll begin again in half an hour."

*

Honey was left alone for half an hour, her bum smarting with the flogging and the hook in her anus, her back arched, her neck and head stretched upwards by the posture collar, her breasts smarting too, and her nipples aching from the twists Madam Julia had given them. She wanted to scream with pain, but she was too well-trained by now to move a muscle. But she knew she couldn't bear her bondage much longer, and was determined, when her deportment training resumed, to perform perfectly and be released from it.

*

Actually, she didn't perform perfectly. She dropped the book one more time, and received another tit-whipping. But she managed nevertheless to circumnavigate the room several times with the book on her head, and her master was satisfied.

"Well done, Honey. You've performed well enough for today, and I think we can remove your bondage now. You are my favourite slave, by the way." He gave her a little kiss on the cheek, and flicked her clitoris with a finger. Honey was over the moon with joy.

CHAPTER TEN :

RIVALRY

There was another pleasant surprise awaiting Honey.

"It would be the best thing if you rested now."

Honey expected she would be taken back to her small, dark, cubic prison, but instead she was made to crawl – and freely, without being led by a nose-leash! - to a bedroom with a shower annexe also adjoining Mr Walpole's office. In it, there was a comfortable double bed. She was told to shower, and then, when she was warm and dry, Mr Walpole fitted a chastity belt on her.

"I don't want you coming before I've given you a good seeing to," he said before telling her to get into bed. She was given an aphrodisiac. The blankets were tied firmly down, as they had been in the hospital ward. Then Mr Walpole left, he had a great deal of business to attend to. Honey luxuriated in the warm clean sheets. She twisted her curvaceous little body around, feeling the unforgiving metal that prevented her from plunging her fingers into her sex, and waited impatiently for her master to return. Eventually, he did enter the room, bringing a paddle, unlocked the chastity belt, and whacked her already sore bottom before each of the many times he entered her moist, compliant flesh.

Then she was allowed to sleep peacefully for the rest of the night.

*

In the morning, James Walpole fingered Honey's sex while he was served breakfast in bed by a female slave item, maid type. The maid was topless and wearing a miniskirt with a cute, stiff, frilly petticoat and a little frilly apron and no knickers. Walpole wondered whether to have the maid for afters, or Honey again, or perhaps both. Oh, how he did love sex! He cut the bread and butter into soldiers, dipped them into an egg, and popped them into Honey's mouth. He fed her, then ate himself. She was really enjoying things, of course. That was how it should be. Domino alternated pain and pleasure judiciously, in order to control the minds of the slave stock. Walpole popped another aphrodisiac pill into her mouth. Then he tickled her clitoris and sex-lips and made her suck his fingers and taste her own juices.

Walpole's mobile on the bedside table burst into life. He grabbed it.

"Yes? All right, yes, I'll be there. Just give me time to shower and get changed.... No, I understand."

He leapt out of bed, sent the maid away, showered and was out of the room in a bewilderingly short time, Honey thought. She felt frustrated. She was on heat, and desperately wanted a fuck. She knew she mustn't, she shouldn't, masturbation wasn't allowed unless it was explicitly commanded, she would regret it, but she found her hands sliding down to her crotch, and was soon plumbing the depths of her sex....

*

Madam Julia walked into the room and threw the counterpane aside.

"Well, what do you know? What do we call naughty girls who wank themselves off in private?"

"I'm a dirty little slave slut, Madam."

"And what do you think should happen to dirty little sluts?"

Honey knew perfectly well what happened to dirty sluts. Mr Short had had occasion to teach her that in no uncertain terms quite a few times. She recited the words she had learnt: "Please, Madam, tawse me hard on my cunt and cane my arse, so that my unacceptable behaviour is corrected."

"Get up."

Honey was ordered to spread her legs, lean back as far as she could without falling over, with her hands behind her head.

She received eighteen strokes downwards on her pussy, delivered by Madam with a heavy leather tawse divided into three thin tongues, and then another eighteen strokes upwards, biting her loins, burning into her crotch. Then she had to touch her toes, and was given eighteen hard strokes of the cane on her posteriors.

After that, her sex was drooling juice and she wanted to wank more than ever. Out of the question, of course.

"Stand to attention! What do you say?"

Honey recited the words: "Thank you, Madam, for correcting my impertinent, sluttish behaviour. I will strive hard not to be a bad mannered disobedient slave slut in future, but if I am disobedient again, I should be very grateful if you would correct my behaviour with the severity it deserves."

Honey was ordered to shower, clean her teeth, and then led into Mr Walpole's office. She was made to stand to attention again: hands behind head, head up, straight back, straight legs, tits out. There was another slave there similarly positioned. Although Honey did not know it then, it was none other than Bimbo, the Bulgarian slave acquired by Victoria Stratton in London.

Both of the slaves eyed each other up, wondering which was the favourite of their master. They were not allowed to speak, of course. Honey had to concede the other one had her charms. She had a beautiful face, with a clear olive complexion, and glistening, smoky dark hair. She was big-breasted with a nice rump, as well, Honey thought ruefully. Her pubic hair had not been completely removed. There was a little tuft at the top of her slit, which had been dyed bright red. Presumably Domino thought red went well with her complexion, and as usual, Domino was right. Her sex-lips like Honey's were swollen and glistening with moisture, so she'd probably been given an aphrodisiac too. Honey consoled herself with the thought that the other girl was far too big and clumpy to be really attractive to Mr Walpole. Suddenly she noticed that the other one was staring at her crotch and blushed with embarrassment when she realised her rival was gawping at the punishment marks on her pussy.

She caught her rival's eye and there was no mistaking the little contemptuous grin.

"She'll know why I've been thrashed down there, of course," Honey reflected miserably. A pussy-thrashing was the standard punishment for wanking.

The two slaves were made to stand to attention for a good hour and a half, for Mr Walpole was in a meeting with Victoria Stratton and the trainers, including Mr Short.

*

Eventually Mr Walpole came back, holding a bundle of files, looking rather preoccupied. His desk scrambler telephone rang. He dumped the files on the desk.

"Yes? Yes, I think that's been sorted out now... No, I don't think we need a new pony-club venue in Texas, it would cost the earth, and the one we have is quite secure... No, the one we have is really quite secure, you tell him that... Yes, I am quite certain about that... Oh, is he? Well, pay him off then... Of course he'll take the money, a little reminder of past peccadilloes... Exactly... That's what I think... I'll trust your judgement on that one... My thoughts exactly... I'm glad you agree... Yes indeed... Well, I'm glad to hear things are going well at your end... Yes indeed, and to you too, goodbye."

Mr Walpole looked round at the two slaves, as if they were distractions he would really prefer not to have to bother with just at that time.

"Oh, you two. Oh, Honey! You've been masturbating again! When will you learn? I'll talk to you later. In the meantime, both of you, stretch your legs out sideways, and touch toes. Left arm to right toe, right arm to left toe, go on!"

The two slaves obediently did as they were told.

Ms McGillicutty came in and gave him a memo.

"Oh right. Well, I'll have to deal with it, won't I? All right, Ms McGillicutty, I'll see the customer in a moment. Now Honey! Bimbo! down on all fours, come with me."

The two slaves obediently crawled to the training room.

"Now you see that cage? In it at once! Look sharp Bimbo!" he added, as the taller girl seemed to hesitate at the prospect of sharing such a small space with a rival.

It was a matter of a few moments before the two slave items were locked in the cage, and Mr Walpole had disappeared out of the door, too involved with Domino business to give them a second glance.

*

Honey never was able to decide whether her imprisonment with the other slave was by accident or design. Did Domino manipulate them into that situation deliberately, or was it, after all, an accident? Her master's preoccupation with business seemed genuine, but you could never tell.

The two naked slave items, both of them on heat, were pressed together in the uncomfortable steel-barred cage.

Bimbo said something in a language which Honey couldn't recognise as being either Russian or Ukrainian and certainly didn't understand.

Bimbo reverted to English: "You wank often? You a dirty slave slut?"

Honey had to agree.

"A dirty little pig you are, yes? Not favourite of Mr Walpole?"

Honey was indignant. "I am his favourite, he's fucked me lots of times."

Bimbo laughed. "He fucks many slaves, even dirty little pigs like you. It doesn't mean you're a favourite. I'm his favourite. He's a powerful man and needs loyal, obedient slaves."

"Not you then. We're not supposed to be talking, remember? Anyway, I am loyal and obedient, most of the time. It was just that he gave me an aphrodisiac, and then rushed off. I know I did something naughty…"

Bimbo giggled. "You're a naughty little pig, you are, yes? Here!"

Without warning, Bimbo plunged her fingers into Honey's cunt, and twisted a nipple with her other hand.

"Ow! Stop that! Stop it!"

But it was obvious Bimbo wasn't going to stop it. She was taller than Honey, and meant to use her strength to dominate and humiliate her rival.

Honey was not easily cowed, however. She might have been small, but she was healthy and well made, and the enforced exercises on the bike and the dildo machine were making her fit and strong.

She scratched Bimbo's face and punched one of her breasts and then for good measure delivered a hard blow to the stomach. There wasn't enough room in the cage for a good swing, but a short stabbing punch hurt quite a lot. Bimbo screamed and furiously tore at Honey's face with her nails and pulled her hair. Honey managed somehow to slide round onto Bimbo's back, get her right arm round her neck and a knee in her back to force her head up and arch her spine. Then she fisted her in the arse with her free hand.

"Who's the favourite, bitch?"

But Bimbo uttered only inarticulate sounds. She was being half-strangled in Honey's headlock.

"Go on, bitch, tell me, who's the favourite?"

Bimbo let out a yell, twisted round, and threw Honey off her back. She punched her in the eye, gripped her biceps tightly and threw her back against the bars of the cage several times. Honey's head lolled about like the head of a rag doll and banged against the steel. She saw stars.

After that, it was clear Bimbo was going to be the victor. Honey kept pinching and scratching with all her might, but to no avail. Within a short time, she found the fingers of one of Bimbo's hands up her arse, and the other fist was buried excruciatingly in her cunt.

Bimbo's body was squashing her, pressing her down sideways on the cold steel floor of the cage, crushing one arm and causing her a great deal of pain. One of her arms was pinned against the floor, the other immobilised by the weight of her rival's body.

"Now, you admit, you're a dirty little pig."

"Please –"

"Admit!"

"I am a dirty little pig. I am not Mr Walpole's favourite. You are. You are his favourite and I am a dirty little pig."

Whether this admission would have satisfied Bimbo was fated never to be resolved, because at that moment Mr Walpole returned.

"Hey! What are you two doing? Assistants! Trainers!"

*

With the two slaves kowtowed at his feet, Mr Walpole played the DVD of the event. Although they had not been aware of it, a CCTV camera had been recording everything that had happened while the two slaves had been imprisoned in the cage. Then he said: "Hm!" and replayed it. After it had finished the second time, he lit one of his favourite Balkan Sobranie cigarette.

There was a silence while the two slaves touched the floor with their noses, and Mr Walpole puffed idly at his cigarette.

Eventually he spoke.

"Well, Honey, are you a dirty little pig?"

"Yes, Master."

"Look at both of you, disgraceful sluts. You've scratches and bruises all over your faces and bodies. Your hair's a mess. Bimbo, you've managed to give Honey a black eye. It's a wonder you didn't crack her skull open."

"Sorry, Master," Bimbo said repentantly.

"You certainly will be. Both of you. I thought we had trained you out of the horrible things I saw you doing to each other. Apparently not. Don't you realise you're property, and have no right to damage each other? How do you expect us to offer you to customers if you look like something the butcher sells as dog food? You should be ashamed of yourselves, and of course, Domino will make you ashamed of yourselves in no long time. I'm afraid to say, it's the punishment theatre for you two."

A yellow jet of wee immediately issued from between Honey's legs onto the flagstones of the punishment room.

"Oh lovely. Your thighs all wet and stinking of urine just completes the picture, Honey. Right. Up! You can stand to attention on the dais of the main refectory until lunchtime, and then watch the other slaves eating their lunch. I think a little fasting will do you good."

*

Mr Walpole handed the care of the two naked slave items to Mrs Collins, who carried a long bull-whip curled in her right hand. Honey took one look at that whip and was very careful to do exactly what she was told.

The two slaves were placed at the edge of the dais of the refectory, in attention posture: hands behind heads, tits out, back straight, legs straight, stomach in, buttocks clenched, to wait for several hours until the slaves came for lunch. Even when lunch was over, they would probably be made to stand there till after dinnertime, Honey thought miserably.

Most of the slaves – those that were not the favourites of any of the directors – ate in the main refectory of the Domino building. They were overlooked by trainers who took their meal on the dais, a raised platform at right angles to the lower table at one end of the refectory. Complete silence by the slaves was required throughout the meal, and an eagle-eyed assistant trainer carrying a heavy rubber tawse walked about the refectory to ensure the rule of silence was observed. Any miscreant who was observed talking – even if it was only a whisper to ask someone to pass the salt - was immediately thrown over the table, bare rump up, and given a flogging with the tawse.

Eventually – it seemed like a long age – the slaves were ushered in by trainers to their midday meal. They were seated at benches, and the food was served to them by maid-slaves of both sexes. Although they were not allowed to speak, Honey was aware of a sudden levity in the refectory, as if something had attracted the attention of the slaves. Suddenly, she found all the slaves were staring at her and her erstwhile rival. She saw herself through their eyes, and understood. They saw two slaves standing to attention, obviously destined for the punishment theatre, bruised and scratched and with dishevelled hair. She had a black eye. Some of them could probably smell her urine, and she had whip marks about her cunt, meaning she'd been wanking in private without permission. No wonder all the slaves in the hall were smiling. If they had been allowed to laugh they would have done, no doubt. Honey felt deeply ashamed. But she could do nothing except stand to attention and endure the mockery, if she didn't want to get severely whipped again.

The rest of the day was dreary for both slaves. Intimate contact with her Master and the other dominants of the Domino Club had led Honey to be able to anticipate the punishment policy Domino would adopt. As she had guessed, they were made to stand to attention throughout the day until after dinner was over. The smiles of the slave-diners were even broader when they realised the two reprobates had been forced to stand there all day. After dinner they were taken back to the punishment room by Madam Julia, bound with leather straps side by side over a punishment horse and given a hard paddling. Then, with limbs aching with fatigue and very sore hindquarters, they were led to their small, dark cells. A chastity belt was strapped on Honey, she was pushed into her cell and the door clanged shut. She would stay there, shut in darkness, until it was time for her to be prepared for her performance in the punishment theatre.

CHAPTER ELEVEN:

THE CAT FIGHT

Over the next few days, Bimbo and Honey were trained in cat-fighting, each separately, by trainers who were specialists in that skill.

"You know, Honey," her trainer told her while she was sucking his cock at the end of training, "it's true that Bimbo has the advantage of height over you, and I think she's going to be given the better odds, but in my personal opinion, you've got a very good chance of coming out the winner."

Honey knew her main job was to concentrate on swallowing the trainer's sperm as smoothly as she could when his cock jerked and splashed into her mouth, but she noted his words and took comfort from them.

*

Before Bimbo and Honey could be punished in the theatre, they had to be made up by the skilled female make-up artists Domino employed. This was because they were to perform and not just be put in bondage and shocked or whipped. The make-up was part of the ritual humiliation all those forced to perform in the theatre had to undergo.

In the make-up room, they were made to stand, wrists chained together and legs forced apart by steel rods with cuffs at either end that were locked round their ankles. Hooks at the end of chains hanging from the ceiling were attached to the chains securing their wrists. The ceiling chains were pulled up by pulleys so their arms were lifted high above their heads until they stood on tip-toe. They were hosed down with cold water and given an aphrodisiac to make their sex lips swell and glisten. Then the artists got to work.

Hair gel was applied to their hair and rubbed in thoroughly. The hair was teased out in long dishevelled streamers, so both of them looked like mad maenads. Honey's black eye was emphasised with black and purple cosmetic paint; red paint was applied to their scratches, and blue to their bruises. Their backsides were turned a beautiful glowing pink by blusher.

"Now we come to your cunt, my dear," Honey's artist said and smiled.

"She really loves her work, you can tell," Honey thought.

"First of all, I think, we'll have to highlight those punishment marks. They've faded slightly."

She knelt down and carefully painted the marks red, following them up the mount of Venus and the lower belly, and down across the perineum and the lower buttocks.

"There, I think that's it. Now all the audience will know what your favourite hobby is, won't they? And I think your sex lips need to be a bit redder... and they could do with a bit of gloss, so the audience knows you're on heat.... That's it.... Perfect. Now for the pièce de resistance. Your face. You'll really appreciate this."

The artist busied herself with foundation cream and rouge and lipstick and the other accoutrements of the cosmetician's art, all the while humming softly to herself. Finally she attached a little bell to Honey's nose ring and held a hand mirror up so Honey could appreciate the fruit of her labours.

Honey had to admit her face had been made up with great skill. She had been made to look like a ridiculous tart, with long false eyelashes and a great deal of eye liner, little circles of rouge on the centre of both cheeks, brilliant red lipstick thickly applied, and a beauty spot, such as might have been worn by an eighteenth century courtesan, below the eye that was uninjured. Then there was that silly, tinkly bell hanging just below her nose. Honey had known her performance in the punishment theatre would be humiliating; she hadn't realised just how humiliating it would be. A tinkling turn of the head showed her that her former rival had been made up in a similar way.

More humiliation was to follow.

Julia Collins came to the door of the make-up room, carrying a heavy whip.

"Are those two nearly ready now, Carole? We're running a tight schedule. Mrs Stratton's asked me to check," she said.

"Oh yes, all done," Honey's make-up artist said, wiping some cosmetic from her fingers with a rag. "Look at the little darlings. What do you think?"

Madam Julia took one look at the two chained and shackled slave items and burst out laughing. "Congratulations. You've both excelled yourselves this time. They look a picture."

The slaves were released from their bonds.

"Now you're in Madam Julia's care."

Honey wasn't sure that "care" was the right word, especially as Madam Julia drove the slaves before her, occasionally flicking their posteriors with the whip, not hard enough to mark them more than slightly, but heavy enough to sting and remind the two slaves of their place in Domino's scheme of things.

*

Madam Victoria was waiting for them in a large room used as a practice theatre.

She strapped them into dildo electrode harnesses.

"They'll give you shocks where it hurts during the rehearsal, but you won't be wearing them on stage, because we want the audience to see your naked cunts, don't we? Especially yours, Honey. I hope you remember your deportment exercises. Put the heels on," she said, indicating shoes with six-inch heels. "Now this area - are you looking? - we'll use as a practice stage. I want you to walk about it with a perfectly straight back and raised chin just as you did when you were wearing posture collars and had those hooks up your bums. O.K., let's try it."

Bimbo stumbled a bit at first and received the usual punishment in an intimate orifice, but Honey was pleased to find she had more or less mastered the basics of deportment, so long as she wasn't required to balance a book on her head or wear that horrible collar or a hook inserted in her back passage.

When the slave items had walked round the stage a few times in the required manner, Madam Victoria called out, "So far, so good. Now you'll do it again, except this time I want you to place your right hands on your hips and swing your arses about as you walk. Begin!"

The slaves did what they were told, and this time it was Honey who received the shock. Her belly clenched, she doubled up, her nose bell tinkling.

"You were punished because you weren't wiggling your bottom enough, Honey. Now let's try again. Imagine you're the sexy favourite of Mr Walpole," Madam Victoria told her.

"That's not likely now," Honey thought forlornly. However she did what she was told, like the obedient slave she tried to be most of the time.

Madam Victoria clapped her hands and laughed.

"Excellent, Honey! You did the arse-wiggling to perfection that time. You'll amuse the audience no end."

Bimbo and Honey were told they would be expected to fight in a wrestling ring after their initial perambulations round the stage. The slaves' dildo harnesses were removed, and thimble-sized flesh-coloured plastic cups were attached to the tips of their fingers with superglue. This was to prevent them scratching each other. To prevent them damaging each other's eyes they were made to wear visors. A metal stem from the visor rested on the nose, so it wouldn't be broken, and a guard in the mouth protected the teeth. They were made to wear high-heeled boots, though, which probably could do a lot of damage to an opponent, Honey reflected.

Bimbo and Honey were whip-driven to the wings of the stage of the main theatre. When they got there, there was another performance still going on. Apparently a male slave was being punished for making sexual advances to a female without permission.

"He probably hadn't done more than kiss her cheek," Honey thought. In fact, it would have been difficult for him to do much more, because surveillance at Domino was very strict. But any unauthorised communication between the sexes was a crime at Domino, where all slaves were property and any unauthorised sexual advance was interpreted as trespass on Domino's property rights.

The fight between the two – the man and a woman who, Honey assumed, was the victim of the assault – was drawing to a close by the time Honey and Bimbo arrived in the wings. He was naked apart from the bondage equipment he was forced to wear; she was wearing only a pair of thin rubber hot pants, so tight that her vaginal and posterior cleavages were plainly to be seen; and a pair of long, laced, fetish boots. The floor of the ring was inch-thick in mud, and the man was covered in it. Honey felt her juices flowing at the sight of him. No doubt that was partly the result of the aphrodisiac she had been made to ingest. He was over six feet tall and with the body of an athlete, broad shoulders and bulging biceps. His cock and balls were pushed forward, tied in an Arab strap, the better to present a good target for the petite female slave who was besting him. His groin was covered with an abundance of shiny black pubic hair, thick and curled, and his big testicles were tight, heavy with semen, beneath his impressively long and thick penis. His arms were tied behind his back, leather straps tightly securing each elbow to the wrist of the other hand. He was wearing a rubber occlusion helmet, which blinded, gagged and deafened him so he was helpless and had to endure every assault his petite female opponent made against him.

His opponent placed a leg behind his, and carelessly pushed him backwards. He fell on his back in the mud with a heavy thump. Then she kicked his protruding cock and balls and stood on them, to the delight of the audience. There was rapturous applause. Honey felt a warm feeling in her belly, and spontaneously applauded also. That was how slaves should be treated! That was how she should be treated, as she knew she would be, in a few minutes. Quite right too!

The female slave came upstage, and bowed. The applause was renewed. She bowed again, and then retreated behind the closing curtains. In spite of demands for an encore, she did not reappear.

A voice came from the speakers at the side of the stage:

"And now – what you've all been waiting for! – a catfight!"

There were cheers and applause.

"The two slaves you're about to see have been quarrelling with each other about which was the favourite of our boss – Mr Walpole." There were giggles from the audience. "Don't take my word for it, have a look at the screens," the voice went on.

Two large screens at each side of the stage showed Bimbo and Honey in sweaty embraces, scratching and fisting each other. There were bellows of laughter.

"Now they'll fight it out on stage – and we'll see which should be the favourite."

There was a lot of clapping as Bimbo and Honey were

brought on stage. They were walked round the ring by two assistant trainers Honey didn't know. Each assistant trainer held a chain leash linked to the ring in the slaves' clits. Honey held one hand on her waist and wiggled her arse for all she was worth, just as she'd been trained to do. The laughter was tumultuous. She could well imagine why. When she thought what she looked like, she blushed under the heavy make-up she was forced to wear. But the humiliation was stimulating, too, partly because of her conditioning, partly because of the aphrodisiac, so she was even more humiliated to feel her sex-lips and clitoris swelling, knowing that they were plainly in view.

The slave-audience was allowed to bet on the outcome of cat-fights: one reason why they were so popular. Slaves didn't have any money of course, but they could wager privileges, awarded as points. They could gamble as many points as they liked up to two hundred. Major privileges cost more than minor ones, naturally. Thirty points would get them off two hours deportment training, for example, and ninety a six hour P.T. drill. Their obligatory daily spankings could be reduced, at five points a spank. It was for the slave to decide how to spend the points. On the other hand, losing meant extra arduous tasks for the slave. Again it was for the unfortunate slave item to decide whether to have extra whippings, more P.T., or whatever.

"I wonder which of these stupid tarts is going to win. Don't you?" the voice from the loudspeaker asked

"The fat-arsed bitch with the flayed cunt!"

"Nah, she's too short. The dark-haired slut's going to win!"

There were various, raucous opinions expressed from the audience.

"We'll soon know, folks. The odds are three to two on the dark-haired slave item and ten to one on the other. It's time to place your bets."

The slave audience couldn't move, being chained in their positions, but assistant trainers came round, taking bets. When that had been completed, an assistant trainer signalled to the man with the microphone, and the cat-fight commenced.

*

The two assistant trainers led the cat-fighters to opposite corners of the ring. Bimbo was led to the blue corner, Honey to the red corner. The bell rang, and the two slave items rose to manoeuvre round each other and grapple. Bimbo had the advantage of height and was the clear favourite with the audience, which howled encouragement when, at the first clinch, Bimbo hurled Honey down onto the mud floor.

"That's it, slut, throw the cow down!"

Honey's head spun and she saw stars. She stayed facedown in the mud for a few seconds, and then rose unsteadily to her knees. Immediately, Bimbo kneed her in the face and made her nose bleed. Honey went down in the mud again to cheers from the audience. Before she could rise a second time, Bimbo was on top of her, with one knee in the small of the back and her arm round Honey's throat, choking her and forcing her head up.

Most of the audience had a lot of points riding on Bimbo. They were not slow to give her advice:

"Come on slut, twist her tits off!"

"Pull the bitch's hair out!"

"Fist the baggage!"

"Give the tart a good kick up the arse!"

Bimbo didn't need any advice. Honey's back was arched backwards, and she showed her agony on her face as first her left nipple, then her right, was twisted. Then Honey's head was lifted up by the hair and she was forced to kneel, then she was pushed back down onto her hands and knees, alternately dragged round the ring by her hair and given a good kicking on the rump. The audience applauded and shouted their approval, though their advice didn't stop:

"What you waiting for, you silly cow? Come on, fist the baggage!"

"Slap the bitch's face! Slap her jugs! Get on with it, slut!"

But Bimbo judged that kind of assault would be premature. Her strategy was to keep Honey too dizzy and punch-drunk to be able to fight back: the same strategy she'd successfully adopted when they had been fighting in the cage. She gave Honey a final bruising kick, lifting Honey's posteriors and causing them to wobble deliciously. There was laughter. Then she forced Honey up by yanking at her hair with both hands, and while Honey was still off-balance, swung her round the ring by the hair as if she were a highland throwing hammer. Honey's nose-bell tinkled continuously.

With her head forced down, with her hair pulled, some of it out of her scalp, thoroughly disorientated and off-balance, it wasn't long before Honey had stumbled and fallen down into the mud once more, only to be yanked up again, hurled round and thrown onto the ropes.

Although standing up now, Honey was too groggy to attack, to do anything but grip the ropes tightly and look blearily at her opponent. Bimbo had her at her mercy now. A glimmer of exultation filled her soul, and she grinned at Honey. They both knew who Mr Walpole's favourite was going to be, Bimbo thought. She walked towards Honey and casually gave her a stunning slap across one cheek, and then a backhander across the other. Now was the time to close in, throw Honey down in the mud again and fist her, thus demonstrating her complete dominance of her and winning the game. But just then Honey was saved by the bell signalling the end of round one.

*

The assistant trainers freshened up both fighters, and Honey could think clearly for the first time since the beginning of the match. She knew that Bimbo must be far ahead on points, and unless she could seize the initiative in this round she would lose – after that, she would be too exhausted and weak to turn the tables on her opponent, even assuming her opponent didn't gain outright victory in the second round by forcing a submission out of her and fisting her. She did have one thing going for her in a way – Bimbo would think she was as good as the winner already, and Honey hoped she could turn that overconfidence to her advantage. All too soon the bell signalled the next round.

Unhesitatingly Honey charged at her opponent, placed a leg behind her ankles and gave Bimbo a heavy shove with her shoulder. Bimbo fell flat on her back. Immediately, Honey jumped on her belly, the vicious heels of her boots digging into the other girl's flesh, then leaped up and came down hard on the other's body. Her rump rammed down on Bimbo's boobs squashing them and she was kneeling astride Bimbo, pinning Bimbo's arms under her knees. For a change, she had Bimbo at her mercy.

Honey wasted no time exploiting the situation. She couldn't punch Bimbo in the eyes because of the visor, but she repeatedly delivered hard slaps to her cheeks - hard and fast, that was the secret, Honey thought – stinging slaps – slap-slap-slap – mercilessly and continuously for a couple of minutes, while tears of pain and frustrated rage came to Bimbo's eyes, and her cheeks blushed scarlet with slap marks and anger. Then Honey pummelled her rival in the mouth and nose under the nose-piece, so blood dribbled from her mouth and nostrils. At every one of the slaps and blows, Bimbo's nose-bell rang as if in protest.

Except for the fact that the rules made it necessary, there

was no reason really why Honey should move from this position which gave her such an overwhelming advantage. But a fighter couldn't be forced down on her back for more than three minutes (three fifths of the length of a round); by that time the fighter forcing submission had to actually secure outright victory by fisting her opponent, or get off her prone body – though that wasn't the same as saying she was obliged to allow her opponent to rise.

An assistant trainer acting as referee told Honey she had to move.

Honey knew that the way she rose from her comfortable seat on Bimbo's bouncy jugs was critical. The slightest error of judgement would allow Bimbo to gain the advantage once more. This was going to be tricky. She gripped hold of Bimbo's hair with both hands, half-rose into a crouching position, and jumped on Bimbo's belly again. Bimbo let out a squeal of pain as Honey's tall heels dug into her flesh beneath the navel. Lack of circulation in her arms prevented her from moving them immediately Honey released them, a fact she had been counting on. Honey did a backwards somersault, pulling Bimbo's head up by the hair, then with a further heave she got her onto her feet, and then digging her shoulder into her enemy's midriff she flexed her legs and threw her opponent over her head.

Bimbo was too dazed to resist after that. Honey leapt on her, and worked her fists into the almost inert Bimbo's lower orifices and looked up at the referee. Honey was the winner.

The audience was subdued in its applause. There was no doubt Honey was the superior fighter, but that meant numerous extra P.T.s and deportment trainings and spankings for most of the audience....

CHAPTER TWELVE:

THE PUNISHMENT OF BIMBO

Both the slave items were sent to the ward for the next few days and their wounds were attended to. They were not allowed to communicate with each other. Naturally they were put in chastity belts, to ensure neither of them did what Honey remembered with shame she had done that time Mr Walpole had deserted her.

However, Mr Walpole did come to see her on the third and last day she was in the ward.

He sat by her bed and fed her grapes.

"Congratulations on your victory, Honey. You are my favourite as I told you before. You're a really remarkable girl, you know, and I'm sure we'll get a very high price for you when you're sold."

Honey felt a warm submissive feeling in her belly. She had pleased her master! "Thank you, Master."

"Bimbo will be punished for losing the fight. Part of your reward will be to witness her punishment."

Honey was overcome with feelings of gratitude and pride. "Oh, thank you, Master."

*

"Kneel to attention, Honey, hands behind head, that's right. Now observe. This is for your benefit as well as Bimbo's."

Bimbo was brought in by Madam Victoria, who was carrying a paddle and holding a leash attached to Bimbo's clit ring. Bimbo was wearing a branks, a rasp-like tongue-piece stilling her tongue, and an upward-pointing spike beneath her chin preventing her moving her jaw.

She kowtowed before Mr Walpole and therefore before Honey, who was kneeling at his feet. Bimbo's dark hair fell to the floor, and her breasts heaved.

"And how has this slave item been behaving herself, Vicky, since her defeat?"

"Very petulantly, James, I'm sorry to say. I had to have her put in the branks to prevent her being punished for any further ill-tempered remarks. She's got a long way to go before she's acquired the submissiveness we expect of all our slaves, I'm afraid."

Bimbo tossed her black hair back and a little insolent growl came out of her mouth, forcibly closed by her branks, which amazed Honey.

"Ah, I see how it is."

Mr Walpole reached down and lifted Bimbo's chin. She was forced to look into his eyes for a moment. Her expression was angry and resentful and she twisted her head away.

"You impudent girl!" Madam Victoria gave Bimbo six hard spanks on her posteriors with the paddle.

Mr Walpole lifted her head again. There was no evidence of contrition. The same anger showed in her eyes.

"Well, I was hoping I could be merciful to her. She did put up a good fight after all. The audience enjoyed it, and she was winning in the first round. However, I see a severe punishment is in order. Suspend her from wrists and ankles for twenty four hours. She'll have to receive a few good canings where it hurts. Then we'll see how impudent she is."

Evidently Bimbo had not been anticipating such a severe punishment. She gave some loud pitiful squeaks and moans, without affecting Mr Walpole's decision in the slightest.

"How firm and masterful he is!" Honey thought. "He's going to make Bimbo regret her insolence. Quite right, too! I've never seen a more impudent slave." But then Honey remembered uncomfortably that she'd been rather like Bimbo once.

*

All the time Walpole was working at the computer terminal, he made Honey kneel at ease at his feet, sitting on her ankles with her hands on her thighs. She had to learn to stay perfectly silent and still, with her legs parted so that her sex was on view and with her back straight and her chin tilted upwards, so her breasts were shown off to their best advantage. She was doing very well and his intuition that she would be ready for sale long before the allotted six months were up was proving sound.

While he was working he was made subliminally aware of her quiet, still presence by her natural scent. He never allowed the slaves he trained to wear the sort of artificial slave scent Honey had been made to wear when she was first introduced to him. In his opinion there was nothing more subtly erotic than the fresh body smell of a newly washed, naked girl.

When Walpole had finished his work at last, he looked down at Honey for the first time for several hours, to find her looking back at him, adoration in her eyes. She really was a remarkable slave, as well as a beautiful one. He smiled at her, and told her to get up and bend over his lap. She did it willingly enough. She had obviously learnt that a spanking was invariably followed by sexual use, which she engaged in with unfeigned pleasure and moans of undisguised delight.

Honey carefully positioned herself on her master's lap just as Walpole had instructed her. She was an intelligent girl, quick to learn. She curved her back and pushed up her posteriors so that they were well-presented and so that her sex was not in contact with his clothing and couldn't leave it damp.

Walpole stroked, moulded and squeezed Honey's buttocks dreamily for a minute or two and then her gave several hard hand spanks which caused ripples in the soft flesh and made Honey's bottom blush. He stroked her warmed bum fondly, then took a light paddle out of a drawer of his desk and spanked her bum hard again for a couple of minutes. She gave out little squeaks of pain which delighted him. Then he stood up, lifting her up and putting her over his shoulder in a fireman's lift. As he did so, he noticed her sex had blossomed and was moist. His suit would probably get damp after all but that couldn't be helped. He carried her into the adjoining bedroom and placed her carefully face-down on the bed. She was too well-trained to have to be told not to move or make a sound till he was ready. After taking his clothes off and hanging them up he enjoyed her for the next three-quarters of an hour, alternately entering her arse and her cunt. There was no greater pleasure a man could have, Walpole thought, than reaming a submissive girl's snatch while she throbbed and moaned with delight.

*

When they had both showered and Mr Walpole had changed, he ordered Honey on all fours and clicked a leash into her nose ring.

"Now we'll go and see how Bimbo's getting on."

Honey's eyes glistened with excitement. She was thrilled at being able to witness the degradation of her rival, and felt honoured and proud that she had been allowed that privilege.

*

When they arrived in the punishment room, Mr Walpole tied the leash to a ring in the wall, told Honey to kneel up at attention, hands behind head, chin up, tits out. He inspected Bimbo, but only briefly, because he had work to do. He said he would come and collect Honey later.

Punishment rooms were usually kept quite dark, unless the TV cameras were recording for the Domino website, which they weren't at the moment.

Bimbo was suspended from a beam running across the ceiling of the gloomy cell, doubled as she had been in Victoria Stratton's flat on the first night of her capture. Her wrists and ankles were chained to a single hook, a steel bar attached to the ankle cuffs keeping the legs somewhat apart, so they framed her torso below. Her face, turned ruddy with the strain of her posture, was forced between her legs by a rubber strap which ran behind her neck and across the back of her thighs, and then was buckled tightly behind her neck again. Lower down, a chain ran through her tit rings round her legs and was padlocked behind her back, so that her breasts were stretched and squeezed between her legs. Another strap, broader than the first, ran tightly round her legs and lower back, pressing her belly to her thighs.

The sight delighted Honey: the degradation was so artistically done, and the overall impression was very comical indeed. That bright red face, still in its branks, positioned just above the stretched and squeezed boobs, and then the red-lipped sex with its tiny tuft of red hair, and the little puckered anus below!

Dimly in the gloom Honey could see that Bimbo was not alone in her plight. There was a whole line of slaves similarly strung up in more or less the same way. Bimbo's neighbour was male. His pathetic little willy was contracted in his shame and balanced atop his scrotum, like a tiny head resting on a pillow. His testicles bulged because cord was tied tightly round the part which joined his torso. Perhaps because he was male, Honey thought, the artist who had positioned him had stretched his anus by inserting a thick dildo into it. The whole effect was very satisfying, and Honey felt her vagina blossoming again.

It was the custom at Domino for staff to visit the punishment rooms in their breaks to amuse themselves, much as aristocrats in the eighteenth century had visited Bedlam, the London lunatic asylum, to laugh at the antics of the inmates.

Honey became aware that two of the staff were walking along the line of slaves, chatting and laughing together and occasionally stopping before a slave to taunt and tease her. As they approached in the gloom, Honey could see one of them was Madam Julia. The other, whom she didn't know, was carrying a paddle. Madam Julia was carrying an elegant whippy cane suspended from a loop of cord with a tassel over her right wrist, and in her hand, Honey was astonished to see, she carried a toothbrush. An odd instrument of chastisement, Honey thought.

They came to the suspended male slave next to Bimbo.

"Ah, this is Juicy, Sarah, the impudent young buck I told you about," Madam Julia said. "Not so macho now, are you my darling? There, there." Madam Julia brushed away a lock of curly black hair that had fallen over his brow, and pouted at him. He croaked slightly behind his branks.

"Yes I know, you want to tell me you're very, very sorry, don't you? But you can't, can you? You can't do very much at all, in fact. And you're so, so very uncomfortable, aren't you, my little pet? Hung up like that, with that horrible fat dildo stuck up your arse. So unmanly. Never mind, I tell you what, I'll give you a little pleasure."

Madam Julia began to stroke his penis slowly with the toothbrush. So that's what it's for, Honey thought.

As Madam Julia brushed it with the stiff bristles of the toothbrush, the slave's prick grew in length, and the little purple end began to glisten. The slave seemed to be straining forward, and pleading sounds were coming from his forcibly closed mouth. "Ah, so now you feel a little bit better, do you, you naughty boy? But, you know, here at

Domino all pleasure has to be paid for." Madam Julia winked at Madam Sarah.

Madam Sarah walked over to the slave and delivered swift hard spanks on his buttocks with the paddle. Honey knew from her own experience that being able to see the strokes being delivered made the punishment ten times worse. The slave's penis contracted once more, until it was only a shadow of its former self.

"Feeling small and insignificant again, my dear?" Madam Julia patted his cheek. "Cut down to size, are you? Well, that's what you deserve, isn't it? Your cock will grow when I tell it to, and shrink when I tell it to, and you'll learn to obey the commands of a woman. That's how it's going to be from now on. We have a very rich lady in the States who's ordered you. She expects obedience from all her slaves. She's an old and respected customer of ours, so you wouldn't want to let Domino down by being obstreperous any more, would you? No, of course you wouldn't. Now let's try again."

The titillation with the toothbrush and the spankings were repeated several times, until at last Madam Julia seemed to get bored with her toy and on the slave's latest erection delivered a hard cutting stroke on his cock with her cane.

"So much for that. Let's move on. Oh well if isn't the cat-fighter! And a very rude girl she is by all accounts. Did you know, she's even rude to Madam Victoria and Mr Walpole, Sarah?"

"Is that so? No, I didn't know that. That's what I call real impudence. Even Juicy would never do that."

"That's the one who defeated her over there," Madam Julia said, looking directly at Honey, who was still kneeling obediently to attention, of course. "Mr Walpole must have brought her here. Let's have a little fun with them both."

Madam Julia walked over to where Honey was kneeling.

"Hello Honey," she said pleasantly. "Come to enjoy

watching Bimbo suffer, eh? I must say, that's not very sisterly of you. I think you two ought to kiss and make up."

As she was saying this, she unhitched Honey's leash, detached it from her nose ring, and reaffixed it to the ring on her clitoris.

"Now down on all fours! Crawl towards Bimbo! At the double!"

Madam Julia held the leash short in her left hand and pulled it up, so that Honey felt it taut in her anal crack and tugging on her clitoris. She was forced to hold her buttocks high and received a few little stinging taps from Madam Julia's cane to encourage her to move quickly until she was directly in front of Bimbo.

"Hup! Stand! Good girl. At ease. Now then, Bimbo, you're probably feeling quite glum and lonely at the moment so I thought you might appreciate some sisterly affection. Honey, bend down and lick her cunt."

Perhaps Honey should have been prepared for this order in view of Madam's previous remarks, but she was not. Her surprise caused her to hesitate a second too long and she felt the burning pain of Madam's cane across her hindquarters.

"I don't like having to give an order twice," Madam Julia said mildly.

Honey did what she was told. She felt the toothbrush stroking her own sex.

"That's a good girl, Honey. You've got the idea. Hold Bimbo's thighs, it'll give you more purchase. Stick your tongue right in there. Good. Now move up a little and suck her clit. Excellent! Bimbo's really enjoying it, you can tell."

Bimbo was moaning uncontrollably and her sex was oozing love-juice.

"That's the way. Now I'm sure Bimbo would appreciate it if you twisted her tits a little. No, don't lift your head.

Keep up the good work down there and let your hands feel their way to her tits. That's it. Aren't her jugs soft and squeezy? Squeeze them a bit. That's very good. Her tits are standing up like soldiers. Right, take hold of them and give them a good twist."

Bimbo yelped in pain.

"That's right! Again! And this time don't stop till I tell you!"

Bimbo yelled in agony and shuddered into orgasm. Honey tasted juices flooding into her mouth. There were peals of laughter from the two lady trainers.

"Oh my, but that was funny!" Madam Sarah said at last. "Honey, come here my dear. Let me wipe your face with a tissue or Mr Walpole will be wondering what we've been doing with you."

While Honey knelt in front of Madam Sarah and lifted up her face like a child to have it wiped, Bimbo was made to watch as Madam Julia stood in front of her and swished in twenty hard swipes with the cane, leaving a pretty ladder of tramlines across the stretched buttocks. It was only the first of many canings she would receive before her punishment was over.

CHAPTER THIRTEEN:

THE HOUSE PARTY

When eventually Madam Sarah took Honey back to Mr Walpole's office, he frowned to see the red stripe across her behind as she kowtowed before him.

"She's been disobedient has she?"

"Nothing serious, Sir. We were having a little fun and games and she was a bit slow to suck Bimbo's cunt, that's all. She seems a very obedient girl most of the time. Quite gentle and charming."

"Hm. I don't think Bimbo would agree with you there. A fiery nature is hidden beneath that demure exterior, eh, Honey?"

"Yes, Master." Honey had to agree. Saying "Well, sometimes," or "Perhaps," would sound like a contradiction and might be taken for insolence.

"I'm pleased with her progress. There was that lapse which forced me to return her to the punishment theatre, but I think that was mainly that wretched Bimbo's fault. How's she coming along by the way?"

"Receiving her second caning as we speak. She's not enjoying herself at all."

"Good. I want her arse quite raw by the end of the punishment session. It's the only way to deal with a slave like her. I haven't seen that degree of insolence for a long time."

"She'll have it beaten out of her quite soon, I should think."

"Good. Sarah, I've got something to tell you of a pleasanter nature. All the trainers will be informed formally by memo of course, but you might as well be told now. You'll have noticed how busy I've been over the last week?"

"He certainly has been," thought Honey. He had been called away quite a few times in the middle of their lovemaking. She'd never been tempted to be naughty again, though. She'd learnt her lesson there.

"I think we've all been missing your advice and supervision, Sir," Sarah said diplomatically.

"It's because of the numerous board meetings I've had to attend, and dealings with new customers. Then we have a new deal with the mafia, who've agreed to take older slaves – customers' ex-wives taken in part-exchange who can't be sold as slaves in the ordinary way. Domino's business has been expanding exponentially in the last quarter. The upshot of it is, our profits have doubled. And because we're a mutual trust, not a limited company, that means the salary of all our staff is going to be raised – quite considerably, I have to say."

"Oh my, Sir, that is good news."

"I thought you'd like the sound of it. And there's another thing. I've decided to arrange a country house party at Scheherazade to impress our new customers. We might even pay the travel expenses of the more important ones. I think it will help to consolidate our success. We'll arrange pony races there and so on. And we'll have some of the better trained slave items as toys of course. Naturally a lot of the trainers will have to stay here to look after the slaves who aren't going – but I'd like you to come, and Mrs Collins too."

"Oh, that's a wonderful idea. Have you chosen the slaves who're going yourself?"

"I thought the trainers would be best placed to do that. And Vicky of course. But this one will be my choice."

"He means me!" Honey thought.

Madam Sarah placed a hand on Honey's well-presented rump. "Oh yes, this little darling's an obvious choice."

*

As part of her reward for victory in the cat-fight Honey had been temporarily let off the training on the dildo machine, the exercise bike, the deportment exercises and the P.T. When Mr Walpole didn't want her, she'd been allowed to luxuriate in bed, and even been supplied with quantities of books and magazines to read – only what Mr Walpole called "appropriate" ones though – books published by Silver Moon, and magazines that concerned themselves with the domination of submissive female slaves. She greatly enjoyed reading these, and in her imagination placed herself in the position of the submissive females she read about. Until her period came, Mr Walpole had locked her in a chastity belt to ensure that her imagination didn't run away with her.

*

Scheherazade was James Walpole's country house in Western Sahara, fairly near the port of Ad Dakhia. In his twenties, Walpole had been an enthusiastic ecologist, and since he combined idealism with considerable entrepreneurial skill, he had set up a company to make the Sahara green. The idea had been to use wave, wind and solar power to desalinate sea-water and pump it into the desert. There tamarisk trees would be grown as a crop. These succulent plants exuded a sugary substance called manna, which could be fermented into an alcohol called mannitol that could be burnt as a biofuel, a substitute for the fossil fuels which would become more and more expensive as the years rolled by. As a twenty-six year old scientist, Walpole had high hopes of greening the desert, providing prosperity for the local population and making a considerable profit for himself.

He did succeed in improving the local standard of living,

and consequently had been highly respected by the government and local headmen to that day. His wider scheme failed, mainly because of the machinations of the oil companies, who saw his enterprise as a threat to their own businesses.

However, once when he was on a business trip to Ad Dakhia, he had been accompanied by a pretty blonde airhead who was his girl-friend at the time. While they had been drinking glasses of sweet mint tea in a café, he had been approached by a local businessman, who asked him in a whisper whether he was prepared to sell the girl and how much did he want for her? They agreed on a price and she was sold, never to be seen again in the western world despite the diligent searches of her family.

It was this experience which inspired him with his second important business idea, which proved much more successful than the first....

*

Scheherazade was set in extensive fertile grounds. There was a private airport too. Square miles of groves, woods, flower beds, lawns, copses, fields and bridle paths surrounded the elegant country house built in a futuristic manner by a talented but hitherto neglected English architect . All the greenery was due to the skill of the landscape gardener, Walpole himself. The water to irrigate the grounds was pumped from the sea and through desalination units; solar, wind and wave generators providing the power. When visitors to Scheherazade approached it from the air, they saw the green acres suddenly cut off by a tall electrified partition fence punctuated by watchtowers, and on the other side, nothing but desert. No slave could hope to escape from Scheherazade.

Slaves, bondage equipment, rubber occlusion helmets, instruments of chastisement, not to mention quantities of Viagra and aphrodisiacs, couldn't be transported to and from West Africa or anywhere else by commercial airlines, of course. Domino had its own fleet of planes. Domino's wealthy customers, who often arrived at Scheherazade in their own private jets, were surprised to see these were piston-engined machines – renovated Douglas DC-3s and Fairchild C-119 "Flying Boxcars" – and sometimes queried Walpole about it.

"Why those old jalopies, James?" one customer, Mario Cevasco, a mafia boss, asked. "Why, they went out half a century ago! I mean I know you Brits are into tradition and that, but still…."

But Walpole had his own reasons. Planes propelled by airscrews were relatively inexpensive to run and anyone who knew how to overhaul a car or a motorbike could maintain and repair them. They were robust as well, capable of carrying loads far heavier than official specs allowed; and they had no difficulty landing on the short runways of the sort of out-of-the-way private airstrips that Domino favoured.

It would be strictly standing room only in those planes which carried slaves. The slaves were lined up in parallel lines, each only a few inches away from her neighbour. Chains suspended from the ceiling held cuffed wrists above heads; legs were splayed out and ankles locked in metal stocks bolted to the floor. No doubt the slaves endured discomfort during their journey, but nothing that need worry anyone. Hygiene was ensured by plastic tubes taped to nether regions and leading to vacuum pumps which took away waste matter. No, really, Walpole thought, the slaves had little to complain about. In any case, they couldn't –

steel branks firmly gagged them and ensured they looked forwards and kept their heads up. Looking forwards and upwards – that was the right attitude for a slave to have when contemplating the future as a useful addition to an owner's menagerie.

*

Within a week, the house party was in full swing. There had been a few isolated sales of slaves, but no auction as yet. That would come on the last day: a deliberate ploy to keep the guests involved and interested to the end and prevent any anticlimax. The only things being auctioned at present, or sometimes offered as prizes in the various competitions that were being organised, was a great deal of equipment: bondage, instruments of chastisement, and various ingenious electrical and electronic devices. One interesting device particularly held the attention of the assembly of dominant ladies and gentlemen: the "SheSqueeze", a dildo which electronically measured vaginal contractions and played a tune or rang an alarm buzzer when a certain pattern of contractions was recognised by the microchip inside the device, indicating orgasm had been reached. It had been invented by one of Domino's boffins. Its purpose was to ensure that the orgasms slaves had when they were being spanked, whipped or shafted anally were real and not faked.

Mr Mario Cevasco was very impressed with the house party. Originally, he'd been a little dubious. He had swished the bloody Mary about he was holding in his hand.

"You gonna palm us off with those old broads, James, when you got all these pretty little cunts here?"

"If you want the young ones you can have them, you have to pay extra for them that's all. There was a price we agreed."

"Yeah, I suppose that's so. Still...."

"Look, Mario. Come with me. I'll show you a fifty year old woman you'll want to fuck."

"This I got to see to believe."

"Come with me then."

Mr Cevasco drained the last of his drink, and followed James Walpole.

*

They came to one of the numerous cells in the basement of Scheherazade.

"Oh Jesus!" Cevasco said when he saw the inmate.

"I thought you'd like her," James Walpole said smugly.

It was clear that whoever had positioned the slave had wished to inflict the maximum humiliation on her. There was a steel pole erected in the centre of the cell to just below waist height. At the top of it the slave was lying horizontally face upwards on a steel surface that supported her back. Her arms were stretched down and her wrists manacled to the pole. A wide hinged steel band was wrapped round her thighs, which were folded over her torso so that her buttocks and sex were presented for the attention of anyone who wanted to make use of them. In fact, all three orifices were readily available for use, because a steel gag was clamped round the slave's mouth and locked into place at the back of her neck. The mouthpiece was a short circular tube which forced the mouth wide open. The circular mouthpiece gave the slave a ridiculous expression of surprise as she looked goggle-eyed at Cevasco and Walpole. The worst part of her torture was the way her head had been tucked between her legs. A steel rod led from the posture collar at the base of the gag across the back of her knees, forcing her head forwards and pressing her thighs onto her body. Her lower legs stuck up absurdly behind her head and were held in position and forced apart by another steel rod attached to ankle cuffs.

"Meet slave item Bumfluff, a wife we took in part exchange. She's fifty, but she's got a body as trim as a young woman's and she's not bad-looking. Her former husband is an English stockbroker. Bumfluff was the very prim and proper headmistress of a private girls' school, so naturally Domino took a great deal of care to degrade the arrogant bitch as much as possible."

"How do you do that?" Walpole could see Cevasco was genuinely interested.

Walpole shrugged. "When she first came I had her head shaved as well as her body hair. Then she was washed with disinfectant and set up as a urinal for male members of staff."

Cevasco chuckled. "You don't say? I guess she didn't like that much."

"I don't know, I never asked her. She graduated from being just a urinal to being a cock-sucker and pussy-licker as well, when I had her sent out to Scheherazade. She crawled about on a leash attached to her clit and begged members of staff to be able to serve them with her mouth. If her services weren't required or were unsatisfactory for any reason, she'd be slapped across the face or booted up the backside. I suppose she must have drunk quite a few pints of spunk and piss every day."

Cevasco laughed. "The dame's had a rough time then."

"It's all part of the training. Now she's got used to serving with her mouth and tongue it's time for her to learn to serve with her other orifices as well, hence her present rather uncomfortable position. You'll notice that rack of canes along the wall there? We encourage guests who want to use her to give her a good hard caning first, so she associates the pain in her bum with the pleasure of sex. It'll help to develop a proper sense of subservience in her."

"O.K. Can I try her out?"

"Of course. Be my guest."

Cevasco gave Bumfluff a caning with a whippy, three foot long cane that left thin red stripes across her behind. She grunted as the rattan instrument cracked down on her broad rump, causing it to wobble and ripple in a quite satisfying way, Walpole thought. Then as a preliminary to penetrating her lower orifices, Cevasco sat astride her thighs and stuck his cock in her mouth.

James Walpole took a last look at the gurgling, scarlet face of Bumfluff, formerly Mrs Eleanor Brown, headmistress; smiled and left, so that Mario could get on with what he evidently wanted to do.

*

It was important that valued wealthy customers should thoroughly enjoy themselves and think their visit to Scheherazade was worthwhile, hopefully ordering more slave items – perhaps more than they had intended to buy at the outset. Therefore a whipping contest had been arranged for the guests. That was always popular.

While the guests were still taking breakfast the next day, the whipping-girls were prepared. On James Walpole's orders the slaves were not to be gagged, and only new, relatively untrained slaves were used, so the chastiser, and everyone else, would be able to savour the delightful sounds of subservience: cries for mercy; grunts; sighs; groans; little squeaks and shrieks and from time to time a scream of pain.

The contest was a chance for some of the guests who were old hands with a whip to show off their expertise. Some of them possessed an awesome whip artistry. The contestant who won would be awarded the title of Whip Master (or Mistress) of the Year and would be given the whipping-girl as a prize.

The whipping-girls were secured to stout timber A-frames: their wrists were held by rubber straps to the apex of the frame high above their heads and their legs spread apart and strapped by the ankles at the bottom. Further straps secured their elbows and knees. A broad belt circled their waists and tightly bound them to the waist-high crosspiece, so their posteriors were nicely presented for the lash. There was a fat plug up each slave's back passage, with wide sideways projections at the end, to keep the posterior cleft open. That was important, for it enabled the skilled user of the whip to show his expertise by landing the lash in an upward stoke into the cleft and between the legs onto the slave's sex.

A SheSqueeze had been fitted in each vagina to measure its state of arousal and any orgasms that were experienced.

Points were awarded for the accuracy of each stroke and the number of orgasms the slave had.

*

In the morning, the guests were entertained with a pony girl race and mud-wrestling. Lunch was a barbecue on one of the extensive lawns, served by maids. They were wearing tight rubber miniskirts and tops. The frilly petticoats that showed beneath the hem of their skirts swished as they walked around, serving their guests. They were topless and the guests were encouraged to enjoy the display of swaying and wobbling titflesh in any way they cared to.

Twelve girl-slaves had been positioned since early morning at the whipping frames; that number of guests had indicated a desire to take part in the contest. Most of the guests were fairly new to this type of sport, but there were two who, James Walpole knew, were very skilled at the art: one was Mario Cevasco, the other, the aristocratic English lady Marianne de Vere, whom Victoria Stratton had shown round the training farm in Guatemala. Although she was here primarily to buy new hunters and racing ponies, she was skilled with a whip, and not averse to buying a whipping slave too. Cevasco and de Vere didn't like each other in the least; it had taken all Walpole's skill to keep them apart or at least stop them from needling each other.

Cevasco had informed Walpole he thought de Vere was "a stuck-up broad," whereas de Vere had told Walpole "in all confidence" that she thought Cevasco was "a common little man. Do you know, I heard he was a criminal."

"Oh, Lady de Vere, I'm sure that can't be true," Walpole had said. "One should never judge Americans by appearances. They may seem to lack politesse but Mr Cevasco comes from a nation that doesn't believe in formality. And he's very skilled with a whip."

"Hm. We shall see."

*

The whipping frames were at the bottom of a landscaped knoll, a rising lawn, on which had been set deck chairs for guests who were not taking part in the contest. The height would give the guests a good view of the contest. After luncheon, the deck chairs slowly filled up with laughing chatting guests, armed with parasols and opera glasses.

Eventually Walpole's voice came through the speakers as he introduced the contestants and explained the rules of the contest.

"We'll begin with two simple strokes across the buttocks: a forward and then a backhand stroke. Contestants, on your marks! And now, when you're ready!"

Ten female backsides rippled and reddened as they were caught with thin plaited leather thongs. Two of the more inexpert contestants missed their targets: one slashed his victim's thighs; the other hit the small of her victim's back.

There were cries of condolence from those in the audience who were the supporters of these two:

"Bad luck, Christopher!"

"Better luck next time, Jenny!"

The two reluctantly handed back their whips to the referees, James Walpole and Victoria Stratton, and retired from the game. Their two slave-targets were released from their frames and led off.

"Now, the same strokes across the thighs. The forehand stroke must hit the right thigh only; the backhand stroke should only hit the left."

This time, only seven of the contestants inflicted accurate strokes. Two of the others managed to hit both thighs at once, one missed the thighs altogether, and hit the buttocks again.

"Well done, you seven. Now we come to the more difficult strokes. The thighs were spread out, but let's see if you can do the same with the buttocks as the target. When you're ready, place an accurate stroke on the right buttock only."

The slave targets yelped and flinched and their naked rumps jounced as the whips cracked down again. But the stroke was a difficult one, and two of the contestants were eliminated this time, hitting both buttock-cheeks.

The next stroke was to find only the left buttock, of course, and one of the remaining contestants failed to do that, leaving only four contestants.

The next two tests were to find the right and then the left tit, and after that only Mr Cevasco and Lady de Vere were left.

"Now we come to the most difficult stroke of all," Walpole announced. "The crotch crack. The contestants must whip vertically, landing the thong in the buttock cleavage, and bringing the lash up between the legs into the slave's vagina."

Mario Cevasco grinned, and cracked his whip in the air.

"You're just a vulgar show off Mr Cevasco," Marianne de Vere said disapprovingly.

"I can lick any little cunt I like with this whip," Cevasco said. "Maybe yours."

Walpole thought it was better to cut this interchange short.

"All right. When you're ready, go!"

Both the slave-items received a vicious cut between their legs. They yelped and wiggled their bottoms in a way the audience found most amusing. Victoria Stratton, who had been standing at the front of the slaves, declared that both the slaves' vaginas had been lashed.

"O.K. That round was a dead heat. It will have to be repeated until one of the contestants misses a stroke or one of the slaves comes to orgasm."

The strokes were repeated a number of times. They were all deadly accurate, and neither Cevasco nor de Vere could be faulted. Eventually, however, the buttocks of the slave who had been the target of de Vere's whip juddered.

"I think I espy an orgasm there," Lady de Vere exclaimed triumphantly.

Sure enough the SheSqueeze buzzed, and Victoria Stratton confirmed that Lady de Vere had succeeded in bringing her slave to orgasm.

Cevasco threw his whip down and stalked off. The prizes, a rather wonderful layered cake with cream filling, and the girl-slave herself, a cute big-arsed garçonne, were presented to Lady de Vere. The audience applauded tumultuously.

*

After hanging on a hook in one of the punishment rooms at Domino's establishment in London for twenty-four hours, Bimbo was broken in as a submissive slave. Nevertheless, Victoria Stratton was a perfectionist in all matters of discipline and so took her along with her to Scheherazade. James Walpole was surprised.

"I thought she could be prey in a hunt, James."

"Hm. I wasn't planning on a hunt. Just putting the pony girls in some races, that's all. In any case, we've got to be careful, Vicky. We have to impress our guests. They pay a very great deal for our services and expect efficiency and professionalism. Quite right too. An outbreak of impudence by Bimbo is the last thing we need."

"Oh, that won't happen. She's learnt her lesson. She's obedient enough now. It's just that, well, there's still something missing in her."

Walpole took a drag on the Balkan Sobranie he was smoking and smiled sardonically. "Tell me more."

"She obeys because she's cowed and afraid. That's not good enough. She must want to be a slave. She must know her place and want to be there. She must get a little warm masochistic feeling in her belly whenever she's dominated by a superior."

"Yes, that's Domino's philosophy... but a hunt...."

"Being prey in the hunt, and the training for it, is just what she needs. And then there's that little darling favourite of yours – "

"Honey?"

"Yes. She'd make an excellent hunter."

"Surely not. She's not tall enough. Hasn't the stamina. Anyway, she's being trained as a bed-slave, not a pony-girl."

"She's got the stamina all right. Her performance in the cat-fight proves that. And some experience as a hunter won't do her any harm, even if it's not her vocation. And she's got lovely tits, and a really lovely bottom."

"What's that got to do with anything?"

"Just imagine it, James: what she'll be like in harness. A tit-bar will make those big boobs of hers flop together as she runs; they'll heave together with exhaustion and the bit will make her drool on them. And that pretty bum of hers, well-whipped and rosy-hued. You'll have customers bidding tens of thousands against each other when they see the DVD."

"I see what you mean… but she hasn't been trained. And the house party only lasts a week."

"She learns fast. She's very intelligent. After a week of training she'll be up for it."

"O.K., Vicky, you're on. I've always been able to rely on your judgement in the past. We'll arrange the training of those two – and the other hunters and prey as well of course."

CHAPTER FOURTEEN:

TRAINING FOR THE HUNT

"Honey, I've decided you're going to take part in a hunt in a week's time. What do you think of that?"

Honey wasn't in a position to think very much about it, since she was tightly bound at the time with her master's cock up her back passage, and in any case couldn't say anything since there was a gag in her mouth.

James Walpole mentioned the hunt again while he was entering her sex. She wondered what a hunt was, but she was still gagged, so she couldn't ask, and anyway the divine feeling of her master's cock slipping deep inside her was occupying her fully.

*

"Bimbo, my little pet, it's been decided you should take part in a hunt. How many more?"

"Five, Madam, please."

"Wrong. Six. Seven, since you've made a mistake. Isn't that so?"

"Yes, Madam," Bimbo said glumly.

There was another spank with a paddle. Bimbo was lying over Madam Sarah's lap.

"How many now?"

"Er...." She had to get this right: her behind was on fire. "Six more, Madam, please."

"Bimbo, move your cunt up. I don't want moisture on my dress."

"Sorry, Madam." Bimbo arched her back.

She received another hard spank.

"Five more please, Madam"

"As I say, you're to take part in a hunt. You'll be prey."

"Oh." Bimbo flinched. "Four more please, Madam."

"Do you know what being prey in a hunt means?"

"No, Madam. Ow. Three more please, Madam."

"You're allowed to ask, my dear."

Bimbo had learnt enough by now to know that being "allowed" to do something meant that she was ordered to do it.

"What does being prey in a hunt mean, Madam? Ooh! Two more please, Madam."

"You'll be put through training to increase your stamina, on a treadmill and so on."

"Eek! One more please, Madam."

"And then you'll be chased through the grounds. If you manage to remain at liberty for twenty-four hours you'll be let off some training and punishments, like this spanking for example."

"Aargh! Spanking completed, thank you Madam."

*

Bimbo was disappointed to learn that the trainer mainly responsible for preparing her for the hunt was to be Madam Julia. Madam Sarah was strict, but only inflicted punishments and disciplines she thought were required. She had a way with slaves, she said, a gift of empathising with them and an understanding of their psychology.

"I love all my slaves to bits," she used to say, and Bimbo tried to remember that when Madam Sarah was energetically applying some instrument of chastisement to her posteriors.

Madam Julia, on the other hand, seemed to delight in causing as much pain and humiliation as possible and showed considerable skill at reducing slaves to helpless bondage objects. Bimbo had often been on the receiving end of her taunts and jibes, though she had up to now been spared much physical pain from her, having mainly been under the supervision of Madam Sarah. However, before she was conveyed to Scheherazade by Madam Victoria, she had been in a good position to witness Madam Julia's continual degrading repression of the wretched male slave, Juicy.

Juicy had once made the mistake of being impolite to Madam Julia and showing a certain male contempt for her as a female trainer. She had never forgiven or forgotten his original attitude and his life had become a constant miserable round of punishments and humiliations. Bimbo had been hung from the a hook for twenty-four hours, but she knew her neighbour in misery, Juicy, had been hung there for forty-eight, during which time his balls had been squashed into little ovals in a cruel vice, his buttocks whipped raw, and the cane vigorously applied to his cock. He had also been forced to learn a humiliating confession by heart. There had been a strong motive for learning it, for the thin wax taper which had been inserted into his urethra and had been burning slowly down, would not by removed until he was word-perfect.

His penis and testicles, being the part of him that made him male, were often the preferred object of Madam Julia's attentions. On one occasion she fastened him into a chastity belt, with the penis squeezed into a metal tube lined with tiny inward pointing pins. Then Bimbo had been borrowed from Madam Sarah and ordered to caress him. She had to french kiss him, rub her boobs into him, fondle his balls and stick a finger up his bum. It wasn't long before he was in agony as his hard-on was crushed by the metal tube.

A favourite trick of Madam Julia's was to put Juicy into a demeaning deportment frame. He was gagged with a branks attached to a metal posture collar. A steel rod was screwed into the collar at the back of the neck. The rod was supported by a projection from the back of a belt and ended in a hook which disappeared into the unfortunate slave's back passage. Metal braces over the elbows and knees and manacles fastening the arms to the belt ensured that Juicy stood rigidly to attention. Then Madam Julia injected him with Viagra. She caned his penis until his erection disappeared, then she waited for it reassert itself, and caned it again. This would go on until she got bored, when she would leave him with all of him standing rigidly to attention, including his very sore cock still with its Viagra-induced erection, which he was unable to terminate in the natural way. Sometimes she would place him in the refectory so that all the other slaves could enjoy his plight as they were having lunch or dinner.

It was this formidable lady, who could reduce a macho male to a whimpering wreck, who Bimbo learnt with trepidation was to prepare her for the hunt.

*

"Stand to attention, Bimbo."

Immediately Bimbo did as she was told: chin up, tits out, hands behind head, back straight, legs straight, belly in.

Madam Julia held a riding crop behind her back. She inspected the slave silently, slowly walking round her. Madam was not nearly as tall as Bimbo was, not much taller than Honey. That wasn't important of course. A horse was much bigger than a man, but it obeyed the man because it was only a horse. Bimbo was only a slave. She wasn't resentful of that fact any longer, only very afraid of being disobedient.

She was whacked across the behind.

"Buttocks clenched," Madam Julia said mildly, as if telling a small child to eat its greens. Madam continued her silent inspection, until, standing in front of Bimbo, she smiled and said, "Whose idea was the little red tuft of pubic hair above your slit?"

"My first trainer's, Madam, Mr Short."

"I thought so, it seemed like Ronnie's handiwork. It suits you. Red goes with your olive complexion very well."

"Thank you, Madam."

Madam Julia stroked the slave's hair. "Later, when you're due to be sold, we'll have to think what hairstyle suits you best. Longer than it is at present, I think…. But we can't do anything about that yet. Just let it grow." Madam seemed to be talking half to herself, in a dreamy sing-song way. She abruptly changed the subject. "Do you know what a hunt is?"

"Madam Sarah said I was to be chased through the grounds, and if I could stay without being caught for twenty-four hours, I should be given privileges."

"That's it, in a nutshell. It's not usual for a slave to remain at liberty that long, and a naked slave would find the Sahara cold at night, but nevertheless, it has been done. But for you to have a hope of succeeding, your stamina needs to be increased by exercise. I'll have to take you out for a run everyday. You'll have to get used to the iron-soled pony clogs you'll wear. And then you need to spend several hours on the treadmill as well. We'll soon have you as fit as a fiddle."

*

Later, Madam Julia took Bimbo to the stables. Ponies were being put in harness for their afternoon exercises. Madam Julia led Bimbo past them without comment to the mews where there were means of transport of bewilderingly different types. Some were light flies suitable for a single pony-girl to pull; there were racing carriages designed to be hauled by a team of six; sedan chairs intended to be lifted aloft by four slaves. Sedan chairs were not intended for racing of course; they were mainly for customers not interested in pony-girl racing, but who liked dominating sweating naked slave items as they were carried along in style. There was also an extraordinary chair at each side of which, attached to the chair by rigid metal rods, were metal corsets combined with posture collars and steel occlusion helmets.

Bimbo stared at it.

"You are allowed to ask me what it is, my dear."

"What is it, Madam?"

"Slaves are put in those corsets and steel occlusion helmets with their arms fastened behind them and of course drive the chair. You see those pedals at the feet of the chair? If the occupant presses one of them, say the right one, the left slave gets a shock in her bottom, which is a signal for her to run faster. If the other slave hasn't been given the same signal, the chair moves to the right. If both slaves get a signal in their bums at the same time, the chair moves faster but straight on."

Bimbo thought it was ingenious. "But what device makes the chair move slower, Madam?"

"Oh there's no device for that, except the driver's whip. A slash across the pussy is the usual signal."

"I'm sure it's a beneficial discipline for the slaves," Bimbo said piously.

"That's as may be. Now we come to the hunting bicycles. Here they are. Bicycles are often used in hunting. Can you think why?"

"Is it because they're more efficient, Madam?

"Quite correct. Even a strong hunter pulling a fly wouldn't be able to keep up with a reasonably fit prey-girl. Consider yourself for example: firm buttocks; thighs; calves; small waist and belly; excellent stamina - and your prey training regime hasn't even begun yet. The fact that the hunter had to pull her master or mistress along would mean she wouldn't have a chance of catching up with you and you would always escape. Of course, one could yoke a team of two or more hunters together, and that's the solution I prefer, and I think Mr Walpole too, but then they have to be well matched in height and strength, and that's not always possible. One shouldn't yoke an ox with an ass, as the Good Book says."

It had never occurred to Bimbo before that the Bible had anything relevant to say concerning slave hunting.

"Now look at these slave bikes. As you see, there are two tandems on either side of the car; four cyclists in all. The wheels are wide and very big to facilitate cross-country riding; the suspension is pretty sophisticated too. And the bikes can be geared differently to suit the stamina of different slaves, so the slaves don't have to be matched so exactly as when they're yoked together."

To Bimbo, the bikes had one thing in common with the exercise bike that she regularly spent a miserable hour or two on every day: there were the same cruel steel crossbar saddles, so hard on the twat and haunches. Dangling from each of them was a lead ending in a penis-shaped plug, which was obviously to be inserted in the slave's back passage, with its trailing stud-inlaid crotch and waist straps. Bimbo guessed they would make quite a sight, those naked toiling slaves, gleaming with perspiration and entirely under the control of the dominant man or woman who drove them across field and through copse surrounded by a pack of hounds, the wheels of the bikes bumping up and down as they pursued the hapless, frightened prey-slave. Bimbo's dismay must have shown on her face, because Madam Julia said:

"I see you disapprove, Bimbo."

Bimbo knew she mustn't show disapproval of any arrangement organised by her superiors; on the other hand, she mustn't be suspected of lying either. In her confusion, she hesitated. To her surprise, Madam Julia said:

"I agree with you."

"Oh – er – yes, Madam." What did Madam mean?

"All these new-fangled contraptions…. You're quite right, my dear, to despise them. Hunters running in harness are best. A couple of slave-girls in harness, their juices flowing over tight crotch straps, drooling through their bits on heaving boobs fastened in tit-bars and flopping together, with well-whipped rosy arses and glistening with sweat – there's nothing like that." A dreamy look came in Madam Julia's eye.

"Uh, no Madam."

*

For the rest of the day Bimbo was exercised on a treadmill. This was not the sort one would find in the average gym. It was the nineteenth century prison variety and filled a room. Small bells had been clipped on Bimbo's tit and clit rings and these tinkled prettily as she trod the endlessly rolling steps that passed under her. Toiling on the treadmill was exhausting, humiliating and painful, which was the intention of course. The only plus point, if it could be called one, was that Bimbo was dosed with an aphrodisiac on Madam Julia's orders. She had to learn to love her humiliation and pain. But even the aphrodisiac was a sort of torture, because she was never allowed to come. During her training as a prey-slave, she often begged Madam Julia to give her a seeing to with a strap-on, but madam only smiled and said that her dear little slut would have plenty of opportunity to orgasm after the hunt.

While treading on the mill Bimbo was put in a rubber occlusion helmet which simultaneously gagged, blinded and deafened her. She was not told the reason for this, though she could guess. Wearing the helmet, it was impossible for her to know whether she was being supervised. Of course, in any case, slackness was automatically punished the same way it was when the slave was on the exercise bike: a dildo electrode was plugged into Bimbo's anus, held in place by the usual uncomfortable and tightly bound stud-inlaid crotch and waist straps. If the treadmill ceased to rotate at what Bimbo's superior judged to be an acceptable speed, the mechanism would ensure she was shocked in the backside. Also the rate at which her tit and clit bells tinkled would give a supervisor in another part of the training quarters a good idea of how hard Bimbo was working. Nevertheless, a personal supervisor standing behind Bimbo with a whip added a human touch which no machine could emulate. Madam Julia was a skilled whip artist and could land a stinging blow precisely on a tit or upper thigh or buttock cheek, or place a lash between the naked legs, burning cunt and arse cleft simultaneously. Not knowing whether she would be lashed for slackness or not kept Bimbo quite literally on her toes, pushing down the steps for all she was worth.

*

Meanwhile, Victoria Stratton was showing James Walpole around the training stables and bridle paths, where Honey was being trained as a hunter. Honey had just been out for a run with one of the regular trainers, and was brought to a halt, panting and lathered in sweat, outside the stables where Stratton and Walpole were standing. She was blinkered, and her hands were fastened behind her back, wrists buckled to elbows. Her breasts were even more pronounced than they usually would be, because they were squeezed by tight surrounding straps inlaid with sharp little pins.

Her driver cracked the whip across her buttocks as a reminder, and she immediately put her feet together.

Walpole smiled. "You've got my property well-trained, I see." He fondled the depilated flesh around the tight, stud-inlaid crotch strap, fingering the end of the dildo that stuffed his favourite slave.

"She's coming along nicely, Sir," the driver said.

"Oh good…. You know, Vicky, I'm still not convinced. You've got her nicely broken in, admittedly. But she's not ideally suited to be a hunter. She's a bit too small at 1.6 metres, and her big tits are a problem, too. She should be a show-pony, surely?"

"She's small I agree, James, but she's got strength you know – well, you saw the cat-fight – and her training has made her even fitter. You should see how she positively runs round the treadmill, like a little mouse on a wheel. She'll make an excellent hunter, she really will, when she's paired with another girl of the same build – and I've found just the one. She's being washed down by the groom at the moment, but she'll be here shortly."

"But those huge tits…."

"Not a problem, with the tit-bar. You don't think so either, do you, Honey?" Stratton said, fondly squeezing Honey's left boob.

The bit clamping her tongue prevented Honey doing more than making a squeaking noise, which Victoria Stratton took as agreement.

Not a problem for Vicky, James Walpole thought, but rather a problem for the slave. The reins led down from the bit through the end of short chains dangling from the girl's nipple-rings, which were connected by a steel bar. When the pony was galloping along, the tit-bar made the boobs bounce nicely together, and any pull on the reins ensured they were yanked in the direction the driver wanted to go. It was a ferocious torment for a big-titted girl like Honey.

"Oh she enjoys herself, with that dildo up her, and the aphrodisiac she's been given. It's true, in the actual race, we'll have to remove the dildo, it would prevent her running at top speed, but that tight crotch strap will still give you pleasure, won't it, Honey?"

Honey gurgled behind her bit.

"Yes of course it will, my lovely." Victoria Stratton patted the pony's rump affectionately.

"Her arse is plugged as well, of course. Ah, Honey's partner is ready to be harnessed," Victoria Stratton said. Honey's team-mate was being led by her groom towards the pony-trap. "Driver, can Honey go for another little run, with Mr Walpole at the reins? She's not too exhausted is she?"

"Oh no Ma'am, she's a sturdy little pony. She's got another half an hour's run in her, at least."

The new slave, Bouncy, was the same build and height as Honey, the same hour-glass figure tacked out in the same way, her firm high breasts secured by a tit-bar, and the same round, broad, pneumatic buttock cheeks, perfectly formed for pleasurable spankings and whippings, divided by a similar tight stud-inlaid crotch strap. She was a southeast Asian girl, and James Walpole admired Vicky's choice of slaves, as he had so often in the past. The pair went perfectly together, the different skin and hair colour, the Russian blonde beside the dark Asian girl, made for a pleasing contrast.

The two pony items were harnessed together. The groom linked Honey's left tit ring to Bouncy's right by a chain, so all four breasts would swing together. Since they were blinkered, tongue-clamped, with their naked arses presented to the whip, their boobs squeezed and their crotches divided by tight pin-inlaid straps, their nipples carrying the rigid tit-bars, their lower orifices stuffed, and with their wrists buckled to elbows behind their backs, the harness gave the driver total mastery over his steeds.

*

James Walpole could screw any slave item he wanted, and they had become for him so much perspiring heaving flesh.

Although he would never have admitted it to anyone, he had grown to fear that he had become jaded. Honey was a little different, it was true, but it was only when he was driving the pair of ponies along the bridle path that he began to enjoy himself in a way he had not for quite a long time. The pair of pretty posteriors took the whip well, and the little squeaks issuing from the ponies' tongue-clamped mouths as they were driven right or left, their breasts swinging obediently in the direction their driver pulled them, amused him greatly. He decided to satisfy himself that they really did have the stamina to be hunters, as Vicky had said they had. He used the whip mercilessly, until the two jouncing naked rumps were blushing and striped with red welts. He made the items gallop faster and faster, expecting one or both of them to stumble, but neither did. They kept up a good speed for a quarter of an hour, the sweat glistening down their backs. Then he pulled on the reins, and made them canter, then trot, then gallop again for the last five minutes of the exercise.

*

When he jumped down out of the pony-trap, Vicky was waiting for his verdict.

"Well?"

"You're perfectly right, Vicky, they'll make hunters."

"I'm sure you'll enjoy driving them in the hunt."

"Ah, no, I won't do that. Mr Cevasco was put out by losing the whipping contest, so I think I'll have to let him be driver, so he has a chance of winning Bimbo."

*

Walpole inspected Bimbo in her cell on the night two days before the hunt.

"Well, Julia, how's she coming along?"

"Very well, Sir. Her running speed has increased

amazingly over the last week. She's a match for any of the hunters. Look at her now. I've been standing behind her, whipping her, so she knows she has to climb those steps at a gallop."

Bimbo, fitted in her rubber occlusion helmet, was climbing the treadmill for all she was worth.

"Very good. Excellent, in fact. Julia, you're a genius. Expect promotion when your career review comes up later this year."

"Oh thank you, Sir." Julia Symonds blushed with pleasure.

"It's what you deserve. Now, her teeth can be cleaned, of course, but apart from that, she mustn't be washed until the hunt. Her scent must be as strong as possible for the hounds. Mr Cevasco has got to have a good chance of taking her."

"Of course, Sir."

CHAPTER FIFTEEN:

THE HUNT

It was the day of the hunt, and slave item Bimbo was being prepared for what Madam Julia called "her big opportunity."

A chain was suspended from a hook in the ceiling of her cell, from which manacles were attached to her wrists holding Bimbo's arms above her head. She was forced into a kneeling position on the floor, with rubber straps looped over her upper calves set in the floor and steel hooks pulling her ankle cuffs apart. A steel posture collar pointed her face at the ceiling, and a conical funnel gag had been stuffed in her mouth and held there by flexible steel bands squeezing her cheeks and locked behind her head by a padlock which immobilised a tightly screwed wing-nut.

"Now my dear, just a few extra touches and you'll be quite ready," Madam Julia was saying. She rubbed and slapped sun cream all over Bimbo's naked body, lovingly massaging her breasts and pubic area. Then she squirted a cloud of tiny droplets of moisture from a perfume atomiser all over Bimbo. The perfume atomiser, however, did not contain perfume, or at least not perfume as conventionally understood; it had been filled with Bimbo's own urine, to give the hounds a strong scent to follow.

Bimbo was released from the bonds that had forced her to kneel once she had been forced to drink a lot of water through the funnel, and the posture collar and gag were taken off. Madam Julia operated a pulley which shortened the chain stretching Bimbo's arms, forcing her to rise.

"Right, slave, hup! Now let's get the stiffness out of your legs, run on the spot, come on, one, two, one two! That's right!"

To encourage vigorous exercise, Madam gave Bimbo a

few cracking slaps across the rump and thighs with a studded leather paddle.

After the exercise, Bimbo was tacked out as a prey-slave should be. A visor was placed over her eyes. She knew why. Darts tipped with anaesthetic would be shot from the specially modified air-rifles the huntsmen and women were armed with. The darts were designed so that they would not penetrate the flesh more than a few millimetres, all that was necessary to deliver a knock-out dose of anaesthetic. Members of the hunt aimed for the buttocks, but obviously the eyes of the prey-slaves had to be protected, just in case.

A comparatively loose, light aluminium chain circled her waist, and her wrists were fastened to it behind her back. This was mainly to prevent her climbing trees, which was forbidden by the rules of the game. The chain also incidentally would prevent a slave picking fruit, although Madam Julia had trained Bimbo to bite fruit still hanging from the lower branches of some fruit trees, like crab apple, which had seeded themselves in the wilder parts of the grounds used for hunting and were quite abundant. Although figs and dates still hanging from the branches of trees were inaccessible, Bimbo had been taught to look for fallen fruit, to kneel down and eat it as a wild pig or a deer or some other prey animal would. She had been vaccinated against types of food-poisoning that might result.

*

A casual observer would have had to have been reminded that all the pleasant greenery that surrounded Scheherazade: the leafy woods and sun-dappled glades; the little streams that splashed through rocky hills where ferns and wild tulips grew in abundance; the rolling moors scattered with gorse and heather, had all been designed by man – in fact, by one man, James Walpole; and where thick verdure existed now, there had once been only waterless sand dunes, an arid desert stretching as far as the eye could see.

However, natural though the country round Scheherazade seemed, it had been cleverly designed for the various purposes for which it was used. There were wide flat-bottomed valleys for pony-girl racing, for example, the sides of the valleys giving the spectators an excellent view of the race, and marshy glades in which naked mud-wrestling slaves provided entertainment. Concealed closed-circuit TV cameras were everywhere. This was not only so that those of Domino's customers who did not want to venture into the grounds during the heat of the day could watch the sports that were going on in the grounds, while remaining themselves in the cool air-conditioned house, but also because edited highlights of the DVDs would later be shown on Domino's secure website. Domino was careful to obscure the identity of guests of course.

Much of the countryside around Scheherazade was given over to hunting. In those parts, much of the undergrowth in the woods had been cleared away and trees were planted more widely apart, or never planted in the first place. This made it easier for prey and hunters to see each other, and for the pony carts to travel through the woods without the huntsmen and women having to dismount. Not all undergrowth had been cleared. That would make hunting too easy. The prey-slaves had to be given a sporting chance.

On the other hand, nettles and brambles had been planted to deter the prey along the borders of parts of the grounds where hunting would be more difficult.

Bimbo, naked except for the visor and the waist chain, was led to the starting point of the hunt by Madam Julia by a leash attached to her nose-ring. The sight of her attracted speculative glances from some of the crowd. Bimbo knew they were wondering how easy she would be to capture.

The hounds were brought up, and snuffled Bimbo's

bottom and snatch, so they would remember the scent.

"Remember – don't stop to pee, the hounds might catch up with you. Best to relieve yourself on the run," Madam Julia whispered in her ear. "You'll be given a sporting chance, my dear. You'll have a quarter of an hour's start."

Without warning Madam slapped her across the buttocks with a heavy leather tawse: "Off you go!"

Bimbo ran as fast as she was able across rough heather and gorse ground. The tough grass was trampled down by her iron-shod clogs, leaving a very visible trail for the hounds. But there was a margin of trees further on. She made for them, hoping she could hide in them before the dogs were released; but before she had got half way there she knew she couldn't hold the water in her bladder any longer. She pissed as she ran; her urine left a track on the ground making it even easier for the hounds to follow. Nevertheless, she ran as fast as she could, in the hope of making the stands of trees and eluding the hounds there.

*

That morning, Honey and Bouncy had been harnessed for the hunt. Walpole looked on with satisfaction. They made a smart-looking pair, well tacked out. Once again Walpole reflected that Victoria had a talent for choosing just the right slaves to please customers. These slaves were matched exactly: the same big boobs, neat waists and ample rears, one blond with a perfect peaches and cream skin, the other olive complexioned and dark, and Walpole was amused to see Victoria had followed Honey's former trainer Ronnie Short in the way she had prinked out the genital zones of the slaves. Honey's pubic area was depilated except for a humiliating little tuft dyed green immediately above the slit of her sex. To match it, Victoria had had Bouncy's sex depilated as well, but in her case the tuft was dyed red, which suited her dark complexion.

The pair had been severely harnessed, in a way that Walpole knew would cause them quite a lot of discomfort, but it was all for the best. The comfort of slaves was irrelevant. Tight girths exaggerated their slender waists and looked good. Tight crotch straps would sexually arouse the pair, and sexual arousal kept a slave's mind where her master wanted it and encouraged obedience. The crotch-straps were studded on the inside, and both of the slaves were impaled with dildos. The reins led down from the rather severe bits – bits also studded with pins – to the tit-rings which held the tit bars which prevented the breasts from wobbling about untidily. The reins were fitted through the tit-rings. When the driver pulled on a rein to indicate the ponies should change direction, four breasts would move in the required direction. The posture collar on each of the slaves ensured they looked directly ahead, and blinkers prevented them from being distracted.

There was no brand on the buttocks or thighs of either slave yet of course, because they still had to be sold. But there was a likely buyer nearby viewing the slaves, for Mario Cevasco was looking at the two slaves speculatively with the sort of expression potential buyers had.

"Those two bitches - they're kinda cute aren't they?"

"Would you like to drive them?"

"Sure would!"

"Be my guest then. Hop aboard!"

Cevasco didn't have to be told twice. He loved the power driving a pony-girl cart gave him. Taking the riding whip from a side-pocket in the cart with a certain expertise he slashed the two pony-slaves across the buttocks.

"Gee up gals! Trot on!"

They trotted to the starting position. One of the referees asked for the reins and tied them round the spokes of the cart's wheels, so that neither of the two slaves could move until they were supposed to. To make doubly sure, the referee temporarily loosened the hunters' crotch straps and fastened light chains onto their clit rings, attaching the other ends of the chains to the spokes. Any movement of the wheel would stretch the clitoris painfully.

Cevasco grinned when he saw the broad in charge of one of the prey-slaves slash her across the buttocks. Off the slave went. Two other prey slaves were released at the same time, but it was Bimbo – Cevasco looked at the programme he'd been given and saw that was her name – who caught his attention. He decided then and there he must have her as a prize. The hunt was popular, and there was a large turnout of guests eager to win one of the prey-slaves as a prize, because slaves captured in the hunt were given away to their captors, so there would be stiff competition.

At least the hounds won't have much difficulty following her trail, Cevasco thought with amusement. She was running across the rough like a jack-rabbit, pissing herself as she ran.

Soon the prey slaves had managed to get to the wood in the distance, and disappeared from view. Cevasco didn't much mind that. It was all part of the fun.

Ten minutes later the temporary hobbles on the carts were removed and reins were taken up by drivers.

After a quarter of an hour the starting pistol was fired.

*

Bimbo ran until she could run no more, not knowing where she was going. Her only plan was to keep away from the other prey-slaves – that way all of them would have a better chance of evading their pursuers. Eventually, panting from exhaustion, her heaving breasts and thighs lathered with sweat and soaked with urine, Bimbo came to a little stream trickling through the forest glades, gurgling and sparkling in the sunlight. It looked perfectly natural, although it had its origin in the mouth of a pipe at the top of an artificial hill, and ended up in an equally artificial cave, from whence it was pumped back to the hill underground and recycled.

She dropped on her knees and gratefully gulped down the cool water. Then she lay in the little stream. The water was icy cold after the hot sun. To remove her scent she had to roll over, since the stream was only a few inches deep. Since her hands were bound behind her back, it was a good thing it was, too: any deeper, she would have been at risk of drowning. As it was, she had difficulty rising to her feet against the swift current, and grazed one knee on the pebbles of the bed of the stream. She had another thought. If she walked along the middle of the stream for a while, maybe the hounds would lose her trail. The trouble was, you couldn't go very fast, paddling, and it was noisy as well. There was no wind, and Bimbo reckoned the splashing sound would carry a long way. Then there would be the alarm calls of the woodland birds. Still it was worth paddling for a bit, and she carried on walking down the stream for a quarter of an hour or so – but then she heard an ominous sound – the baying of hounds in the distance.

She stopped still, almost stopped breathing, and tried to gauge how far away the hounds were. It was difficult to tell, but the still air carried sounds a fair distance, so they were probably further away than they seemed. By the same token, though, they might have heard her splashing in the stream. She carefully scrambled up the bank on the side opposite the one she had entered from, trying to make as little noise as possible. She saw some undergrowth ahead of her, and gratefully headed for it.

*

Cevasco knew by a kind of instinct that his hacks could take a lot of whip, though if he had been asked he would not have been able to say how he knew. There were yelps, more high-pitched than stallions', as the lash cracked across two pretty asses. Cevasco grinned to himself. That was one of the advantages of driving mares: their high-pitched screams scared the prey, especially inexperienced slaves. In any case, Cevasco didn't enjoy dominating males nearly as much.

His grin faded as another sulky overtook his. It was driven by that stuck-up aristocratic English broad – what was her name? – de Vere. Grudgingly, he had to admit she had style. Her cart was pulled by two powerful stallions, which was obviously the reason why she had been able to overtake him. She was lashing them viciously across the hindquarters to encourage them to keep up a good speed, and, helpless in their harness, they had no choice but to oblige her by galloping along as fast as they could. They growled and grunted behind cruel steel bits, as muscles flexed beneath smooth flesh already shining with sweat. Penises and testicles had been buckled up in tight leather cock straps. Viagra-induced erections caused their thick shafts to stick out provocatively, and as a little humiliating touch, rings had been set through their foreskins from which hung little bells, which tinkled charmingly as they galloped along and their pricks waggled up and down. Steel hooks which sunk into buttock clefts to stretch their anuses were held up by chains attached to their waist belts. Both rumps were held up high. Ostensibly, Cevasco knew, that was to make them easier to whip. Really, though, a bum hook was a magnificently degrading device, and the torment was as much psychological as physical.

It was a masterly touch. O.K., the English dame knew what she was doing. It didn't mean she was going to take Bimbo though. He wished he'd had the chance to supervise the harnessing and have hooks inserted into the anuses of his own pair. Female bums came in two shapes, apple and pear. Both his mares had satisfyingly ample apple-shaped hindquarters which would have looked good held up by hooks. Still, no good crying over spilt milk. Their rumps looked good anyway, and would look even better after they had been well whipped.

De Vere wouldn't be allowed to find Bimbo before he did. He was determined that tall olive-skinned brunette was going to be his prize. He needn't have worried. Galloping his pair for not more than ten minutes or so he saw ahead of him that the hounds were paddling about near a stream. They had evidently lost the scent. Now finding the prey would depend mainly on skill and a little luck. It was true that luck might not go his way, but at least the fact that the de Vere broad was driving powerful stallions would not give her too much of an advantage. He decided to lead his pair further down the stream to the right, on the opposite bank. A double crack across their backsides encouraged them to plunge into the stream, and another good lashing got them smartly out of it onto the other bank. Cevasco pulled on the right-hand rein, and heads, clamped tongues, and boobs swung to the right, so the two mares were in no doubt which way they had to go, if they wanted to avoid the whip again. Thick undergrowth prevented the pair doing more than a walk, and they were soon overtaken by a few of the hounds, which were running along darting this way and that, still unable to pick up a scent. Suddenly one of them ran towards some undergrowth, barking like mad, and a female prey-slave started out of a clump of bushes. She was a tawny blonde, and her nude body was sanded all over with freckles. It wasn't Bimbo, but Cevasco would have her anyway. Again he lashed the rumps of his pair, not so much to make them trot faster (that wasn't really necessary because three or four hounds were running after the slave and would soon bring her down) but to induce those high-pitched screams that curdled the blood of new, inexperienced prey-slaves.

The hounds brought the slave down as they were trained to do, without biting the prey hard enough to puncture the skin. One ran in front to slow the slave down, another jumped on her back, knocking her belly-down onto the fresh coarse grass. As she sprawled with her face in the dirt, the others gripped arms and legs in their jaws.

As Cevasco's cart came up, he lifted the air rifle from its holster, attached to a metal shaft at one side of the cart, and loaded it with a dart tipped with anaesthetic. He carefully aimed the rifle at the prey's left buttock. Before he had squeezed the trigger though, he heard a "Whoa halt!" at his left. He looked up. It was the de Vere dame again, her two stallions panting and lathered with sweat.

"Mr Cevasco! We've both been following the same prey, I think."

"It would seem so, Ma'am."

"Well, you seem to have beaten me to it. Pity, I wanted that gal. Freckled slaves are so appealing, and I haven't got one. I wanted to add her to my collection. Still, there's no doubt you have the right to her. Go ahead, Mr Cevasco."

Cevasco thought quickly. Perhaps it would be better to play the part of a courteous sportsman. After all, he didn't particularly want this prey. If he gave way now, and she caught Bimbo later, perhaps she would be more amenable....

"No, Ma'am, since you want her, she's yours."

"Oh really?" Lady de Vere flushed. "No I couldn't!"

"I insist."

"Oh well. If you're sure…. Very well, thank you very much, Mr Cevasco."

"Don't mention it, Ma'am."

Lady de Vere needed no further invitation. She aimed her rifle at the prey, and a dart suddenly appeared on a buttock cheek of the slave. The prey immediately lapsed into unconsciousness. Lady de Vere tapped her mobile phone. After a space, gillies came up, hogtied the slave, and tagged her for collection later.

Since Lady de Vere continued along the stream the way they had both been going, Cevasco decided to try his luck in the opposite direction, and pulled the reins round.

Honey felt the pull on her head and clamped tongue, and a taut pain in her nipples when the tit bar swung her boobs to the left, and then left again, as her master ordered his pair of mares to reverse. The dildo, and the plug stretching her bumhole, both held in her by the tight, studded crotch strap that rubbed against her clitoris, were making her juices wet on the inside of her thighs, and her eyes were glazed with lust. She had been treated with an aphrodisiac before the race, and the effect of that and her cruel harness was to keep her mind exactly where her master wanted it. The pain associated with sexual pleasure, and her previous conditioning, created within her a deep longing and need to submit and be controlled by her driver. She wanted nothing more than to surrender to his every whim, and the whip that frequently burnt her rump strengthened her lust and confirmed her desire to be an obedient slave.

She felt the reins slap against her back, a signal to trot on, and she and her olive-skinned team-mate obeyed. She heard the crack of the lash on her team-mate's hindquarters, and Honey's nates involuntarily clenched in anticipation of the lash her own buttocks would inevitably feel in a moment. Even before it came, the pair of hard-worked mares were doing a smart, breast-jouncing canter, the bells on their harness tinkling merrily in time with their strides.

*

It was falling dark. Bimbo knelt down and tried to worm her way into the bushes, past briars and stands of tall nettles. It was difficult with her hands firmly handcuffed behind her back. Her hands were hoisted up her back further than she would like by the waist chain, and that prevented her from protecting herself. She had to force herself not to let out little whimpers and screams as she was pricked and stung. She began to ease herself round a rhododendron bush, so she could peep from it. It was a vantage point which gave her a good view of the green glades sweeping down the valley to the little stream at the bottom. She hadn't heard them for many hours, but now she heard again the faint but unmistakable sound of hounds baying in the distance.

Bimbo waited like this for a long time. Her scratches and nettle stings smarted and she began to shiver now that the sun had dropped below the horizon. She remembered what Madam Julia had said about the cold Saharan nights and wondered whether she had done the right thing in hiding. Perhaps she would have done better to keep herself warm by running, and put as much distance between herself and the hounds as possible. On the other hand, that would have meant setting up another trail, whereas if she stayed here, there was at least a hope the hounds would pass her by. In any case the dilemma became irrelevant, when she saw one of the hounds loping into view.

The hound, an Alsatian, was walking along the bank of the stream, but its nose was in the air, and it was looking around, ears erect. As she hoped, it had evidently not yet found her scent again. She made herself remain still. The slightest sound, and the dog would be on to her.

Soon, more hounds came into view, walking on both sides of the stream, sniffing and looking about, and then she saw the huntsman, riding a sulky pulled by two slave mares, trotting along at a good boob-bouncing pace. Bimbo gasped when she saw them. She recognised one: it was none other than Honey, her erstwhile rival. Bimbo was almost sorry for her now. The tight bit forced into her mouth was making her drool over the fleshy orbs of her breasts: these protruded because they were squeezed by tightly-bound surrounding straps. Madam Julia had shown her straps like those: they were studded, and Bimbo knew they had pins in them which would be cutting into the hapless mare's flesh. Her tits were clamped by a rigid metal rod. The idea was to make the breasts "tidy", Madam Julia had said, to make them bounce in unison as the mare cantered along. She had, on a whim, once made her wear a tit-bar briefly, so Bimbo knew from personal experience how excruciatingly painful they were – all the more so, as the reins led down from the bit to the rings clamped on the nipples, to swing the breasts, as well as the head, in the direction the driver wanted the controlled and helpless slave to go.

The two shafts of the sulky were connected to the meanly tight girths of the mares, to the right side of Honey and the left side of her slave-partner, and Bimbo guessed the girths was probably inlaid with pins as well. And I bet their arses and vaginas are plugged too, Bimbo thought.

The huntsman pulled on the reins to make his two hacks change their course and trot parallel with the stream. Heads and breasts were yanked in the direction the driver intended them to trot and Bimbo winced in sympathy as she heard a crack and a high-pitched yelp as the leather lash of a hunting whip met the flesh of one of the mares' ample buttock cheeks. The long lash snaked round a haunch and left a livid red mark on Honey's depilated pubic area. Then it was the turn of the other slave to get the same treatment. Another yelp and another livid mark. As the two hacks came nearer, Bimbo was able to see that their bellies and pubes were criss-crossed with marks, and she had to admit, ruefully, that the huntsman was very skilful in the use of the whip.

The two hacks were panting heavily and glistening with

sweat, their naked flesh, constricted by the harness, looking strangely neat and proper, as if their only vocation in life was to be slave-mares. Perhaps it was. Because they'd been driven so hard, the friction of the crotch straps and the dildoes stuffing their snatches had done the work they had been meant to do, and the inner parts of the thighs of the hacks would be sheened with juices. They were still too far away for Bimbo to see, but she knew from her own experience, when she had been made to gallop down bridle paths by Madam Julia during her exercises, that their eyes would be glazed with lust. Every lash on the buttocks would make their nipples stand erect and their juices run more. Hot and wet, they would be easy to control, and Domino's object, to make them willing accomplices in their own subjection, was easily attained.

Their driver was in total control. He used the whip expertly, and handled the reins with ruthless skill, so that the naked, sweating female animals pulling his sulky in harness were simply extensions of his will, willing tools who could no more resist him than could his little finger. He pulled the reins viciously to halt the pair. Their heads were jolted back and their large boobs juddered and flattened. Obediently they placed their feet together as they had been trained to do, and waited for their master's next command. Bimbo had never seen such hard-worked mares. Now that the air had turned cooler as dusk was falling, sweat was actually steaming off their backs and loins. With a sinking feeling in the pit of her stomach, Bimbo realised their master was going to be hers too if he caught her. They had perhaps been loaned to him only for the day; she would be his slave for life.

Involuntarily she began to imagine what that would be like. She would be branded, whipped, put in no doubt excruciating bondage, perhaps trained to pull a cart just as this pair had been. And all the time, force-fed aphrodisiacs and with her vagina and back passage stretched and plugged, she would actually enjoy her servitude and long to please her master with her obedient subservience, just as she longed to serve Mr Walpole now.

She came to herself. She had to get a grip. Dusk was falling, and with every minute she had a better chance of escape. As long as the hounds stayed beside the stream and didn't wander too far in her direction....

No sooner had that idea come to her, than some malign genie made one of the Alsatians do just that. There was nothing for it except to be as still as possible and hope the pooch didn't catch her scent. The hound came closer, and Bimbo began slowly to edge deeper into the undergrowth. The trouble was, with her hands secured behind her back, she couldn't do that without making a slight noise...

Bimbo always thought she had been particularly unlucky at that point. Perhaps if she'd had only one set of hounds to contend with, she might have escaped unnoticed. She would still have remained a slave of course, there was no escaping Scheherazade, but she might have avoided becoming the property of the ruthless master she later learnt was called Mario Cevasco.

But though she didn't know it then, her fate was fixed. She heard the sound of a hunting horn behind her, frighteningly near. She looked round, craning her neck awkwardly, but couldn't make out anything. She slithered round scratching her belly on thorns, and tried to peer out from between the stalks of a large stand of elephant grass. She saw sweat-lathered stallions, standing, feet together, not more than fifty metres away, and a dozen hounds yelping and running in her direction. Suddenly a hound pricked up its ears and barked. Stupid! Why had she moved?

Soon the smell of dog was all around her, and hounds were snuffling through the undergrowth. Her nerve gave way at that point. She knew she had to run, and she also knew that running was futile. She barged through the thicket, and raced for all she was worth. The hounds set up a great baying and yelping behind her. It would not be long before they brought her down. A hound ran in front of her, and she fell over it, nose down. Her belly slapped the earth. She felt hounds lightly grip her arms and legs, and one climb on her back. Then the hunters arrived.

*

Lady de Vere smiled to herself as the anaesthetic dart pierced the prey-slave's left buttock-cheek. She was getting a better markswoman with practice. At the last hunt she'd attended, she'd managed to hit a prey-slave in the testicles. Fortunately the wound wasn't serious, but the slave had had to have hospital treatment as a result.

Anyway, this gal had to be hogtied and tagged. Lady de Vere tapped at her cell-phone to call the gillies.

Just then, another huntsman emerged from the brow of the bank of the stream. It was that American, Mr Cevasco. She had thought him vulgar when they'd first met, but he'd proved to be a rather charming gentleman, after all.

"Well, Ma'am, I reckon you've beat me to it this time, fair and square."

"Oh, Mr Cevasco, were you following this prey too?"

"Sure was, Ma'am. But you beat me to her, like I said. Ah well, that's the luck of the game, I guess."

"Did you really want her? Then you may have her, Mr Cevasco. You gave me that freckled slave I really wanted, so it seems only fair I should let you have this one."

"I'd be really grateful, if it's O.K. by you."

"Of course it's all right. One good turn deserves another."

She watched as Cevasco neatly punctured the right buttock and the slave's body went limp.

CHAPTER SIXTEEN:

THE HUNT BALL

Bimbo woke to a swaying rhythm, as if she were being gently rocked in a cradle. As she came fully to consciousness, she realised her situation was not so benign as that. She was gagged, and her wrists were tied to the pole directly above her. Although she couldn't see them, she felt straps binding her wrists, knees, lower legs and ankles to a pole. She couldn't see them because there was nothing supporting her head, which lolled backwards. In fact, the only things she could see were a thick, and very stiff cock and blue-veined balls, bulging out of leather straps. They hovered just above her, so that the smell of them excited her nostrils, and male pheromones began to make the slit between her legs damp once again. She would have moaned, but the huge, phallus-shaped gag stuffed down her throat prevented that.

*

From the French windows of one of the living rooms in Scheherazade, Walpole looked out across a wide expanse of lawn and crocus beds. Beyond the lawn was the rose garden, where, in less busy times than these, he loved to lounge in a deckchair and read a good book, with only three slaves in attendance: one a footstool, one a side-table, and one an ashtray. There would be no lounging in deckchairs today, however. At any rate, not for the Domino staff. Everybody was milling around like ants in a hive busily preparing for the evening's hunt ball while the guests were seeing to the stabling of their hacks or changing for dinner. Meanwhile, Walpole was waiting for the prey-slaves to arrive. They were part of the evening's entertainment so it was pretty important they arrived as soon as possible.

Ah, here was the first one. None other than that awkward girl Bimbo they had had such trouble with originally. Not while the guests had been here though, thank goodness.

Her lower legs and wrists were tied to a pole carried on the shoulders of two muscular male slaves. The sight of the returning prey-slaves was calculated to give pleasure to the guests: the porters carrying the hogtied prey, usually female. The slave porters were completely naked, of course, and for the guests' further titillation they sported the usual Viagra-induced erections held up by leather cock-straps. At walking pace, the tight cock straps stopped their shafts waggling about in an undignified way and at the same time squeezed the neck of their balls and made them bulge out.

This one had woken from the unconsciousness induced by the anaesthetic-tipped dart, but was prevented from protesting about her predicament by the jaw-challenging gag which had been introduced into her mouth.

*

Walpole called Cevasco on an intranet cell phone line (you couldn't be too careful about security) to ask him whether he wanted his new slave branded. Cevasco did. Somehow Walpole wasn't surprised to learn that.

"Well, you'd better come down to the prison cells then, Mario, and choose your brand mark. There's quite a selection to choose from."

"How do I find the prison cells?"

"Where are you now?"

"Just driving my two mares up to the stables."

"O.K. I'll go there and take you to the cells myself. I need to supervise the branding in any case."

*

The two mares Cevasco had been driving were being hosed down when Walpole got to the stables. They were shivering and involuntarily pissing themselves with shock. My, my, they have been hard-worked, Walpole thought. Whip marks led all across their buttocks and the front of their thighs and across their pretty little pussies. There were red marks where their harness had cut into their crotches, their waists and around their breasts. They looked bedraggled as they were hosed down with cold water and were trembling as it splashed across their hot flesh. Never mind, Walpole thought, the cosmeticist will soon have them looking charming again. Cream would be massaged into their flesh to reduce and partly disguise the red marks of the harness and the whip, they would be drenched in some erotically-smelling scent and their hair shampooed and brushed.

Honey managed to look cute even in her present bedraggled state, Walpole noticed. She was still his favourite.

"Mario, let's go and have a cocktail or two while the little darlings are prepared. It'll give you a chance to chat to the other guests. Plenty of time to visit the prison cells after that. The bar's this way."

"Lead on, James."

*

The prison cells were not at all like the dungeons of some fantasist's imagination. Rats, starved prisoners hung up by their wrists, racks and masked warders wearing studded collars were noticeable by their absence. The cells were pristine clean, smelling of disinfectant and lit by brilliant strip lights. Domino couldn't afford to allow its valuable slave-stock to suffer from disease or serious injury.

Bimbo found herself forced to stand rigidly to attention in one of them, facing the wall. She knew she was going to get some awful punishment; she didn't know what. She supposed it would be another caning. She had done nothing to deserve a caning, she thought, but that didn't seem to matter – she was familiar enough with her discipline now to know that her masters and mistresses could cane her when they liked, how they liked, where they liked. She was a slave – she knew that now, accepted it, and – if she was honest with herself, not only accepted it, but rather liked it – no, she didn't just like it, let me be honest, she thought, it gives me the hots, it makes my pussy wet.

Bimbo was standing rigidly to attention because her bondage forced her to. Her feet and lower legs half way up to her knees were encased in a stiff cone, rather like the one her former lover, Stefan, had been put in when they were at Madam Victoria's flat. The cone kept her feet and legs together and perfectly still. It was screwed onto a sort of four-wheeled cart, for some reason. A vertical steel rod ran up from the cone between her legs and was bolted to a piercing at the perineum. Bands of steel attached to the rod braced her legs at three inch intervals all the way up them and forced her to stand up perfectly straight. A massive dildo, held in place by a steel arm connected to the vertical rod, stretched her denuded snatch.

The upper part of her body was kept still and rigid by the steel corset she had to wear, which crushed her waist and raised her bulging breasts. The breasts were lifted up from beneath by the metal corset and simultaneously squashed down by a steel clamp so they bulged outwards. The rings piercing her nubs were threaded through a T bar which jutted out from the corset. Her boobs were painfully squashed, lifted, and stretched, no doubt for the amusement of the onlookers who would watch her being punished, Bimbo thought.

A tall, and very uncomfortable posture collar lead to a mean, tight branks that held her head rigid and introduced a long thick phallus-shaped gag into her mouth so that her jaws were forced wide open.

The discomfort behind was even more awful than the

discomfort in front. Her wrists and elbows had been braced with steel bands and her wrists attached by a short chain to the posture collar, also of steel, so her forearms were forced together up her back. The way her arms were bound behind her severely arched her back, and pushed her breasts out even further.

Her bum had received the attention of her dominants as well, needless to say. A hook probed her back passage and hoisted her buttocks up. She'd never worn one before, but she remembered seeing them on the stallions of that imperious lady who had brought her down in the hunt. There was another device, though, that she wasn't familiar with. She couldn't see it, but it seemed to be a horizontal bar held up by adjustable sliders on either side of her corset. It cut into the gluteal area beneath the anus, squeezing her buttocks outwards like a pair of ripe plums.

All in all, her discomfort was immense, but she was forced to maintain the humiliating posture devised for her without uttering a sound or even twitching – and she would stay like this, she realised, for as long as they wished. She was entirely in their power. Her vaginal muscles squeezed the dildo and her pussy became wet as that realisation gave her a thrill, but, paradoxically, there was also a thrill of fear and she dribbled a drop of urine too.

*

She had been alone in the room for quite some time, facing the wall, forced by her frame to stand rigidly to attention, with buttocks jutting out provocatively, when she heard two male voices. She recognised both of them: the recognition made her do a little pee out of fear again – and yet there was another little shudder of lust too. One of them was her former master, Mr Walpole, the other, that terrible man, whom she knew would be her next master: that lady gave me to him in the hunt, she remembered.

The voice that she recognised as Mr Walpole's said, "Here she is, Mario."

"Ah, ass presented for treatment. Just like it should be."

That seemed in character for Mr Cevasco all right, Bimbo thought.

"The branding irons are over here. Select the one you want."

Branding irons! That couldn't be right. She wasn't going to be branded was she? She would have protested at that point, but of course the gag prevented more than a grunt.

"Did you hear that little piggy noise? Bimbo's obviously looking forward to the experience, Mario."

"She'll have lots of things to look forward to as my slave... Hm, let me see... I think, this one. 'C' for Cevasco. Er... I guess she's going to be branded on the lawn, right?"

"She's going to be branded on the arse, Mario." Walpole laughed. "Yeah, we'll take her up to the lawn. We'll bring the branding iron up with us."

In front of all those ladies and gentlemen, too! The thought of that humiliation aroused Bimbo sexually, and her pussy dripped juice. She knew her conditioning made that happen. Not for the first time, she felt a grudging respect for the efficiency of Domino's psychological techniques.

The reason for her being mounted on the cart now became apparent.

James Walpole took a remote control device out of the pocket of the cart. "You need this, Mario, to direct the cart. So I'll take the branding iron for the moment, and you have this."

Cevasco took the device and frowned. "How does it work? Oh, I guess I press this – "

Bimbo felt dizzy as the world spun round her.

Walpole laughed again. "No, you need the button there, for forwards, and the others for left, right, turn round, reverse, and stop, see?"

"O.K. Got it. Right. Forwards we go!"

The cart immediately charged into a wall of the cell and came to a juddering halt. Bimbo swayed and felt slightly sick.

Walpole collapsed in guffaws.

"Aw heck, I just did what you told me."

When Walpole had recovered, he said, "Sorry, Mario, my fault. I should have said, you don't have to keep the button pressed down. You just press it once, and then when you want the cart to stop, you press the stop button. Then press another button to change direction. Is that clear now?"

"Uh, I guess so."

"Right. Then let's get the slave up out of the cell, up the ramp, and onto the lawn. You're going to be a star, Mario. A lot of other customers will want to see this."

I'm sure they will, Bimbo thought. And they'll want to buy slaves they can brand themselves as well. And it will make good television. Bimbo knew she was a selling point. That realisation made her pussy wet again.

*

When they got to the well-mown croquet lawn, they found quite a number of Domino's customers strolling about. They were admiring all the naked slave flesh on view, calculating how much of it they could afford. When the rigid form of Bimbo, with buttocks squeezed out and well-displayed for branding, rolled onto the lawn, she caused quite a stir.

The branks prevented Bimbo from looking around, but out the corner of her eye she thought she saw something that looked like a barbecue grill. She knew it wasn't though.

Three of Domino's staff holding TV cameras focussed on her. That didn't concern the dominants watching the show. They knew they would be edited out of the version prepared for Domino's website, Bimbo supposed.

"My, look at that one!" a Chinese gentleman from Hong Kong said to Lady de Vere.

"She's a healthy gal, ain't she?" Lady de Vere replied. "I brought her down in the hunt, you know, but I gave her to Cevasco."

"That was very generous of you."

"Well, she's not my sort of slave, really. I prefer the garçonne type – like this cow here." De Vere delivered a hefty kick with her riding boot to the buttock cleft of a pretty, small-breasted, big-buttocked brunette with a pageboy hairstyle kneeling on all fours at her feet. "And, anyway, Mr Cevasco kindly gave me a freckled slave in exchange. I'm adding them to my collection, you know."

"Well, I wouldn't have minded having her."

"Too late for that, Mr Lin, but there are plenty of other slaves of her build around. Ask Mr Walpole, I've always found him very understanding and able to come up with just the slave the customer requires."

"Do you want to brand her, or shall I get an assistant to do it?" Walpole said to Cevasco, studiously ignoring the interest Bimbo's sudden appearance had created.

"You kidding? 'Course I want to do it."

"O.K.," Bimbo heard Mr Walpole's voice say. "An assistant is heating the iron right now. It'll take some time. It has to be white hot. Otherwise, it causes the slave unnecessary pain."

Oh, well, thank you very much for your concern, Mr Walpole, Bimbo thought.

"You know, this is the ultimate in domination," Mr Cevasco said.

"How do you mean?" Mr Walpole's voice seemed uninterested.

"Well, you know, a broad being branded on the ass – as my property. With that brand, she'll know who's the boss, won't she?"

"She sure will, Mario." Even Bimbo caught the irony in Mr Walpole's voice, in spite of her not being very adept at English. But she didn't think Mr Cevasco did – he was American, after all.

Eventually, the brand was ready: a white-hot silver "C".

"It's all yours," Walpole said.

The crowd gathered about seemed collectively to hold their breath as Cevasco raised the branding iron.

"Now which will it be, the left or the right?" Cevasco mused to himself

"The left buttock is the traditional place for a brand mark," Walpole said.

"I know, I know, you're disturbing my concentration," Cevasco said irritably.

Mario Cevasco stamped Bimbo's left buttock with the brand mark. There was a slight hiss. There was intense pain. Bimbo juddered. The crowd of ladies and gentleman clapped and cheered.

He's right, Bimbo thought to herself. I'm just property. I know my place for sure, now.

*

The hunt ball was in full swing. Naked slaves were displayed around the sides of the ballroom and on the patio and lawn. They'd been set up in deliberately enticing positions in the hope of seducing Domino's guests into purchasing them – Victoria Stratton had been a senior manageress in a large supermarket chain before she had taken more lucrative employment with Domino, and knew all about how to encourage impulse buying.

Some slaves, their legs spread wide apart, had manacled wrists pulled up behind them by chains suspended from the ceiling, forcing them to bend over and display well-whipped buttocks and genitals, metal number tags dangling from clitoris or cock, and bells from the tits of the females.

There might as well have been a notice: PLEASE FUCK ME – except of course it would have been superfluous.

Some of the guests were perhaps too modest to wish to fuck a slave in company, so for them slaves had been arranged so they could be whipped, or simply ogled at. Some were hanging from chains, their wrists manacled to a bar above their heads, their mouths plugged with ball gags, their ankles manacled together. The displayed crotch parts were sometimes painted with body paint, the pubic hair sometimes removed, sometimes shaped and dyed. Other slaves were tied to fences of chicken wire, similarly displayed, front or back, ready to be whipped or caned.

Desert nights were cold, but overhead electric heaters kept the nude slaves on the lawn or patio warm for the comfort of any master or mistress who wanted to play with them.

It was there, outside the French windows on the patio, beneath a crescent moon in a black sky dusted with a million brilliant stars, Honey found herself strapped over a metal hurdle; her legs spread apart by a rigid rod attached to her ankle manacles. Her jaws were forced apart by a huge gag that filled her mouth. The steel wires that held it in place drew her lips back. Her arms were bound behind her back, the wrist of each hand fastened to the elbow of the other. While her rump was held up provocatively by the hurdle, the forward part of her body was held immobile by two wooden boards locked together. They were a pillory for her tits, which were squeezed through two holes in the boards. They gripped her boobs tightly, and made it impossible for her rise up, or move very much at all.

Honey could see the stars between her legs; but she couldn't see Madam Julia at first, though she recognised her voice:

"Ah, Honey, my dear, I knew you were somewhere out here. Isn't it about time you made up with Bimbo? All that cat-fighting, and then you were one of the pair that took her in the hunt, so I'm told. Yes, I really do think it's time you two came to love each other."

Between her legs, Madam Julia came into view, and Honey saw her sip a cocktail thoughtfully. She saw Madam Victoria join her.

""You know, Vicky, I think Bimbo and Honey would make such a sweet pair. It would be, well, good television – and the punters would like it. You know, Bimbo humping this little blonde one. Don't you think?"

Madam Victoria put her drink down on Honey's left buttock. The glass was cool on her sore rump. Madam Victoria lit a cigarette and considered the matter.

"Cevasco won't like it. He wants to screw her himself."

"He'll have plenty of opportunity to do that, now that Bimbo's his property. We only want to borrow her for an hour or two. I've a shrewd suspicion when he sees the loving couple he'll want to buy Honey too. She's a little darling after all. You know, if I weren't one of the staff I wouldn't mind buying Honey myself."

Honey weed a little when she heard that Mr Cevasco might buy her. She didn't want to be the slave of the ruthless master who had driven her so remorselessly in the hunt – or did she? She trembled, and her pussy became wet again. Her trembling caused Madam Victoria's glass to slide off her buttocks, and smash on the patio.

"Oh, bad girl!"

Madam Victoria took hold of a tawse hanging from her belt and slashed Honey forwards and back again across her rump. Vip! Vop! "Naughty girl!"

Honey's bottom hurt like hell. It wiggled, giving the dominant ladies some amusement. Madam Julia smiled. "You see, Vicky, the little one's worked up already. Bimbo humping her will be a real hit with the guests."

A male slave was ordered to sweep up the broken glass,

and the two ladies went into the house. Their voices faded and Honey was left alone again, to consider her likely fate.

*

Madam Julia's prediction proved correct. Cevasco made no objection to his property reaming Honey's snatch. In fact, he expressed a desire to watch Bimbo ploughing the little blonde girl's gash himself.

Bimbo was led out of the house, warders' electric prods nudging her where she had to go. The "C" branded on her left buttock cheek caused much amusement with the interested guests. She was still wearing the branks, but the dildo gag had been replaced by a steel tongue clamp. Her arms were helplessly crossed behind her back. A chain from her left tit ring was secured to the manacle on her right wrist behind her back, and similarly, another chain ran from her right tit ring to her left wrist. But it was the device at her crotch which mainly caught the attention of the sniggering onlookers – a strap-on dildo of elephantine proportions. One end of the dildo entered Bimbo's pussy, stretching it outrageously. Juice dribbled down the inside of Bimbo's thighs. The petite blonde whose beautifully formed naked ass was upended over a trestle was in for a real treat. So were the onlookers, whose eager anticipation was apparent from their gloating, happy expressions. Walpole, who had changed into a smoking jacket, a cigarette drooping from his languorous fingers, joined the crowd, and noted the expressions. Pity the TV cameras couldn't record them, he thought. Julia had come up with a good idea here, he thought. Our sales are going to exceed all expectations. Walpole had mixed feelings about using Honey, though. He didn't want her damaged.

"Here we are, m'dear," one of Bimbo's escorts said. "Now, stuff her cunt." He lodged the massive shaft at Honey's entrance and made sure it was poised to penetrate.

When he was satisfied he pushed his electric prod into Bimbo's anus. The shock made Bimbo start, the crowd laugh and Honey try to scream as the huge thing slid into her, stretching her to her limits. Bimbo knew what would happen if she didn't perform properly so she went to work humping Honey without delay. Jerking her hips back and forth, shaking the petite body in front of her as she rammed into it. A cheer went up from the crowd.

Cevasco came up with an idea.

"Hey, James. Have my slave stuff the blonde one in the ass."

"She's your slave now, Mario. Give the order yourself, if that's what you want her to do."

"O.K. You heard that, slut? Poke the little pig-girl in the ass."

Bimbo pulled back and the huge shaft sprang up as it was released. Honey gurgled and groaned as she was emptied. With her hands pinioned she couldn't re-position it but Cevasco stepped forwards and lodged it firmly against the tightest of Honey's entrances. He briefly considered dolloping some lube onto her anus but thought that the shaft had enough pussy juice on it to suffice. He stepped away and slapped Bimbo on her backside. She immediately obeyed and jerked her hips forward. The crowd held its breath as they watched honey's anus stretch and stretch while she mewled and gurgled through her gag. Then slowly the huge shaft began to vanish inside the slave's back passage. There was a louder muffled sound from the petite blonde as she tried to scream through her gag. Spontaneous applause broke out among the crowd as Bimbo's pelvis at last came to rest against Honey's flogged posterior.

Cevasco grinned. "That's it, my beautiful slut, give her a good shafting up her rear. You've got all the crowd's attention now."

Bimbo set up a steady humping rhythm. It made good television, as Julia had predicted. All the onlookers enjoyed the spectacle, except one, James Walpole. A vague feeling of anxiety overcame him. It wasn't that he felt sorry for the slave who was being used in this humiliating way – it was just there was a danger she might get damaged. There was more to it than that, as well. Most slaves Walpole enjoyed were so much meat, and didn't touch his feelings at all – but Honey was different. She was cute. She'd roused him out of the jaded state he now knew he had fallen into. He loved having his way with her – taking her in all three orifices. He wanted her – badly – as his own property and realised at that moment that he couldn't sell her. She must be kept as his privately owned sex-slave. He'd make her pregnant too. He wanted children and she was the type who'd make a good breeding mare. Of course, the high price Honey would be sure to command if she were sold would be lost, but that couldn't be helped. Domino was doing well, very well indeed, much better in fact than he could have predicted even a year ago, and what was the point of wealth if you had to forgo every slave you fancied?

"Mario, that's enough. I don't want Honey damaged. Tell your slave to stop now."

"Aw heck, James, the fun's only just beginning."

"No, Mario, Honey's too valuable, exercise your mare on another slave."

"Look, I've been thinking, I'd like to buy Honey, she's a nice piece of ass."

"No that's impossible Mario, she's already been promised to someone else."

"I'll pay more."

"You don't know the price."

"Hell, James, I'm not short of bread."

"No, it's not the money, it's just that I can't sell her to you. You know, there are other considerations…"

"If I wasn't such an amiable type of fella, I might take that as an insult."

"Oh, please don't do that, Mario." Walpole had a sudden inspiration. "Why not have Bimbo ream Bumfluff?"

"Bumfluff? Oh you mean that old broad we're contracted to buy?"

"Yes. We've got her arse-up in the main hall. And we've trained her to beg to be fucked. It's really funny. She gets a good reaming and if she doesn't beg hard enough for it she gets caned across the backside with a little whippy cane. And then she has to say thank you for the caning. Come along. I'll show you."

As Walpole hoped, Cevasco was distracted from his desire to buy Honey.

"O.K! You!" he said to Bimbo, "come along now!"

Obediently, Bimbo withdrew her dildo from Honey's arse. There was a sucking sound. Walpole winced slightly, but no great harm seemed to have been done.

*

Bumfluff, formerly Mrs Eleanor Brown, headmistress, was enjoying her new rôle as a comic turn for the entertainment of the dominant ladies and gentlemen who were guests at the hunt ball. She was not gagged as she had been before; her trainers had successfully impressed on her that it was wise for her to show enthusiastic approval for whatever her masters and mistresses chose to do to her. She'd been conditioned to become sexually aroused by pain and humiliation. In fact, she's coming on well, Walpole thought.

Apart from the lack of a gag, she was in the same diabolic frame she'd been in before, when Cevasco had given her a good whacking with a cane and screwed her: arse and cunt presented to view as she lay on her back, her head forced between her legs, and her limbs poking up above her head. Her trainers had finessed her humiliation though, Walpole was pleased to see. Her face was made up like a clown, with an elaborate spiral pattern painted on her depilated head. A little bell was hanging from her nose ring. There was another bell at her clitoris, not large enough to hinder her vagina being entered. Her sex lips had been painted a bright magenta, and brilliant red and green circles and stars had been painted on her buttock cheeks too.

Bumfluff was such a comical sight she'd attracted quite an audience. Someone had begun a game of smacking her across the face, to make her nose bell tinkle. Then some one else had the idea of inserting fingers in her vagina, to shake her clitoris bell.

"I've got an idea, let's play a tune. You smack her face, then I'll play the bell on her clit."

"You ought to make her beg," someone else said in authoritative tones. This was none other than Lady de Vere. "Slaves get above themselves once they find a way of pleasing their masters and mistresses. You ought to make her beg, to bring home to her her insignificance."

The rest of the dominant ladies and gentlemen thought that was quite a good idea too.

Eventually the game got going with a vengeance:

"Please shake my bells, Masters."

Smack! Tinkle.

Tinkle, tinkle. "Ur! Thank you, Masters!"

While this merry scene was taking place, a thought occurred to Walpole: "Are you going to have Bumfluff branded too, Mario?"

"No. She'll be used as a hooker, back in the States. Branding wouldn't be appropriate."

"Oh, I see. Anyway, time to have some fun with her. Hello, Bumfluff," Walpole said cheerily. "Looking forward to a reaming, are you?"

"Oh yes Master; very much Master."

There was general laughter among the company.

"Thought you would be, slut. And I suppose you'd like to feel the tawse on your cunt, to make you all hot?"

"Oh yes, Master, please."

There was more laughter.

"Do you remember Mr Cevasco? I'm sure if you ask him nicely, he'll oblige you with a good pussy-whipping."

"I'd like that very much, Master. I enjoy having my cunt whipped."

"Of course you do, slut. Well, ask Mr Cevasco nicely, then. He'll be your new master after the ball, so you'd better do all you can to please him."

"Please, Master, smack my cunt with a tawse. Smack it hard, because I want to know you're my dominant master."

Cevasco didn't need any second invitation. He took a leather strap handed him, and laid into Bumfluff's sex-gash. Bumfluff whimpered, and her little nose bell, and the bell at her cunt, tinkled again.

"Thank you, Master," she cried, each time the tawse came down.

After he had had fun with Bumfluff, Cevasco ordered his newly branded slave, Bimbo, to hump her "up the ass."

The television people will really go to town with this one, Walpole thought. He was right. The cameras hovered long over Bumfluff's comic make-up, the look of desperation and sheer enjoyment on her ridiculously made-up face, then zoomed in on Bimbo's thick dildo reaming her hindquarters. The long, black dildo seesawed in and out of Bumfluff's back passage, and when, for short periods, it came out entirely, it left a large distended hole where the anus remained distended for a few seconds.

"Now enter her cunt, Bimbo," Cevasco said.

Bimbo did so, and the television cameras caught orgasm and ecstasy on Bumfluff's clown face, which, on viewing it afterwards, Walpole thought were some of the best shots of subservient sex ever taken.

CHAPTER SEVENTEEN:

THE WHIPPING CONTEST

Bimbo humping Bumfluff attracted a great deal of attention from the dominants at Scheherazade. There were many admiring glances cast at the long limbs, high round buttocks and generous breasts of the dark-haired beauty, and, despite Bimbo having already been branded, many enquiries and offers of purchase, which flattered Mario Cevasco a great deal. He refused them all of course. He still nursed a resentment at the way Walpole had refused to sell him Honey, though. She was a cute little thing, and Cevasco was determined to win her, one way or another. In his own world, when Mario Cevasco wanted something, he got it: maybe he had to play the game by different rules here at Scheherazade – but he was going to have a darn good try at getting the little blonde doll. He had an idea. He walked over to Walpole who was chatting to Lady de Vere. She was holding a leash in her hands, attached to the collar of her newly acquired slave, who was kneeling as usual on all fours at her feet, the better to show off her ample rump.

"Say, James, you won't change your mind about letting me buy Honey?"

Walpole gave Cevasco a worried look. Cevasco guessed Walpole had hoped he'd been able to distract a simple-minded American with the game with Bumfluff. He hadn't been able to. That was a problem for Domino, Cevasco knew. It was Domino's policy to give all its wealthy customers satisfaction, and Cevasco, who was a very important customer indeed, needed to be kept happy.

"Er... no, Mario, I can't," Walpole said.

"Why not? Who's this customer who's so much more important than me?"

Walpole hesitated. "As a matter of fact, Mario, it's me. I want Honey myself."

Cevasco stared at Walpole for a second, then burst out in laughter. "Well if that don't take the cake! O.K., O.K., now I understand. Well, I'm not gonna go away in a huff and cancel all the orders for hookers my organisation has made with you, that wouldn't be good business. We're quite satisfied with the service your organisation provides on that level."

Walpole looked relieved. "That's very reasonable of you, Mario."

"But I guess you've no objection if I buy that other slave – what's her name? – who formed the pair with Honey in the hunt?"

"That would be Bouncy."

"Bouncy, that's it. Well I guess you've no objection to me buying her?"

"Of course not – and she's very like Honey in height and build. The reserve auction price is $90,000, but what's $10,000 between friends? I'll let you have her for $80,000. She's very well-trained and subservient. Your type."

"I prefer blondes."

"Dye her hair then."

"Nah – her complexion's all wrong – too dark. I'll keep her hair its natural colour."

"As you wish. Do you want to brand her?"

"Not just yet. Let's have a game first. You put in Honey, and I'll put in Bouncy, and the winner takes the other slave as a prize. If you win, you take Bouncy back and get to keep my $80,000, and if I win – "

"You take Honey?"

"You got it."

"What sort of game? A race do you mean?"

"No, I reckon both of 'em have been hard-raced already. They need a rest from galloping for a bit."

"What then? If you want me to play poker or anything like that I'm afraid I'll have to decline. I'm hopeless at card games."

"Nothing like poker. Or strip monopoly. Actually, I was thinking of another whipping contest."

"You'd beat me there, I'm out of practice with the whip. My favourite instrument is the cane you know."

"No, the whipper isn't tested. Just the slave."

"How?"

"Simple. Wouldn't you say that both of those little dolls are well-trained masochists?"

"Of course. Domino wouldn't be doing its job otherwise."

"So we plug their twats with those SheSqueeze dildos. The owner of the first slave to get three orgasms is the winner."

Walpole smiled slightly. "All right. You're on."

All through this dialogue Cevasco had been aware that Lady de Vere was hovering nearby. She broke her silence: "I say, what a jolly idea. I'd rather like to join in too."

"No, Lady, this is between me and James here."

"Oh, Mario, where's your gallantry? Lady de Vere can join in if she wants to."

"Oh hell, O.K. But you might lose that big pink butt, you know."

"It's a risk I'm prepared to take, Mr Cevasco. After all, I won Cheeky in the last whipping contest, so losing her won't be a financial loss. If I do lose her, maybe I'll buy her back anyway, if the winner agrees."

*

Walpole set about organising the contest. It was decided that each contestant could choose the punishment frame and instrument of chastisement he or she wished. Assistants erected the punishment frames according to the requirements of the contestants. Walpole asked Victoria

Stratton to be the referee. On the whole, Walpole was not too sorry that Cevasco's desire to acquire Honey had worked out this way. He was pretty sure that Honey would win the game, or he was no judge of slave-flesh. When she got going, orgasms blew through her like wind through sails on a stormy sea. That was one of the reasons he wanted her for himself. The game would be popular too, and no doubt attract quite a few spectators.

Walpole went to find three spare SheSqueezes. He decided to preset them with three different tunes, so there would be no doubt which slave had orgasmed. With a grin, he chose excerpts from what he considered appropriate pieces.

*

Within an hour or so, the assistants had managed to construct the punishment frames according to the contestants' requirements. Predictably, Cevasco's was the most sadistic. He had preferred a frontal position for Bouncy. Her forearms were bound behind her on a horizontal bar just below the level of her breasts, each forearm pointing towards her body.. She was kneeling, with her thighs splayed out, and her lower legs bound together too, with each foot touching the inside of the knee of the opposite leg, so her legs formed an equilateral triangle. This posture forced her to arch backwards, emphasised by the fact that the steel posture collar round her neck, which was of a quite staggering height, was attached by a taut cord to one of the uprights supporting the horizontal bar to which her forearms were tied. Her head was forced back so much that she was forced to look up at the sky. An adjustable leather strap from the same upright held a chain of beads that ran down and dug into her crotch and up again to another adjustable strap attached to another upright at the front. To complete her discomfort, a rubber-coated metal bar opened her jaws, and was savagely pulled back into her mouth by wires that reached round the back of her head and were attached to the back of the collar.

Cevasco's obviously relying on the pain and humiliation of the frame to induce orgasm, Walpole thought, and the beaded chain will rub against her clit every time she shifts when he whips her. Walpole had grudgingly to admit that it was a good strategy – but he thought a little too fussy. All those straps and uprights will get in the way of a good swing of the whip.

Lady de Vere was obviously counting on the sensitivity of her slave's rump. The big-arsed slave, Cheeky, had been placed in a position where her backside was the obvious target. Actually, when he won the contest (Walpole had no doubt he would) he wouldn't mind owning that slave. She had a sweet square face, and rosy cheeks, with the glowing complexion that some brunettes have. Although her bottom was big, she was quite slim. He could imagine having fun dressing the little garçonne up in an open-necked shirt and tight hot pants, spanking her, and then taking her between those two big bouncy cushions of her bottom, doggy style. He could imagine Lady de Vere probably liked doing something of that kind too, with a strap-on.

De Vere's slave was bent over on a wooden platform to which was attached a tubular aluminium frame, that arched over the vulnerable naked slave. Her legs were splayed apart and her arms and legs anchored with manacles to the platform. A horse-hair rope led from a leather belt round her waist, through her legs, cutting into her sex-slit and buttock cleavage, and up again to be attached to the back of the belt. The belt was hoisted up by a pulley suspended from the aluminium frame, pulling up the slave's buttocks for any treatment a dominant mistress chose to administer to them. Her bum-up posture was emphasised further by the short chain leading from an iron ring in the floor to her posture collar, pulling her head down and pointing her rear skywards.

That's quite good as well, thought Walpole. But it concentrates too much on the slave's rear. It would be difficult to whip her tits accurately, for example, with that frame. But then, he had to concede, Lady de Vere knew her slave better than he did. (He was beginning to regret he'd had no hand in training her, leaving that to Vicky. He was far too busy, nowadays, for some of the simple pleasures of life.) Perhaps the slave's bottom was an especially sensitive erogenous zone that would induce orgasms without stimulation elsewhere.

Walpole himself had gone for the traditional stout timber A-frame as in the case of the first whipping contest, when Lady de Vere had won her little garçonne. Honey, the little darling, had been strapped to it. He had chosen it partly because it was familiar to his favourite slave. She knew what to expect, and she would perform for her master, Walpole hoped, exactly as he required.

Her wrists and elbows were held by the rubber straps to the top angle of the frame, and her legs spread apart and strapped up by the ankles and knees. Hindquarters were nicely presented for the lash by a tight belt round the waist, and, as before, a thick butt plug with sideways projections at the end kept the posterior cleft open for the lash.

"Very nice," said Walpole. "I think we're ready." He asked one of the assistants to call Ms Stratton over, to keep score.

"Oh no I almost forgot." He rummaged in a shoulder bag he was carrying. "The assistants will have to loosen some straps for the moment, and stuff these SheSqueezes in their little pussies. Now let me see, I think I'll have the one that plays an excerpt from the Halleluiah Chorus myself; you two decide between yourselves which piece of music you prefer."

No piece from Italian opera had been included, so Mario Cevasco had no preference, but Lady de Vere chose the Trumpet Voluntary, which left the Marseillaise for Cevasco.

"Right," James Walpole said, when this last manoeuvre had been accomplished, "now, I think the lady should go first, Lady de Vere, and it's for us men to decide which of us goes second."

"I really don't mind, James."

"Then, since you're a guest, Mario, you go second, I'll follow on. Six strokes each, at each round, I think. Six is the traditional number, for some reason. I've often wondered why."

Interestingly, Walpole thought, all three contestants had chosen to use single-lash whips: Lady de Vere had chosen a riding whip, Cevasco a bull whip, and he himself a rubber flogger. Well, that was logical. Whips could find parts of the body less flexible canes, birches, tawses, straps, paddles and riding crops couldn't reach, and were more accurate, less likely to get hitched on parts of the punishment frame, than cat o' nine tails.

By this time, Victoria had arrived – having been directing another event elsewhere on the lawn. She briefly went through the rules.

"The score is assessed at the end of the round. In the event of a dead heat, the game continues until, at the end of a round, one slave has the lead in orgasms. Whipping is the only form of stimulation allowed. Anything else – for example, inserting the whip stock into the anus or vagina, will lead to the disqualification of the contestant. Whipping the genitals is allowed, however."

As she said this, she thought the expressions of the contestants revealed something of their characters: Lady de Vere was listening with polite attention; James was wearing a faint cynical smile; Cevasco showed barely suppressed impatience.

"If all that's clear, we can begin. Who's first?"

The order did matter, although Victoria doubted that the two guests would understand why. Hearing the cracking of the whip and the screams and gagged gurgles of a slave being punished caused nervous anticipation in the ones who were due for punishment next. The sheer anticipation of the same punishment, the realisation that it was going to be meted out very soon, made it more likely a slave would orgasm when her turn came. The contestant whose slave was to be treated with the whip last had a clear advantage. Victoria wasn't surprised to learn that her boss had arranged things so he went last. Neither did it cause her too much astonishment to learn that Lady de Vere was to go first. She'd always thought James had a weakness for big bottoms. He was a bottom man, definitely.

"Lady de Vere?"

Lady de Vere was certainly an expert when it came to using a riding whip. The first two strokes lashed her slave across her broad rump, leaving two artistically contrived exactly parallel red marks. The strokes must have been painful, but the slave only gasped. After that, de Vere concentrated on vertical strokes. Two downwards, slashing into her slave item's buttock cleft. At that, the girl started to whimper. The last two were extremely skilfully done: the lash snaked between the slave's legs, so that end of the lash, moving faster than the speed of sound, cracked against her sex-slit. The slave howled in pain.

Lady de Vere's artistry brought spontaneous applause from the onlookers; but there was no orgasm.

"Mr Cevasco," Victoria said.

Victoria knew, from the last whipping contest, that Cevasco's artistry was the equal of Lady de Vere's, but today he was obviously relying on the brute force of a bull whip, and the sadistic punishment frame he had put his slave into, to do the work for him. He might be making a mistake, Victoria thought. Cevasco aimed for the genitals right off, but the whip was caught in the beaded chain that cut through them, and didn't do his slave any harm at all. The first two strokes were wasted in this way, and it was Cevasco, rather than the slave, who grunted with annoyance. Changing his tactics, he brought the second two strokes down across his slave item's breasts, jutting skywards and obvious targets. She began a deep, gurgling groan beneath her gag, that became a high-pitched scream. He used his last two strokes of the first round of the game on his slave's thighs. She gurgled beneath her gag again, and shifted her rump, moving the beaded chain through her vagina and causing it to frig her clitoris. Suddenly, the triumphant tones of the Marseillaise were to be heard from the SheSqueeze buried deep in the slave item's sex-slit.

"Mr Walpole," Victoria said. As she said this, she noticed that the inner thighs of the slut slave Honey were already glistening with juice. Victoria fleetingly thought what a perfect little blonde masochist Honey was. No wonder she was James's favourite – and no wonder Mario Cevasco wanted to own her too.

Victoria knew that her boss had no great skill with a whip. She approved of his strategy of going to root of the problem: he applied the rubber flogger energetically in the first two strokes on his slave item's snatch. The Halleluiah Chorus was immediately to be heard.

The next two strokes reddened the attractive posteriors of James Walpole's favourite slave – and for the next two, he brought the heavy flogger down vertically into his slave's buttock cleft, as Lady de Vere had done. Amazingly, there was another blast of the Halleluiah Chorus. That little doll goes like a banger, Victoria thought.

"At the end of the first round," Victoria said, "the score is: Lady de Vere, nought; Mr Cevasco, one; Mr Walpole, two."

"Well, I reckon I underrated you, James. I'd thought I'd win this, hands down," Cevasco said.

"Do you want to concede? Then you get to keep that slave of yours."

"Hell, no! I'm still in with a chance."

"I won't concede either," Lady de Vere said. "My filly will orgasm in the next round, I'm sure."

"She'll still be behind, if she does," said Walpole.

"'Behind' being the operative word," chortled Cevasco.

"No," said Lady de Vere, a trifle uncertainly, "I'll stay in for now."

Victoria was a bit sorry for Lady de Vere. She was an English lady of the old school, and Victoria rather admired her, particularly as she was so skilful with a whip. It didn't seem right for James to fleece her in that cynical way he had. Like taking candy from children. I shall have to talk to him about it, Victoria thought.

"Would you like some refreshments before we continue?" Walpole asked his guests.

Victoria knew why he said that. To let the slaves cool off. That would give him a clear advantage in the next round. She wasn't going to allow it.

"No, that's – er – against the rules. The game has to continue straightaway."

James Walpole looked at her crossly, but said nothing.

Lady de Vere saw no reason, evidently, to change her tactics, and this time, Victoria was secretly pleased to see, they paid off. After the second stroke that found her slave's quim – the fourth altogether – the Trumpet Voluntary was to be heard at last, but that still left Lady de Vere trailing, as James had said.

Mario Cevasco didn't make the mistake he had made the first time round, instead lashing his slave's thighs and buttocks, to make her shift her weight and rub the chain of beads through her pussy. Victoria noticed it was glistening with her juices. She was sobbing, her eyes were glazed, she was transfigured by pain and lust. On only the second stroke she orgasmed, and then again, three strokes later.

And how will the little sex-bomb do this time? Victoria wondered, when it came to James's turn. Not as well as the first time, it would seem. Although James applied the rubber flogger as enthusiastically as ever, for some reason Honey managed only one orgasm this time.

"So, at the end of the second round, Lady de Vere has one point, and Mr Cevasco and Mr Walpole three points – a dead heat, which means there has to be at least one more round to decide the winner."

After having been on the receiving end of twelve of Lady de Vere's lashes already, the little garçonne was well and truly on heat, coming to a juddering, bum-trembling orgasm right at the first stroke, and then again at the sixth. On the other hand, Bouncy couldn't repeat her performance of the round before no matter how hard her buttocks and thighs were beaten or the chain of beads rubbed through her cunt. She managed one orgasm only, though that was a fairly dramatic one, accompanied by a gurgling scream and her whole torso, pinioned though it was in its sadistic frame, trembling and jouncing, breasts wobbling, a flood of juice at her groin.

"I say, she puts on a good show, doesn't she?" Walpole remarked.

"'Good show?' Hell, the bitch has lost me this game." In his frustration, Cevasco raised his arm to strike his slave again with the bull whip, but Walpole laid a hand on his shoulder.

"What are you doing, man? You haven't lost yet. If you strike her out of turn you'll disqualify yourself."

"Oh, yeah, I guess so."

It seemed Walpole had decided the best strategy was to target all six strokes at Honey's sex-slit. It paid off. The blonde masochistic sex-bomb was as responsive as Lady de Vere's slave had been, when de Vere had adopted more or less the same plan of action. As the rubber flogger snaked between Honey's legs and stung her muff, Victoria and the contestants were treated to a fine display of buttock-trembling, the juices flowed, and the slave-slut came to orgasm twice once more.

"Well, that's been an interesting game, but the result is now clear," Victoria said. "Lady de Vere has three points, Mr Cevasco four, but Mr Walpole is the winner with five points."

This time neither Cevasco nor Lady de Vere were to be deterred from giving their slaves a thorough arse-whipping.

"Stupid – useless – cow!" Lady de Vere said, bringing her whip-lash cracking down across bare posteriors after each word to emphasise her point. "You don't deserve me as your owner." With that remark, Lady de Vere stalked off.

*

"Vicky, Domino isn't a charity, you know, and our guests aren't children. They both knew perfectly well they risked losing their slaves."

"Well, it wasn't very sporting of you to treat poor Lady de Vere that way. Making her go first more or less guaranteed she was going to lose."

"It made it slightly more likely, that's all, and if she's going to gamble slaves in whipping contests, it was her business to know, or to find out, that order is important. Anyway, the main reason she lost was that her slave isn't quite broken in yet, and she should have known that, too."

"I still think you were taking unfair advantage of your professional knowledge. You just wanted Cheeky for yourself. Don't try and tell me otherwise."

"I'll take great pleasure in completing her training,

certainly. Then I'll sell her back to de Vere, if she wants her. You talk about de Vere as if she were hard done by. You of all people should know that isn't the case. Remember all those BDSM parties. She's one of the richest women in Europe, and she has, literally, dozens of slaves at her beck and call – "

" – well, but even so – "

" – mares and stallions for riding and buggering with her strap-on; butlers, maids, chauffeurs; slaves kept sweating on treadmills in her dungeons and never allowed to see the light of day; bed-slaves of both sexes, females with bouncy bums and breasts and juicy cunts and muscular males with long thick dicks. I don't think she'll miss Cheeky for long, somehow."

*

James Walpole wasted no time breaking Cheeky in. He had one of the cells in the basement of Scheherazade made out as a school room. Cheeky was put in a school uniform: white shirt and school tie; the tightest of tight thin rubber hot pants which showed clearly the cleavage of posteriors and quim (not very scholastic, but very effective at keeping the slave conscious of her principal assets in the eyes of her superiors); and little white socks and sandals. She was left alone unsupervised without a chastity belt, but the prominent CCTV cameras discouraged masturbation, despite her daily dose of aphrodisiac. In any case, her slender waist was locked between two planks of wood, acting as a sort of body stocks, so she couldn't touch herself down there. She had to write long essays on the importance of obedience and respect, and was punished with the cane for spelling and grammatical mistakes and any untidiness. There were plenty of spelling and grammatical mistakes because her native language was Lithuanian, and since she had to write out everything with an old-fashioned nib pen which had to be dipped into an inkwell, blots and untidiness were pretty common too.

Apart from the P.E. lessons, her visits to the ablutions and her sessions with her master, she spent all day sitting at her desk facing one wall of the cell. The bench was hard, and her bottom ached, but she couldn't rise because of the body stocks. Her feet were locked in stocks as well, and a posture collar attached her to the back of a high-backed chair.

*

Her master was late today. He usually came at about four o'clock in the afternoon, but it was half-past four now. She had been slow to bend over the caning block that morning to receive her daily caning, and was now desperately trying to complete six hundred lines:

"I must show obedience at all times, doing whatever I am told by my superior at once."

There were seventeen words in that long sentence, and writing it out six hundred times, why, that was over ten thousand words she had to write. She'd never do it in time, and trying to rush it would make it worse, then she'd scribble and blot the page. Of course, she knew she'd been set up to fail. It was very clever, really. After the hours of discomfort and boredom, her master's use of her came as a relief. She looked forward to the shafting she'd get: however temporarily, that relieved the craving that always built up between the sessions with her master. Spankings always came before sex, so she looked forward to them, too. In fact, she usually orgasmed when she was being caned or spanked now, far more often than she had done when she was owned by Lady de Vere.

She heard her master's footsteps in the corridor, and felt a little thrill of fear and sexual arousal in her belly and groin.

"Hello Cheeky! Looking forward to a good spanking?"

"Yes, Master!" Cheeky realised that, recently, she'd actually meant what she said, and she knew her master could catch the sincerity in her voice.

"Let's see how hard you've been working…. Well, your handwriting has improved, at least. But there's not very much of it, is there? Not more than five hundred lines here, not nearly as much as you were supposed to write. That's not good enough, is it?"

"No, Master."

"Still, you're coming along. There's nothing wrong with you a good, hard, bare-arsed spanking won't cure." Walpole unbolted the stocks and detached the slave collar. There was a teacher's desk in the cell with a broad wooden paddle and a long, heavy, two-thonged leather tawse on it, and there was a chair behind it. Walpole sat on the chair. "Over my lap, Cheeky."

Cheeky wasn't going to make the mistake of hesitating this time. She was over her master's knee like a shot. She received a slap on her left buttock's ample mound. In spite of the fact that it was just a slap with the hand, and she was still wearing her hot pants, the unexpectedness of it made her gasp.

"Fingers touching floor, Cheeky, you should know to do that now, you've been told often enough."

"Sorry, Master." She had been told too, how could she be so forgetful?

Her master placed a hand firmly round the nape of her neck, forcing her head down, and began a slow rhythmical hand-spanking, first on one shiny rubber-clad buttock, then the other, then one bare thigh, then the other. Through the rubber, even on the flesh of the thighs, the spanking wasn't very painful, and had a gentle hypnotic effect, warming her rump and making her feel sexy. Eventually, when the slave's bum cheeks felt to her as if they were as big and as red as pumpkins, she was ordered to stand, take off her shirt and tie, and lower her pants. The undressing revealed her jugs, modest but with quite evidently erect nipples, a moist depilated pussy, and the pink, glowing orbs of her prominent nates, criss-crossed with faint marks, memories of countless earlier canings and spankings.

"Over my lap again, slave."

Instant obedience, and this time Cheeky didn't forget to touch fingers to the floor. She also carefully remembered to raise her bottom, so that her moist sex-slit wouldn't be in contact with her master's clothes.

The rhythmical hand-spanking continued for a while, but was more painful now that the palm of her master's hand was in contact with the unprotected flesh of her backside. She felt the twin orbs ripple and wobble under the impact of increasingly hard spanks; and knew that the sight excited her master, for she felt his penis stiffen under the weight of her naked body. She felt flushed and proud that, although she was just a slave, she could please her master like that.

Suddenly, the spanking ceased. Her master gripped her rump with both hands, nails digging into the generous flesh, forced the cleavage apart, and probed her anus with a finger.

"Time to get you hot and hungry, Cheeky."

"Yes, Master." God, she was hot and hungry enough for sex now. But she knew her master wouldn't have sex with her until she orgasmed from an experience of real pain. She was being trained to accept pain and humiliation as her lot, she knew that.

She felt her master lean forwards, and guessed he was reaching for one of the instruments of chastisement on the desk.

The heavy paddle came down on her hindquarters and knocked all the breath out of her body. Then again, and again, and again so many times she lost count, and soon she was in an agony of pain, and ecstasy as well. Her whole body shuddered as her rump was lifted up by the hard strokes, then it quivered without the prompting of the paddle, and she howled like a she-cat and came in an emphatic, juddering orgasm.

Walpole laughed. "Well done, little slave slut. Now let's see if you can give your master a repeat performance."

He leaned forward again, presumably to replace the paddle with something else – Cheeky remembered the heavy, two-thonged tawse.

"Spread your legs wide, slave."

Oh, golly, he was going to thrash her snatch. But she had to do what she was told, that went without saying, and soon the burning leather tawse was belaying her sex-lips.

It was not long before she was howling with pain once more, as her cunt gushed juice, and she was liberated in a shivering masochistic abandonment of joy, pleasure she would never have believed possible in an earlier life, before she had been captured as a slave, that now seemed as distant as a dream dreamt years ago.

"Good. That's very good. Now stand up, slave."

Cheeky did so.

"What do you say?"

"Thank you very much, Master, for spanking me, and giving me two orgasms."

"Do you want me to fuck you, slave?"

"Oh, yes please, Master. Please fuck me." Cheeky knew her master would not doubt her sincerity.

"Very well, then."

Walpole kicked off his slippers unbuckled his trousers, took them off, and the thong that was, with difficulty, hiding his manhood. His slave was pleased to see his penis was fully erect, and, as soon as it was released from its light bonds, pointing at twenty degrees to the ceiling. Here was undeniable proof her master was pleased with her!

"Bend over your desk. Splay your legs."

"At once, Master."

Cheeky felt her master's finger, lubricated with ointment, probe deeply into her back passage. Then his cock plunged into it, and, impaled by his shaft, she orgasmed again, her buttocks shivering and shaking. When his penis came out, she felt her anus stayed wide for some time. Her master went away for some minutes, but she didn't dare move or turn round to see what he was doing. Then she was impaled once more, where, she thought, every woman wants to be. Again there was the delicious shivering joy, and blissful orgasm, and once more, a delightful surrender to the powerful presence of her master and owner.

She howled like an alley-cat each time she was shafted. James Walpole penetrated her in both of her lower orifices twice more over the next hour, without once allowing her to move from her position, buttocks up over her desk.

"I've decided I'm not going to sell you to Lady de Vere, even if she still wants you, or put you up for auction. I'll keep you for myself, and brand you with my own brand."

CHAPTER EIGHTEEN:

THE SLAVE AUCTION AT SCHEHERAZADE.

The penultimate day of the house party arrived, and with it, the slave auction. Most of the guests had been taking note of slaves they would like to acquire, and were looking forward to this last event eagerly. Of course, most of Domino's slaves were sold online, but an electronic slave market could not compare with the old fashioned sort. The cheap musky slave perfume, slapped onto the slave's flesh to disguise the odour of fear-generated sweat and urine, the slave cowed and trembling and vulnerable, or proudly selling herself into subservience, naked thighs and buttocks and genitals showing evidence of treatment by the cane and whip, all this was wonderful to behold. The internet version could never hope to match it in excitement and erotic charge.

Walpole glanced at the programme, which gave the names of the slaves to be sold beneath their photographs and vital statistics including intimate details such as the size of the genitals and elasticity of the anus. Lot one was a girl of Middle-Eastern appearance, with long, black, straight hair, plaited in a single strand behind her back, called Perky. The marketing department hasn't been particularly imaginative in the name, thought Walpole.

Stratton and he were sitting at the back of the auction room, Walpole with his arms stretched carelessly along the backs of seats, a Balkan Sobranie cigarette characteristically held between two long languorous fingers, and his feet resting on Honey's back, as she crouched on all fours in front of him. Victoria Stratton was sitting erect, worried perhaps that something might go wrong even now.

"Fine figure of a girl, that," Walpole remarked, indicating the photograph entitled: Lot 1, Perky.

"Where did she come from? She looks Arabic."

"She is, well North African anyway. We bought a job lot of them from a Berber tribe. They were selling at a bargain price so we didn't vet each one, mustn't look a gift horse in the mouth and all that, but actually quite a lot of them turned out to be very pretty indeed."

"Why were they a bargain price?"

"There hadn't been any time to fatten them up when we saw them, so the locals thought they were unattractive. They like their women plump. And then again, of course, their standard of living is low, so the money we offered seemed a lot to them."

"And I suppose we make a big profit on them?"

"That remains to be seen, but I'm hoping for ten thousand percent at least on the good quality ones, like this girl. The less attractive ones we'll sell off to Mario as hookers. Hello, it looks as if the bidding's about to start."

*

Perky was led on the stage at the front of the auction room by her trainer. Except for certain items of sophisticated bondage, her collar, sandals, and a tight belt round her waist, she was quite naked. Her trainer was holding a chain leash attached to the collar in his left hand, and a broad wooden paddle in his right. He handed the leash to the auctioneer, who put the end loop over a hook at the side of his desk. Then the trainer stood behind the slave, who was looking cowed and humiliated, forced to stand naked in front of all those dominant ladies and gentlemen.

"Look happy!" the trainer said, accompanying that injunction with a hard spank with the paddle.

There was a loud clap as wood met buttocks, a sudden jolt and bouncing boobs. Perky gave a yelp, more in surprise than pain, then smiled obediently. Domino's slaves looked forward to the opportunity to serve their owners. The audience chuckled good-humouredly.

After the chastisement with the paddle, Perky looked like a girl who enjoyed displaying herself to her lords and masters. She was standing on tiptoe, legs splayed so that the audience had a good view of her depilated quim, arms behind her back, tits well out, chin up, lips slightly apart, and mouth wide in a warm smile. In short, her whole posture suggested she was proud to be a slave.

As a matter of fact, although Perky's enthusiasm for subservience was genuine enough, three months of Domino's conditioning had seen to that, she found she had little choice but to stand in the way she did. She stood on tiptoe because a tall blunt nail projected upwards from the heel of the insole of each of her sandals; her legs were splayed because the ornamental brass leg irons she was wearing forced them apart; her tits were thrust forward because her forearms were fastened tightly together behind her back at elbow and wrist; her chin was proudly set because a short leather thong tied into her plait was fastened tautly to a metal ring at the back of the tight belt she was wearing. She could yelp when spanked, but was unable to articulate words because a metal clip was fastened across her tongue. And she smiled because she would have received another jouncing spank if she hadn't.

"Ladies and Gentlemen!" the auctioneer said, "the reserve price for this very beautiful girl, Perky, is $10,000. You can see her figure, Ladies and Gentlemen, I don't need to talk about that, big boobs, small waist, and – " At a signal from the auctioneer, the trainer placed a knee on Perky's behind, an arm across her throat, and gently forced her to bend backwards, so that her depilated sex was well displayed – "a lovely big cunt, as you can see, and – turn round Perky," at the direction of her trainer Perky turned round and wiggled her rear, "– as you can see, very delightful posteriors and – if I may ask, thank you –" the trainer stretched out Perky's nates – "an anus used to being invaded by the – ahem – instruments of desire of her superiors. Well, turn round again, Perky. Good. Now, what am I bid for this little sex-bomb? Shall we start at $15,000? Thank you, Sir. $20,000? Thank you, Madam. Thank you, Madam, $25,000."

The bidding went on for a couple of minutes, and became a contest between an Arab oil millionaire and a Japanese electronics manufacturer.

"Do I hear $70,000? Thank you, Sir. 80. 85. 90. 95. Any advance over 95? Going for 95, for the second time, and the third." The auctioneer banged his mallet. "Sold to the gentleman in the grey suit for $95,000."

"So the Japanese got her," Victoria remarked to Walpole. "I bet the Arab is a bit miffed."

"Oh he'll have his chance. We've got nine more lots from that batch of Berber girls to get through. Then there are fifteen blonde Russians. Not this little one under my feet though. Half a dozen other assorted East Europeans, too. A few Thais but no Chinese this year, surprisingly. Quite a few Indian slaves. Mostly from the Himalayan region. There are traditional slave-markets there. Neither the British, when they ruled India, nor the modern Indian government, has ever managed to stamp them out. Fortunately. An awful lot of slaves from the North West Frontier Province of Pakistan, too. We always get a glut of slaves from a region when there is war or political disturbance. And then there are the males, as well."

"Surely as more bidders spend the money they've allotted for buying slaves the price will go down?" Stratton had never witnessed a live slave auction before. Her experience of selling slaves had all been online.

"That's not how it works. Most of the bidders haven't

come in yet. If you've got millions to spend you can afford to be choosy. A girl can be attractive and not appeal to everyone. And a lot of people – in fact most of our guests – will want to buy quite a few slaves."

*

Slave items of many types were sold at the auction. Tall, petite, blonde, brunette, red-haired; little garçonnes like Cheeky, with large posteriors and small breasts; top-heavy girls with enormous tits; girls with hour-glass figures. Walpole waited until the price for a type began to fall, indicating a fall in demand, then sent a message to the auction staff indicating that other slave items of that type were not to be put on offer. They would be sold later, online.

*

Eventually many female slaves had been sold – at very high prices, too, Walpole was pleased to see. None went for less than the $95,000 that Perky had been sold for. The most expensive, at $2,000,000, had been a dark-haired Bulgarian beauty, bought by a Chinese tycoon from Singapore, and a tall blonde Russian girl with a perfect hour-glass figure, who went to the Arab millionaire, as did indeed quite a few other Russians.

"Did you know the word "Slav" gives us our English word 'slave'?" Walpole remarked. "Honey, ashtray." Immediately, Honey turned round and held her head up and her mouth open, so that Walpole could toss his cigarette butt into her mouth. She had by now learnt the art of extinguishing the butt quickly, and swallowing it without retching. Being an ashtray was just another little humiliating duty intended to put her in her place and keep her there.

"Circassians, Ukrainians and Russians have been sold to the Arabs and Turks for generations. There's nothing new under the sun, is there? Honey, footstool!"

Victoria laughed at the completeness of Honey's subjugation as she hurried to obey.

"Ah! Now we've got some boys coming up," she said, glancing at the catalogue. "Now this you must see, James. I enslaved this boy." She pointed at the slight figure being led out onto the brightly lit stage. "He was called Stefan, that was his original name, a Bulgarian I believe, a natural submissive. He was originally Bimbo's partner. You know what? You won't believe this, but the two of them actually advertised for me! When I saw the ad I couldn't believe my luck. Imagine, two attractive submissives just begging to be enslaved. I suppose it's a good thing they hadn't the faintest idea what enslavement involved. They advertised as a couple, but I think the ideas for the ad was his – he was more submissive that she was then. I wondered what to do with him, for a while. I thought maybe I should make him into a big strong boy with a great big prick, but then, I thought no, he's better suited as a sissy boy, with a very little prick. The tiny prick and balls reinforce the slave's determination to please 'her' master or mistress as a sissy, because she can't get satisfaction any other way."

Walpole drew on a cigarette. "Yes, Victoria. Thank you for that explanation. I believe I wouldn't have understood otherwise."

Stratton looked at her boss, who was smiling slightly. "All right. There's no need to be sarcastic. O.K., I get carried away at times. It's a pity I can't get Mr Cevasco to buy Giggles. I once promised Giggles and Bimbo they could stay together as a couple. It would be nice to think I'd kept my word."

"They're only slaves, Vicky," Walpole said. "You mustn't think of them as people."

"Well, I know, but I had quite a lot of fun with them in the early days, when I was first getting to know them. I sort of grew fond of them."

Walpole tut-tutted reprovingly. "Always a mistake. Pay no attention to Vicky, Mario," Walpole said to Cevasco, who had just walked up.

"I reckon I will buy her," Mario decided. He waited almost until the hammer was about to come down for the third time on the bid of a Russian oligarch, before putting in a surprise bid of his own. It was successful, and so Giggles and Bimbo, formerly Stefan and Tanya, were united once more as part of the menagerie of Mario Cevasco.

*

After the sale of women and she-males, he-men studs were offered for sale. Each of the studs was the product of intensive exercise on treadmills and exercise bikes, of the kind that had been used to break in Honey; a course of injections of steroids and testosterone; and surgery to lengthen and thicken the penis and enlarge the testicles. For the auction, they had been given Viagra. Cocks and balls were pushed forward by leather straps buckled tightly round them; they were hard and proud and at full length; so prominent, in fact, no member of the audience could doubt the virility of these slave items.

Lady de Vere was an enthusiastic purchaser of all the types of slave. Walpole was amused to see that she had bought six new slave girls, three she-males, and no less than a dozen studs. (Studs didn't fetch as much as the others, the average selling-price was about $25,000, so Lady de Vere could afford to be prodigal.)

*

Over cocktails the next day, and nearly the end of the stay at Scheherazade for the guests, and for Walpole and Victoria Stratton too – they had to get back to London to organise the online auction – Lady de Vere invited Walpole, Victoria Stratton, and "that dear Mr Cevasco, who gave me that little poppet of a slave girl at the hunt," to have dinner at her private chambers in the west wing of Scheherazade.

At Lady de Vere's request, the maids who brought the meal to her apartment wore nothing but thongs and sandals, and the minimum of bondage equipment – tongue clips with sideways spikes that forced them to smile open-mouthed and prevented them from saying a word, and light aluminium chains attaching to tit-rings and wrist-cuffs. The bondage was there for ornamentation really, rather than serious restriction, just acting as a mild inconvenience to remind the slaves of their place and function.

Lady de Vere was in most respects demure and discreet. Bon chic, bon genre comes naturally to the aristocracy. Displays of wealth were left to the American rich and other vulgar persons who no doubt had earned their money in trade. That was Lady de Vere's attitude anyway – despite the dubious way she had come by her own wealth. However, when it came to her menagerie of slaves, she took every opportunity to show them off. This was not because she wished to show everybody how wealthy she was. She assumed they knew. It was rather that she took a childlike delight in playing with her new toys, and genuinely wished others to share her pleasure.

Lady de Vere had overseen the slave kitchen staff of Scheherazade. The meal itself had been cooked to her very precise specifications. (Not all the slaves taken to Scheherazade were intended to be sold, at least not then, though no doubt they would be auctioned off sooner or later.) Lady de Vere was a very strict task mistress, and slaves who failed to prepare food exactly as she required found themselves with very sore bottoms very quickly.

The meal she had had prepared was a terrine of chicken liver pâté with newly baked bread as hors d'oeuvre, and baked salmon with new potatoes and butter and a salad of dill, coriander, basil, tarragon, cos lettuce, cucumber, and cherry tomatoes. To follow was flaky pastry blackcurrant pie, which was cooked according to Lady de Vere's mother's recipe. This was served with custard made with fresh ingredients. A slave who had tried to make the custard with custard powder was unable to sit down comfortably for a week afterwards.

Not all the food was flown out to Scheherazade at great expense. The country house had an extensive kitchen garden and fish ponds.

Lady de Vere had had some of the furniture in her chambers especially made up for her by the department of Domino that built slave control apparatus.

The trays of food were brought to Lady de Vere's chamber, and laid down on the transparent, glass table top. The table top was transparent so that it was possible to view what supported it. These were four of Lady de Vere's newly-acquired girl slaves, one at each corner, facing outwards. They were completely naked, it goes without saying, and were strapped up in a squatting position, thighs pressed to bellies, vaginas plugged with long thick vibrators which operated silently, elbows and wrists fastened together behind backs, and steel posture collars keeping their heads still and rigidly erect. On the head of each slave was clamped a branks to gag the slave and at the crown form a metal headpiece resembling a mortar board, which slotted into a grooved under-surface of the table top. The slaves had to suffer in silence and stillness, while at the same time being titillated by the vibrators quietly ploughing their furrows.

There were four chairs round the table for Lady de Vere herself and her three guests, and others scattered round the room. The principal component of all the chairs was a female slave, but they varied in their design. Chair slaves forming those chairs scattered round the room were folded over, so that the seat was formed from the slaves' rump and back of the thighs, with the lower legs forming the backrest, and a leather headrest fitting over the feet, neatly bonding them together. A rubber strap, attached to the steel corset each slave was wearing, looped round the back of the knees. The legs of the chair extended from a metal plate beneath the corset, to which the corset was attached by screws. A steel tube running down from the headrest was screwed to a branks clamped over the slave's head, and was inserted into her mouth, forcing the jaws wide and gagging her. The steel tube supported a U-shaped armrest halfway down its length, and the hands and wrists of each slave were enclosed in rubberised cavities at each end of the armrest.

Chairs of this design were intended for sitters who preferred access to the slave's lower orifices, and so obviously weren't suitable as dining chairs – it would have been very bad manners to finger a slave's bottom at table. Hence the different design of dining chairs.

The seats of the dining chairs were the faces and breasts of the chair slaves, who had been specially chosen for their top heavy mammaries, now firmly squeezed through two holes in the base, which formed a sort of pillory. The mouth of the slave was kept permanently open and receptive by a funnel gag, and the sitter could adjust the angle at which the branks held the head for his or her convenience. A metal tube running up the buttock cleavage and between the legs, held the legs almost vertical to act as a back rest, with the feet enclosed in a headrest in the same way as with the other design. Every six inches up the tube, metal surrounds secured the slave's limbs, keeping them perfectly immobile. Two pegs, screwed into the tube, plugged the slave's anus and vagina.

*

The three guests congratulated Lady de Vere on her dinner.

"It was superb, Ma'am. I've rarely enjoyed a meal so much," said James Walpole.

"Yeah, it was great. Eating baked salmon and having your dick sucked at the same time is a great experience," agreed Mario Cevasco. "I must get some of these chairs."

"May I have your recipe for flaky pastry, Lady de Vere?" Victoria Stratton asked.

*

After coffee, Lady de Vere remarked, "I've taken over one of the adjoining rooms as a discipline chamber. I'm putting one of my new acquisitions through her paces right now. I thought you might be amused to have a look at her."

Her guests agreed enthusiastically.

"I thought the prospect of seeing a slave crushed, humiliated and in pain would appeal to you," Lady de Vere said. "It appeals to all dominants."

"I don't think we dominants are very different from the majority of humanity," said Victoria Stratton. "In the old days, crowds gathered to watch heretics being burnt, murderers hanged, and whores whipped."

"No," said Walpole. "The main difference between Domino's customers and most other people is that our customers can afford to do what the majority can only dream about."

In the discipline chamber there was a naked slave girl sitting on what looked at first like an ordinary dining room chair. Her legs were splayed, and her ankles cuffed to the front two legs of the chair. The usual rubber restraining belts looped round her waist and her neck. Her arms were secured round the back of the chair. She wasn't gagged. Some dominants like to hear their slaves whimpering and pleading for mercy, Walpole reflected.

There was a large hole in the centre of the seat of the chair, and through it a long cylinder of ice shafted the slave's depilated sex. Rubber lashes attached to four rotors were giving her naked rear a thorough thrashing. The rotors would whiz round in one direction for half a minute or so, then pause, and counter-rotate. The pain, burning her bum, made the slave squirm and wiggle, insofar as her bondage allowed her to do so, so that her quim was wet with her juices as the ice shaft slid around inside her.

"Domino sold me a pup, Mr Walpole. This slave is frigid."

"I'm sorry to hear that, Lady de Vere. We pride ourselves on having excellent quality control, but occasionally a dud gets through. Slaves are generally forced to have sex, so sometimes frigidity is missed. We'll be happy to exchange the slave for another of your choice."

"That's all right, Mr Walpole. I take great pleasure correcting the slave's behaviour, as you see. I suppose you can see how my machine works? It was invented originally by my husband for punishing reluctant maids back home, and Domino's staff were kind enough to knock one up for my use here."

"The ice-dildo's balanced on a spring, which is pushing it all the time into the bitch's cunt, so I guess as it melts... the spring extends," said Cevasco.

"Precisely," said Lady de Vere. "When the spring reaches its maximum extension, the electric motor cuts out automatically. So the quicker the little cow melts the dildo the quicker her torment is over. Meanwhile, she's in a constant frenzy of pain and sexual arousal, which is just lovely to behold. She won't be frigid after this. And the symbolism of the ice is quite apt, don't you think?"

All her guests agreed that it was. Then they went back to join all the other guests at the leaving party, which was being held in the main hall of Scheherazade, and everyone drank lots of pink champagne.

CHAPTER NINETEEN:

BUSINESS AS USUAL

There was a change in the pitch of the engine's throbbing as it dived into cumulus whose tops were dyed pink on their westward sides by the setting sun. The C-119 descended under rain and into the gloom of a damp English autumnal evening.

Walpole stared out of the plane's window, flecked with raindrops like tears, as the tarmac raced past under the wings.

Although the trip to Scheherazade had not been a holiday, coming back to drizzly weather in England felt like the end of one.

Oh, well, there's a great deal to do back at Domino's headquarters in London, Walpole thought.

The C-119 was one of the first of the fleet to land on the runway of a little airfield somewhere in Sussex, which half the time looked abandoned to casual passers-by driving along the nearby A26, but which was in fact owned by Domino.

There was, of course, a customs officer at the airfield, nominally a servant of the Crown, but long since seduced by Domino. Essentially, in addition to his state salary, he received a six-figure annual stipend from Domino for doing nothing at all, which is not a job many would refuse to take. He was not allowed to know the nature of the merchandise bundled in and out of the small airfield, but every time there was a consignment, Mr Walpole saw to it he was "entertained" by a pretty young lady who fulfilled his every desire. In the circumstances, he thought it was prudent not to enquire too officiously into Mr Walpole's business; but just in case he became too curious, his extracurricular activities were recorded on DVD without his knowledge. Like most people, male and female, who are in what is nowadays the unusual position of having absolute power over an attractive sex-object, he found his creativity blossomed, and the experiences his unfortunate temporary sex-slave was forced to undergo were most inventive and imaginative. Domino personnel whose duty it was to review the DVD recordings were always greatly entertained.

*

The next day there was a board meeting, in which updating the website was the principal topic under discussion; it was an important matter, because by far the greater part of Domino's business was the sale of slave items online. As sales took place, the website had to be constantly updated with new items, and twice a year there was a more complete change: a new gallery, new tableaux, and clips of hunts, pony-races, cat-fighting, whipping contests, mud wrestling, and so on, such as had occurred in the last six months. Naturally clients were pixelled out, unless they specifically requested that recognisable features should remain. Sometimes winners, or the owners of winning slaves, did.

Of the directors, only Walpole and Victoria Stratton had managerial responsibility. They met afterwards in Walpole's office. Walpole smoked a Balkan Sobranie cigarette. Honey was kneeling by his side. Thigh straps were linked to ankle straps, forcing her to remain in a kneeling position, and her wrists were manacled to the thigh straps too. A steel posture collar forced her head up, and a tight, gleaming black rubber helmet enclosed her head, just leaving holes for nostrils and the mouth. She could neither see nor hear. Her jaws were forced wide apart by a ring gag, so she offered her open mouth for use by her master. At the moment he was using it as an ashtray.

"We have to assign responsibility for the various pages

of the website," Walpole was saying. "I shall edit the Scheherazade clips myself – the hunt, whipping contest, pony races and so on. But that leaves an awful lot to be done. Firstly the girl-slaves. I think we'll follow our normal policy of dividing the non-specials into four types: general, big buttocks, big breasts, legs and crotch. Then there are the special types."

The specials were the milch-cows, racing mares, hunters, and the extraordinarily developed ones with enormous mammaries, buttocks, musculature, surgically enlarged vulvas.

"Well, Ronald Short usually supervises the general category, and Julia Collins had the buttocks last time, and made a very good job of it, in my opinion."

"I agree. Oh, and talking of buttocks," Walpole said, flicking ash into the human ashtray kneeling at his side, "I've changed my mind about Cheeky, she can be sold off – in the buttocks category, naturally."

"Sarah Cunningham did the breasts last time, but she says she'd like a change – she wants to be in charge of the specials."

"Fine. I've no objection to that. So that leaves – let me see, breasts and legs."

"I think we should give Thomasina Grey a try on the breasts, she's a new mistress, but very promising."

"O.K." Walpole made a note of it.

"As for legs and pussies – well, Andrew Falck is the obvious candidate. You remember how his screwing machine went down with the crowd at Scheherazade?"

"I do indeed. It fucked the slaves silly. That rubber dildo pumping their pussies – the guests loved it. A good choice, Victoria. We take our engineers too much for granted, I've often thought that. I'm sure he'll make a good job of it…. Now, what else…?" Walpole riffled through his notes. "There are the galleries – two, as usual, rubber bondage and rope bondage, and there'll be an exhibition of caning by Madam Kwan."

"The rubber bondage gallery will be Jack Devine's department, of course?"

"That goes without saying. He's made it his own. It's a big hit, and his slaves sell like hot cakes. In fact, I've put it to the board that Devine should be made a director."

"What was their reaction?"

"Officially, they're thinking about it. But they always follow my recommendations. I've no doubt Jack will be a director before the year is out." The digression caused Walpole momentarily to forget the agenda. "Now then, where was I? The rope bondage gallery will be Mr Suzuki's department of course. I think we have some material on caning already – we can use clips from the time this little darling at my feet was treated to the cane by Madam Kwan – but I think we need something else too. I think Cheeky's prominent posteriors receiving the ministrations of one of Madam Kwan's instruments might be a popular draw."

"I don't suppose you're going to do anything else with your little favourite? I guess you can't really exhibit her twice. In any case, since you're not going to sell her, I suppose you don't want to exhibit her?"

Walpole looked down affectionately at Honey, and flicked some ash into her mouth. "I am going to exhibit her. She's going to be one of Jack's exhibits in fact. Since she'll be totally rubberised and unrecognisable, it doesn't matter about her appearing twice. That's why she's wearing a rubber hood at the moment. To get her used to the idea, so to speak. Of course, I won't sell her. But to be a rubberised object in an art exhibition will do her no end of good. And the guests will have numerous other rubberised statues to bid for, so they won't miss not being able to have her. And what about you? What are you going to do?"

"You know me. I'll be in charge of the male slaves."

"They're a simpler matter."

"True. We sell them as big strong boys with long thick cocks – though not so many of them. Or sissy boys with tiny cocks. A great many. With some of our guests they're more popular than girls."

"Yes. I've always found that a bit strange. But, as you say, dominants get a kick out of dominating them because their male ego is so obviously crushed."

"It's not strange at all. Dominating wimpy men is wonderful."

*

When their meeting was finished and Stratton had left, Walpole rang for a cup of tea. It was brought him by a female slave in a maid's outfit with frilly petticoats beneath a miniskirt. Walpole made a few notes on the desk-top computer and looked pensive for a while as he pondered on the problems that the new virtual slave market and online gallery would present. Then he relaxed, smiled and took a soda siphon from the drinks cabinet. He squirted soda-water into Honey's gaping mouth to swill away all the ash, then inserted his penis into the freshly cleaned orifice, and let his favourite slave caress it with her tongue until he came. Then he tipped her over, so that her knees and breasts pressed on the floor and her rump was upended, and shafted her in both of the orifices presented for his pleasure.

*

Julia Collins was creating Cheeky's presentation when she received a note from Walpole to let Madam Kwan have her after she had finished.

The presentation followed Domino's usual format. There were preliminary shots of Cheeky dressed as a maid in a skimpy outfit, presenting food and drink to various dominants at Scheherazade whose faces were pixelled out; a brief scene of her doing menial chores like cleaning a lavatory; on all fours holding a cane in her teeth; and then her naked in the gym: running, doing star-jumps; leaping over hurdles; climbing up a rope, all supervised by a trainer who carried a bull-whip, and occasionally landed it with expert precision on Cheeky's ample behind, making it ripple and wobble in a most enticing way. There were plenty of bum shots of course, to emphasise Cheeky's principle asset, with Cheeky bent over or sticking her bottom out.

Julia Collins was responsible for writing the voice-over, but it was the slave who had to say it, of course in a convincing way. Typically, there were quite a few takes of the voice-over before the slave got the intonation exactly right, but Cheeky managed to get it right first off: the little garçonne had been a would-be actress in her former, pre-Domino life, so her delivery was completely convincing. It was made easier by the fact that Domino conditioning ensured she believed everything she said:

"Hello, my name's Cheeky. I'm a submissive, totally obedient slave. I've been trained to do everything my owner wants of me. I have lovely rosy apple-shaped buttocks, as you can see. I get wet when I'm chastised, and there's nothing my rump loves better than a good hard spanking before my owner has his or her way with me. I respond well to bondage, and another thing that arouses me sexually is to be totally humiliated. I love being subservient, and grovelling before a masterful owner. I take sex well in all three orifices, and particularly love being shafted between my beautiful, fleshy posteriors."

That completed the initial part of the presentation, but the selling of the slave depended on a detailed overview of her naked body. These were presented to the buyer in three still images: front and back, standing to attention, hands behind head; and one from behind, the slave touching fingers on toes, legs apart. A potential buyer could click on any part of any of the three images, and vital statistics would come up on the screen, as well as the slave's voice-over. For example, if the potential buyer clicked on the anus, as well as the statistics on the screen, Cheeky's voice said:

"My anus can be extended to a diameter of four centimetres. It can take a length of twenty three centimetres."

If the buyer clicked on Cheeky's sex-slit, her voice would say:

"My vulva is eight centimetres long; it can take a length of thirty centimetres, and a width of at least eight centimetres, although a greater width with practice. When sexually aroused, I typically exude about a centilitre of juice in the first ten seconds."

And so on.

*

Jack Devine had been one of the new British Conceptualist artists who had come to prominence in recent years. His first studio had been a bed-sit in a more rundown part of Haringey, in North London, but he had leaped to fame with his "Unwashed Pots" – which, as the title of the work suggested, was a sink with a pile of dirty crockery in it. He had followed that with "Rat in Plastic," which was the corpse of a rat encased in a solid block of transparent plastic. These works and similar ones earned him world-wide fame and a modest fortune: he had become a millionaire before he was twenty-five. But life went downhill for him after that. Instead of producing acceptable art concepts which would have continued to earn him six figure sums from appreciative buyers, he began to create art which was not considered to be in good taste, which was, indeed, thought by many to be pornographic. Female models were encased in rubber and placed in extreme bondage postures. They were then televised and the DVD encoded so it could not be copied. But the market refused to buy. One of the DVDs was impounded by the police as obscene. The art critics of the Sunday newspapers panned his work. Some feminist groups objected. Shocking the bourgeoisie was all very well, but it threatened to lead to poverty. Devine himself was unmoved. Money meant little to him. He lived for his art. His agent gave up trying to persuade him to change to more acceptable subjects, and Devine declined into obscurity.

There he would have remained, had not James Walpole viewed his later work. Walpole was a keen art connoisseur, and decorated his office and home with many examples of contemporary art. Devine's work had interested him, even in the earlier, more conventional period. When he first viewed the DVDs at a poorly attended exhibition in Bond Street, he recognised the true genius of Jack Devine. He bought all of them, at bargain prices, because there was no demand for Devine's work any more, and got to talking to the artist, who was present at the exhibition.

Later, he invited Devine round to his house in Hampstead, showed him the art he possessed, and told him there was a way he could regain his wealth. Devine was not interested at first.

"I won't prostitute my art for money," he said.

"Oh, I'm not asking you to do that," said Walpole. "I only mean you'll be able to practice it on a much grander scale than you've been able to do up to now. The fact that you'll also make loads of dosh is incidental."

"How do you mean?"

"I can provide you with all the models you require – we have a huge selection available, all shapes and sizes, so you'll be able to create a whole gallery of living statues – tableaux I believe you call them."

"Really?" Devine's eyes lit up in anticipation. "But that requires a lot of equipment, and I'm not able to afford it any more. That's the only reason I regret not making money."

"Don't worry about that. All that will be provided free of charge."

"In that case, I agree."

It was in that way Jack Devine was recruited by Domino.

*

The virtual gallery created by Devine was a whole new venture in art. It had never been done before, and had become central to Domino's website – and the website was the main way Domino sold slave items to its customers. Special events, like the auction at the garden party at Scheherazade, and one-off sales, like the slave item sold to Lady de Vere in Guatemala, or Bimbo sold to Mario Cevasco, accounted for only a tiny fraction of turnover.

Six months had passed since the foundation of the virtual gallery, during the course of which quite a few of the items had been sold to enthusiastic buyers. It was time for a complete overhaul. Devine couldn't wait to begin. One of the few drawbacks he found working for Domino was that, for sales purposes, continuous replacement of tableaux wasn't thought desirable. It was better to keep the same statues in the gallery for six months, indicating which ones were sold and which ones still available, and then launch a completely new exhibition in a fanfare of publicity. A launch attracted more attention from buyers and significantly more sales. So Devine had had to content himself during the six months subsequent to the first launch sketching out on paper the new creative ideas that kept bubbling through his mind. Sometimes, it's true, a particular human statue might be created, stored away for the time being in Devine's atelier – but that wasn't really satisfactory.

The gallery as a whole, Devine thought, had to be considered as a single work of art. The statues had to be seen in their relationship to each other. Now at last, the concepts which had been planned on paper could be put into practice – realised in rubber, PVC, plastic, wire and human flesh, and the odd tableau stored away in an equipment cupboard or behind a chest of drawers could be brought out to be mounted and viewed in a proper context.

In the earlier part of his career, before he had been recruited by Walpole, the models Devine used, since they were of course free women, were of necessity kept in their restrictive bondage for only a short time, an hour or so at most, until a DVD had been made. However, slaves could be kept as living statues for an indefinite period, and indeed that was demanded by customers. They were interested in purchasing the tableaux, after all, not DVDs. But this created problems of its own. Slave items needed to be fed and watered, they had to excrete, and they would have to be exercised every so often if they were to remain healthy.

Jack Devine's ingenuity was equal to the challenge which these problems posed. The problem of feeding and watering was easily solved: nutriments and water could be squirted down the mouth of the item. Excrement was more of a problem. Usually, ways had to be found of relieving the exhibit unobtrusively, but sometimes excretion could become part of the tableau's aesthetic function – something the tableau did as part of its being a tableau, as it were. Devine devised a clock mechanism which automatically fed and watered, and opened and shut the anus and urethra at set intervals. He experimented with a process he called "hyperhydration" – filling the exhibit's stomach with water until it was distended, then leaving the urethra blocked for varying lengths of time: after various experiments he decided that half an hour was probably the maximum time advisable. He also experimented with food dyes, to colour the urine in interesting and striking ways: emerald, cerulean, maroon, tourmaline. Then the antique plumbing of the taps and sink in the atelier gave him another idea: he developed a device which fitted neatly over the urethra and gave out a high-pitched squeaking sound when the exhibit made water.

Exercise could sometimes similarly be built in as part of the tableau's function. Devine had exhibits working out on exercise bikes, treadmills, and running machines. He used Domino's standard exercise machines: rotating rubber floggers powered by electric motors automatically started up and thoroughly thrashed the naked rumps of the exhibits if they slacked in their work. But Devine's genius was evident nevertheless. The equipment had been modified so that the mobile tableau could relieve themselves without pausing in their work, and although they were not fully rubberised – part of their aesthetic appeal was the sheen of sweat which glistened on their taut, rippling bodies – they were fitted out in rubber harness and occlusion helmets with a nutrient pipe that plunged into their throat. Devine also decorated them with body paint, and sometimes dyed pubic hair bright red, green or blue rather than shaving it.

*

Devine pondered how to use the item Honey, donated by James Walpole. At first he hesitated. Eventually he decided she would be excellent material for a tableau he had in mind which was to be entitled simply: "Squat."

Honey was made to wear a papier-mâché face mask and high-heeled black boots, but was otherwise completely rubberised, except for the naked pussy, which was depilated, the naked buttock cleavage, and her ringed tits, peeking out of shiny black rubberised orbs. Devine put her in a squatting position (hence the title of the tableau) with rubber garters at the top of the thighs locked to ankle cuffs tightly encircling the necks of the boots. The garters were connected to each other by a rigid steel rod, so that the thighs were forced apart and the crotch parts plainly on view. A tight steel belt encircled her waist.

She was squatting on a square platform over a porcelain receptacle. From the top of a post at each corner of the platform, taut cables ran to rings fixed in the steel belt, so it was impossible for the exhibit to move very far from its upright position – all the more impossible because elbows and wrists were bonded to a steel upright behind the exhibit's back. The rubber helmet the exhibit was wearing completely blinded and deafened her and her mouth was gagged open by a flanged steel rim, into which intruded a pipe that carried water, soluble nutrients and food dye. The feelings of the exhibit, as shown by the expression on her face, were hidden from view, but the mask wore a cheerful grin.

Once a week, Honey changed places with a mobile, and sweated for a day on a treadmill, or an exercise bike, or a running machine.

*

Of course, the gallery itself, and its décor, was largely created by CGI, but all the exhibits were real enough, and there was no illusion in the way the gallery was illuminated – by some of the exhibits themselves. Devine's genius was never more evident than in his creation of the lamp standard tableaux that lined each side of the gallery, Walpole thought.

Each tableau was encased in a rigid, transparent plastic frame, moulded to fit her body, squeezing out her breasts, prising open her anus and sex lips, keeping her rigidly erect, with legs and back straight and chin up. Her eyelids were glued down to protect her eyes from glare. The water pipe for nutrients led up through one nostril rather than plunging into her mouth as in the usual design. That was because there was something else, an electric socket supporting a lamp, screwed into her mouth. An insulated wire flex ran the length of her digestive tract, to a plug fixed in her anus. An extension lead led from that to a wall socket.

When Walpole first saw the lamp standard exhibits, he couldn't believe his eyes.

"How an earth did you do it? A surgical operation?"

Jack Devine laughed. "Nothing that drastic, no scalpels or anaesthetic were used. A small porous bag filled with sweet roughage was attached to a very thin flex. The slave item is made to swallow the bag, it goes to her stomach, through her guts, the food in the bag is digested, and then the indigestible parts including the bag get excreted, pulling the flex with it."

It was Walpole's turn to laugh. "That's incredible! I'd never have thought it possible. You're a genius, Jack. But I still don't quite understand...."

"You want to know how they shit? Well, they don't very much, they receive all their nutrients in liquid form. But the anus plug can be unscrewed temporarily, if necessary. Once every two or three days is usually sufficient. Anyway," he looked at his watch, "I want to show you Honey, it's nearly time."

Mystified, Walpole walked along the rigidly standing forms of the lamp tableaux, until he came to the rubberised form of Honey, squatting on her square platform. Walpole noticed that her stomach was visibly distended. Devine explained that every hour, on the hour, the exhibit was filled up with water.

"At exactly thirty minutes past, the mechanism unplugs her urethra. And that's about – " Devine looked at his watch again. "Now!"

With a high-pitched whistle, as if on cue, a stream of steaming, light blue urine squirted into the receptacle.

"That's funny!" Walpole laughed. "Especially with that mask having such an inane grin on its face. I can see that we're going to get very high bids for that exhibit. I'll have to think again whether I really want to keep her."

"Since her face is obscured, another slave item of the same build and height could be substituted," Devine suggested.

"Hm, I'll think about it," Walpole said.

*

Over the next few months Honey led a bleak life as a living statue, pissing to order, and being forced to drink water every hour on the hour until her stomach was bloated. Then her bladder ached but she was unable to relieve it for half and hour. She couldn't move a millimetre from her excruciating squatting position, with her elbows bonded together, encased in dark rubber, blinded and deafened.

Once a week she was released from her bonds, and forced to toil and sweat on a treadmill or exercise bike. If she faltered, there was a whirring noise as an electric motor started up, and rubber floggers lashed her naked rump. Another slave item took her place as the squat exhibit while she was doing duty as a mobile. When she was allowed to rest – not even slave mobiles could work non-stop for twelve hours – she got a glimpse of the other slave substituting for her, and realised what a ludicrous object she made, squatting and pissing coloured urine punctually every hour while wearing that absurd grinning mask.

How long would her torture go on? Surely her master would release her soon?

*

Her master, however, was uncertain what to do. Out of his harem of slaves, Bouncy, Honey's partner during the hunt at Scheherazade, had become his favourite since the conversion of Honey into a tableau. She had the same petite figure as Honey, firm high breasts, the same pneumatic buttock cheeks, the same hour-glass figure. She was basically Walpole's type.

However, he needed an heir to pass Domino onto, and Bouncy gave him the impression that she was more maternal than Honey. As and when an heir appeared he had no doubt that Bouncy would mother him- or her - well. Honey however needed sex and punishment constantly…

True, she was dark, whereas Honey was fair, but that was an unimportant difference, in Walpole's eyes. So what to do with Honey?

Victoria had no doubts on the matter: "Sell her off James. Have you seen the latest bid? $3,000,000! It's unheard of! I'll think you're going soft in the head if you don't."

Eventually, Walpole went to the gallery and told Devine his decision. Devine nodded, and grinned. "I thought you'd decide on that. I'd do the same in your place."

After Walpole had left, he gave Honey a sleeping pill.

*

When Honey emerged from the haze of sleep, she found – oh, joy! that her limbs were no longer in bonds, or encased in rubber. She had been washed and perfumed, and was now lying in bed between soft, freshly laundered sheets.

"Awake at last, Honey?" Her master's voice said. "Get out of bed and over my lap. I'm going to paddle that pretty little arse of yours till it's rose-pink – and then I'm going to screw you silly."

"Yes, Master, at once."

Honey jumped eagerly out of the bed and ran to abase herself at the feet of the master who had come back for her.

In a brothel in Dendera in ancient Egypt, Hatentita plies her trade as a whore. But she is no ordinary whore – she once claimed the throne of Egypt but her armies were vanquished by the Romans. Now she must remain in hiding, plotting her return to power.

But others have learned where she is and want her under their control. She is abducted and taken to a temple where she is made to serve as the lowest of the low. But her great beauty make her the object of everyone's lust – including the High Priestess. And for the indignities she suffers at the hands of the ambitious and treacherous priestess, Hatentita swears revenge. However, her attempts to escape fail time and again and deliver her up to a succession of cruel gaolers; all of whom take ruthless advantage of her.

Eventually she is taken to an island where rich Romans disport themselves with Egyptian whores and it is there that her final destiny is resolved – in the most cruelly erotic orgies that she has yet encountered.

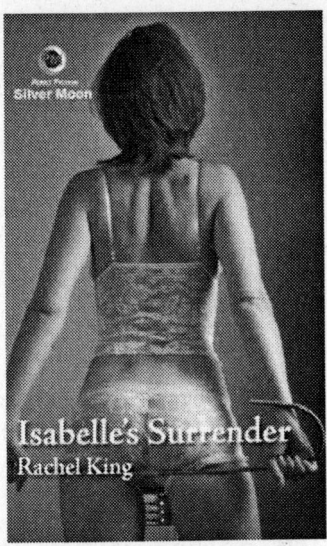

Isabelle is a woman at a crossroads in her life. She knows she needs more than she is currently getting from her sex life.

But when she goes on a cruise to recover from having ditched her last boyfriend, she gets a lot more than she bargains for!

The ship's second officer is a man like no other that Isabelle has met – except maybe one! And for her the cruise turns into a nightmare; one that she doesn't want to awaken from. She is put through a series of breathtakingly erotic experiences at the hands of a consummately manipulative Master, and at journey's end she has surrendered more than she could have believed possible.

Rachel King is a woman who has intimate knowledge of female submission and 'Isabelle's Surrender' is a remarkable debut by a major new talent.

There are over 100 stunningly erotic novels of domination and submission in the Silver Moon catalogue. You can see the full range, including Club and Illustrated editions by writing to:

Silver Moon Reader Services
Shadowline Publishing Ltd,
Box 101
City Business Centre
Station Rise
York
YO1 6HT

You will receive a copy of the latest issue of the Readers' Club magazine, with articles, features, reviews, adverts and news plus a full list of our publications and an order form.